WHAT HAPPENED ON FLOOR 34?

CAROLINE CORCORAN

avon.

Published by AVON
A division of HarperCollins*Publishers* Ltd
1 London Bridge Street
London SE1 9GF

www.harpercollins.co.uk

HarperCollins*Publishers*
Macken House
39/40 Mayor Street Upper
Dublin 1
D01 C9W8

A Paperback Original 2023
1
First published in Great Britain by HarperCollins*Publishers* 2023

A catalogue copy of this book is available from the British Library.

ISBN: 978-0-00-844181-4

Typeset in Bembo by Palimpsest Book Production Limited, Falkirk, Stirlingshire
Printed and bound in the UK using 100% Renewable Electricity at CPI Group (UK) Ltd

WHAT HAPPENED ON FLOOR 34?

After 16 years working as a journalist for many of the top magazines, newspapers and websites in the country, Caroline had her first novel *Through the Wall* published in 2019. It made the bestseller list and was followed by *The Baby Group* in 2020 and *Five Days Missing* in 2022. Her novels have been translated into numerous foreign languages. You'll often find her looking green with travel sickness but still trying to write on a train into Euston from the north west, where she moved for the beaches, house prices and free babysitting.

You can follow her on Twitter here: @cgcorcoran or on Instagram @carolinecorcoranwriter.

To Diana

Prologue

6 March, 2010

I'll tell you where you don't want to be when you are scared for your life and about to run: on the thirty-fourth floor of an empty Canary Wharf tower block. I'll tell you what time you don't want it to be too, for that matter: 2 a.m.

It's March and the birdsong isn't imminent. The world will stay quiet in its blackness for hours yet. My heart thumps like footsteps. Around me, ten or twelve TV screens hang from the ceilings of our national newspaper office, like large, ugly chandeliers. They are silent; as usual they show rolling headlines but it's the subtitles not the presenters that fill me in on what's happening around the globe.

Through the glass – floor to ceiling all around me – London's twenty-four-hour light show beams in. In daylight, you can see everything London has to offer from those windows and people take advantage of that. Friends, family, they traipse up for a tour to treat themselves to a look from the unofficial viewing platform, phones clicking, before the view is slipped into their back pockets and they head off to get on with their days.

Even now, in the deepest of night, London reminds you that she's there. That she has no time for sleep.

I try to breathe slowly. Glance for half a second at that skyline. There's a comfort in it. But you know what extremes are: the best and the worst.

That view.

That drop.

I snap into action. Shove a water bottle into my over-sized Mulberry handbag, an engagement present from Patrick's family. When I lean over my keyboard to log out, my hand slips from it, clammy.

An image flashes into my mind: my missing colleague, our website night editor Will Frost. Gone for more than six weeks now. Not a word about where. But last night, sitting in the seat Will disappeared from, with worn-out old Clarks shoes left under the desk, I finally figured out why.

I look up. No. I'm being paranoid. There is no need to fear anything here, not with all these glaring lights, company in the hum of every resting screen. And then there is London too, awake, alive, just outside those windows. I've always been more fearful on a quiet lane in Surrey at 8 a.m. than in the banging heart of London in the middle of the night.

Except I'm not in the heart of London, am I? I'm in a box. London couldn't hear me if I screamed the place down. I look all around. Check. And then I hear it. The lift, reaching our floor. The cleaners have left and it's hours before any editorial staff are due in. London's heart may beat hard out there, but I swear now that mine hammers harder. Faster.

I wait.

Nothing.

I imagined it, then. That's all. I do that, sometimes: my mind tells me stories.

I have been watching the wires and I know there has been no breaking news big enough to bring people into the office in the early hours. If something happens, the section editors may jump on and post from home but to come in now, at 2 a.m.? That's 9/11. It's Princess Diana's death. It's the 'where were you when that happened' stuff.

But then, the door slides open. Footsteps. The humming machines, waiting for the touch of the morning, are no longer a comfort. Louder.

I was wrong, I'm not imagining anything. And whoever is coming, there is only one person they are coming here for in the middle of the night. I am the only one who would be here. There's no more time for standing still and I head, fast, towards the fire escape stairs. Best to avoid the lifts. Then I hear it again, that tread. Male. You know, don't you, as a woman, the threat of a male tread, coming at speed towards you. When you weigh eight stone and fear is spreading through your body like lava, that tread sounds like that of a giant. I am running now, but I am too late.

Would you believe it? Here I am, about to die, on what was supposed to be my wedding night.

Chapter 1

Six Weeks Earlier

It was January, a Tuesday like any other so I cycled from my flat in Stoke Newington, through a Dalston already whistling with the chat of market traders in thick padded coats and beanies. I skirted the edge of Victoria Park, hit Mile End and then landed on the river around Limehouse, speeding up at that point as I was – typically – late.

In the lift, I pulled my helmet off and let my breathing slow. I took my phone out of my pocket. 6.06 a.m., just over an hour after our night editor Will Frost would have left the building. I pulled the back of my jumper from my T-shirt and let a little air touch my body. I looked in the lift mirror. My cheeks looked angry and slapped.

The door opened on my floor, and I hit the button and walked into the office and there it was: the London skyline. Well, sort of. In summer you could take pictures for your Facebook of the sunrises from the windows but today was the third week of January. The darkest of dark. There wasn't a lot to see. I yawned. Smoothed down the deep brown bob that was always a little rumpled by my helmet. The computer hummed a tune as I wiggled the mouse, and I wiggled my toes in thick black tights into ankle boots, kicking off my commuter Asics under the desk.

Will had left a water bottle behind after the night shift and I tucked that away too, into the top drawer. It wasn't the first time I'd done that. Things were as they always were on our desk, our miniature home. We had these little habits, Will and I.

I sat back in my chair, which still contained a trace of human warmth, and thought of Will, heading home to bed. I wasn't tired by then, exactly, with the adrenalin of the bike ride, but still I felt a shot of envy. I had been sleeping badly lately. I felt it again, in my belly. A jitteriness. A chatter.

I thought about Will pulling a duvet up, up and over about now. Letting eyes fall closed. We are the twain, Will and I, and never shall we meet. We're as intimate as we are anonymous, the night editor, the day editor, Will's shift finishing at 5 a.m., mine – the first one on the team – starting at 6 a.m. That hour in the middle is covered on a rota by a junior member of staff, blurry eyed on a laptop from home.

I looked around. Exhaled. I could treat myself to such luxuries as a leisurely exhale when there was no one there to make me hold my breath in fear. When I looked up, I spotted the Post-it on the side of the screen. That familiar handwriting. 'Homepage could do with a refresh. Everything else on handover email. WF.'

The roll of my eyes was habit rather than annoyance, too. This was standard. Will never refreshed the homepage before leaving so that my day usually started off with a scramble to prioritise a slew of news, heart pounding at how time sensitive it all was, while everyone else – ambling in at 7.30, 8 – got to have a relaxed coffee while they spooned cereal into their mouths at their desks and surreptitiously checked Facebook on their company iPads. My stomach growled and I copied, pasted, copied, pasted, my eyes scanning everything that had been happening in the world. The smatter of the juicier end of politics we covered as a tabloid, the ridiculous, the bizarre, the celebrity break-ups, the football, the award ceremony that went on in LA and the stuff that was pinging in as we went, happening in the world – and over the wires – that very second. Despite how hard things had been for the last few months, news still gave me a buzz.

But then, something stopped me in my tracks. There it was, right at the bottom of the news homepage. One of those stories Will would put up two or three times a week. The ones I *knew* were meant for me and contained a message. I couldn't prove it. If I brought it up, it would sound crazy. But I knew. I felt my fingers shake as I unpublished this one, like I had done so many others. *What is your game, Will?*

All the while, I listened out for my boss, Douglas. Coming into work early, fuelled on a double shot, and coming too for me. Raging, about something, nothing, everything. Not yet, Douglas. Not until I've caught up. My fingers couldn't go fast enough as I scrolled through. Moved, swapped, sorted. 'Thanks again, Will,' I muttered.

The same irritations crop up daily and I've got zero doubt it's the same from Will's perspective. Habits as everyday as a wife smoothing down her husband's hair on his way out of the door. Comfort in foibles; irritation in the familiar.

A major fire in the Midlands, some record-breaking football transfer fee. Then I spotted the big one: someone from *The Only Way Is Essex* had had what was known in these circles of ours as a 'wardrobe malfunction' on a red carpet. Copy, paste. I knew what was going at the top of the page. Above me was the looming chart that told us which stories were a success and how many clicks they were getting in real time. Whether they were going up, going down. Where people were finding them. How long they spent on each story. Where those people 'went' afterwards. Numbers, arrows, flashes of red. Nothing human; no one visible. Just endless, endless data.

It makes your heart pound with adrenalin, with fear, with pressure, with pride, that chart. As something starts to gather pace, or doesn't do what it should do. As you see it soar or sink, and it feels like the same is happening to you. I made sure 'Nip Slip' was in the keywords. Added in seven extra pictures. All the same, just very slightly different angles. Keep readers on that page for a few seconds longer before they moved on; help those stats. Tweak, tweak, tweak, until it sticks. I glanced nervously at the chart. Save. Done. Now a minute to grab a coffee, surely, before I had to come back to see what had happened to the traffic.

My heart rate slowed, ever so slightly. But then, as I went to stand, my phone beeped. Patrick, with a long message about his mother wanting to do a speech at our wedding. *It's not tradition I know but it means a lot to her, could we do it? Do you mind? Sorry to bug you about it in work, I meant to ask you last night xx.*

The feeling in my belly came back. Speeches. Dances. Vows. Being watched all day. My jaw tightened. I hadn't always been like this. Before, I couldn't wait for our big, beautiful wedding. Now, things were different. I physically shook away the thought of why, of what had changed, forcing myself to think instead about Patrick's proposal. Just us in a beautiful log cabin in the Highlands. It had been May but late enough at night that outside was pure blackness and inside was lit only by candles. The fire roared and Patrick poured the champagne. Without me noticing, he slipped a box from under the cushion next to us on the sofa. Then he slipped down onto the floor and I screamed with laughter. The most unfamiliar, familiar moment. The definition of surreal.

I didn't get chance to say yes because the fire was open and where he had jumped down was right in front of it and it was about to burn his back, but half a glass of champagne later I clarified that it was a yes. 'If you hadn't got that.'

We cackled like witches, we were half-mad, and then we phoned Patrick's parents and mine, then our sisters and heard our joy echoed back at us until we realised it was two o'clock in the morning and we should let them sleep.

I smiled at the memory. Perspective. *It's fine for your mum to do a speech, love*, I replied.

Then I went for my coffee. In the queue at the canteen, I didn't need to say a word.

'American-o,' Mo sang to me.

I laughed. He knew my order because I was there for the same thing three times on a good day, more on

8

a bad one. *It's subsidised*, was how we justified it. *We are very important journalists, far too busy to boil kettles*, was the other way. As I walked back into the office, I glanced at the screen on my phone and then the one on the wall; saw the *TOWIE* story starting to gain traction and zoom higher up the ranks.

'BUS CRASHHHHHH!'

I jumped, even though I should have been used to this by now. My boss Douglas had arrived at work while I had been in the canteen and was punching the air in delight at death. At horror. At misery. All of his favourite things. And all before 8 a.m.! I steeled myself, all memories of romance in the Highlands banished.

'LOADS of them dead!' he shouted. I looked up. Yep. A right old glint in his eye now. He twizzled back round to his screen like he was making his entrance on *X Factor*, about to kick off Big Band Week. 'And it's going up! 10! 12! 15! Fucking hell guys, this might be one of the biggest fatalities we've had in MONTHS!'

I stared at him. This is why we loathed him. The only thing he cared about was news. His favourite type though, without any doubt, was miserable news. Grim news. Death. War. Humiliation. That lot were his *raison d'etre*.

'Come on then, Rose, chop-chop,' he said, either ignoring the loathing on my face or too news-absorbed to notice it. I was the day editor, technically in charge of what went on the homepage, despite his seniority. But I was staring at my screen. Paralysed by indecision. It was happening more and more lately. Which angle to prioritise, who should write what, what my headline should be. I used to have the confidence to *know*. To trust in my own instinct. Now, I presumed I would make the wrong choice. What if I got it wrong, what if I got in trouble, what if, what if, what if, what if.

'Get someone writing this then get it top of my mother-fucking homepage, Rosie, what the fuck are you waiting for?' When I jumped, he laughed. Then he frowned at me. 'You got that, Rosie? On it? Hello, earth to Rosie?'

He flicked the back of my head, and then he was off again.

'Seventeen of them dead now! Eighteen! Young people! A recent *retiree!*'

Was it possible for a human to combust? Then, in an awed voice. 'Fuck me. Twitter says one of them was on *Bake Off.*' He looked at me, still unmoving.

'Jesus Rosie, what is *wrong* with you lately?'

I stared at him, sitting down now, spread out with arms behind his head on somebody else's chair. Rotating around on it as big as he could be, and I felt like Thumbelina. Shrunk.

What *was* wrong with me?

I knew, of course.

'Sometimes, that *girl* . . .' Douglas was already bellowing to anyone in listening distance. 'No nose for news. Not a journalistic insight in sight. Sits there staring into space. I do wonder whether I was drunk that day I promoted her. Was I pissed? Anyone remember?'

There was a light, uncomfortable titter. Douglas had moved on quickly though, busy counting dead people and I was expected to do the same. But I was thinking, *No, you weren't pissed.* I pictured the woman who had walked into that job interview nine months ago. Prepped, enthusiastic, smart. I already worked here and it was a big step up, but I had felt ready. Able.

'What would you say if I said we had other candidates who were hotter on news than you?' Douglas had said that day, sitting back in his chair so that the headrest lolled back with him and smirking at me, pleased with the challenging question he had learned on his How To Be A Dick When Doing An Interview course.

I had smiled back at him. Smoothed down the midnight blue silk blouse I had bought for the interview. Glanced at the pictures behind him. Douglas, posing in front of a Range Rover with a private number plate. Holding his stomach in at the beach with – I presume – a wife who was very definitely not smiling. With ten or twelve other men on a boat spraying champagne.

'Well,' I had said, thoughtfully. 'I would say that we hire – very successfully – news reporters who are on it with news. My job would be to motivate them. To get the best out of a team. To strike the right balance of content on the homepage. I would also say that I may not have the background of court reporting and door-stepping that some people have, but I do have news sense. I think I've demonstrated that time and time again in my current job. But I also have a lot of other skills that this role needs, and I'm confident that mix makes me the right person for it.'

I had felt a slight vibration in my belly. I *wanted* that job. I smiled, bright red lipstick, confidence and my eyes trained on his. 'Does that answer the question?'

Douglas stood up and walked to his office door. 'Yes Rosie, it does, and we're done now. We had a lot of external candidates though. All kinds of experience. So don't get your hopes up, love.'

But forty-eight hours later, he had offered me the job.

'What would you like me on, Rose?' asked our junior reporter Eddie, and I snapped out of eight months ago and everything that had happened since that moment, and back into the now. I needed to get it together and get on this story.

'Live blog it please Eddie. Get it up ASAP.'

I spun my chair round and briefed the rest of the team on what was needed, then drank my cold black coffee while I moved their stories round the site and tweaked here and there. Then, drink in one hand, I logged into my emails and read Will's overnight handover.

I felt the usual flicker of irritation. Instruction after instruction after request after job for me to do. None of which was technically a problem – and all of it was part of our role as two sides of the same coin – but it was the lack of warmth in it that always bothered me. We exchanged a lot of information, Will and I. We gave each other a lot of help. We asked a great deal of each other, unable to get to all we needed to during our hours despite them being as long as they were. Push, pull – two sides of the same role. People describe having work spouses; I thought at times that Will was more like a work twin, especially since – according to Douglas – we were the same age, recently turning thirty within weeks of each other. Being civil though, friendly, making the odd joke even: to me that was fundamental. Not to Will.

'Shall we try for a coffee one time, in between our shifts?' I asked, many times. You do, over eight months.

'Need sleep,' came the reply. Or sometimes, simply: 'Nah, can't do.'

Such a shame they hide you away in the night-time, I thought, reading that day's instalment with its absence of greeting or sign–off as usual. *What a charmer.*

I didn't know it would be the last instalment I'd get. The last time we did this dance. Will would come back to the office for a shift that evening, but disappear before there was a chance to write the handover. When I next sat in this chair, there would be no trace of human warmth. No trace of Will Frost at all. Not here. Not anywhere, actually.

Chapter 2

'This would be more effective if you weren't checking the news, chick,' said Rania, our company physio, with her soft Geordie lilt. 'It doesn't help relax those muscles.'

Her hands kneaded into my forearm; my other arm was outstretched, refreshing the news wires. De-tense. Tense. I refreshed.

It was 2 p.m., seven hours since I'd come into work. Other than the bus crash – which, though it galled me to admit it, had done well on the chart – it had been a slow news day. But they're *exactly* the type that get you. Start off slow, end with a high-profile celebrity coming out, a big football transfer or a nipple falling out of a jumpsuit. I couldn't get complacent.

Please don't leave Leicester for Man City. Please don't leave your wives. Just for half a bloody hour, while I get my RSI seen to, can you all for the love of God keep your nipples in your clothes.

I checked my emails with my one hand. Deleted sixty-five of them straight away. Seven more had appeared when I refreshed again.

'You know it's a big enough deal they let me come here at all,' I told Rania, one eyebrow raised. Despite my half-attention, we had formed a friendship since she started treating me a year ago. I had been at the company for two years by then. 'I can't just go off radar.'

She shook her head. 'That place,' she sighed. '*Let* you come. They're the reason you have RSI, the lack of breaks, the relentlessness . . . It's not going "off radar". It's attending your necessary physio appointment.'

But then she picked up where she'd left off last week about an ex who lived in Amsterdam and how he wanted to get back with her, but she has moved on and something about a new lover, and I zoned out, back on the wires. I came to when she physically removed my phone from my right hand and put it in the left one so she could start kneading on the other side. She had stopped arguing with me. Her fingers plugged into minimal flesh and I noticed I had got thinner. There was no intent. Sometimes lately I just didn't know how other people remembered to eat three times a day.

I looked up. As ever, there was the slight smell of sweat in the room. Rania eschewed deodorant and rubbed lemons in her armpits instead, and somehow, on her, that didn't offend. I had no idea how she got away with it at work, but there was always a dim trace of weed too. 'I lived in Amsterdam for a long time, chick,' she said with a wink when I mentioned it once. 'Old habits die hard.' And then she offered me a spliff and I recoiled and repeated over and over that I was at *work* and she fell around laughing because she cleary hadn't been serious. Though, she pointed out, it probably would make a day with 'that fuckwit boss' upstairs a damn sight more bearable. She had only heard about Douglas, of course: though she treated people from the multiple companies who owned or rented offices in this building, she hardly ever saw anyone else from the website.

'Ow!'

She held a hand up – fingers that had just pushed too hard into my skin – in apology. Rania's hands were rainbows, a different bright shade on each nail, and I imagined having the time to paint my nails again. With this job – *your dream job, Rose, remember, your dream job* – I was too exhausted for self-care. The truth is that I was consumed by this place. I was at capacity. At any given second all I had room for was news. All I could make space for was the chart, the wires. But this was what it was, doing your dream job, it was like having a child: it was *supposed* to consume you, wasn't it? Otherwise . . . what was the point?

I often wondered how it was for Will. If we could bond over it, the all-consuming nature of this place.

'How's the elusive *Will Frost*?' Rania asked, as though she could read my mind. She asked as though we were talking about a fictional character. Which, in a way, we were. I winced as she kneaded hard and I heard the bones in my forearm click. I shrugged.

'Still can't get a meeting in. Still no chat over a coffee. Still can't be sure our night editor isn't a computer-generated robot.'

'It could be true!' she said, a voice full of fun. 'A cyborg they wheel in in the evening. That would be SO your place; can't get anyone who can post enough per hour. There's only one thing for it: robot.'

I smiled. 'Robot wouldn't need physio.'

'Or to stop for – ugh, lazy fuckers – toilet breaks.'

16

I laughed. 'Just one problem. Explain the water bottle on the desk.'

'Look, even cyborgs can't bear single use plastic.'

She shrieked with genuine mirth at her own joke, and it was catching. I looked up from my phone for the first time. Rania's eyes creased and I realised I had no idea how old she was. Thirties? Forties? We did this, the kneading of my arms, the battle over my phone, every week. Even went for the odd after-work vodka and tonic. How did I not know that about her?

'I'm sorry I always talk about me,' I told her. 'About this place.' I looked at her tattoo. Sanscrit on her inside wrist, a little glimpse of who Rania was alongside the anonymising medical blue tunic and trousers. 'Sorry I never ask you about you.'

Then it happened again. The odd thing that had been happening to me lately. Sweat saturated my back. I was crying, apologising for it between sobs.

Rania held my hand as I struggled to breathe.

'How old are you?' I managed to ask.

'Old enough to know when someone needs a rest,' she said, brow furrowed. 'Thank God the wedding means you're finally taking time off.'

I didn't say anything. I was entitled to twenty-five days of holiday. But most of the time it felt like it was impossible to walk up to Douglas with a form and expect to use those days on a real-life break. Rania budged me up on the bed and we sat alongside each other.

'I'm embarrassed,' I said, knuckles digging deep in the corners of my eyes. It had stopped now. I felt normal. Nearly normal.

'Look,' she sighed, 'technically I am the building's physio. But chick, everyone knows I'm the therapist. Everyone tells me their troubles. Everyone confides in me. So don't think this is the first time I've seen someone cry on this bed, okay?'

I nodded. It was all I could manage.

'Maybe on these handovers of yours, you should leave a note to Will Frost,' she said with a tentative smile. 'Feels like that dude – apologies, apologies, that robot – could have a few issues to talk through as well. Perhaps it would help?'

I smiled. 'And at the very least, running the site alone all night must mean wrist issues to rival mine.'

'You can bet on it, chick.'

Ten minutes later I left, via the canteen for an Americano in place of lunch. Douglas shouted at me for being away when a rugby player's old tweets had just come to light showing him doing a Nazi salute. I opened my mouth to say it was a pre-booked appointment, that I had told everyone before I went, but he held his hand up to shush me.

'If you're a journalist, you're a journalist,' he said. 'News doesn't wait while you go downstairs to whine about your sore wrist.'

But even as I sat in my swivel chair and Douglas loomed above, as large as the chart, lecturing me, I knew it had been worth it. Not just for the physio, but for the dose of humanity. I sipped my black coffee and tried to let his words wash over me.

Our night editor came to mind again. Where did you get your dose of humanity from, Will, glued to a screen for twelve hours across the dark of the night?

When Douglas finally stalked off to make someone else's life harder, I messaged Will. 'Really would like to do that coffee at some point. It's so weird I've never met you in real life!'

Three years we had worked loosely together. It was in the last eight months though, since I'd been day editor, getting in first, collecting Will's invisible baton, sharing that desk, that the need to know one another had grown in me.

But Will never replied to that message. Not even when it hit 5, 6 p.m. and I knew it would be time to get up, ready for the night shift. Will waking up, pulling on work clothes, even though no one would ever see them. Slipping on trainers for the commute.

Or so I pictured it. Like I say, I didn't see Will Frost in real life. Our night editor could have been a robot. A robot, or anyone at all.

Chapter 3

I was cycling home, weaving my way down a back street in Hackney, when I felt my phone vibrate in my pocket. I stopped to read the message, wobbling with one foot on the kerb.

Patrick. 'We need to leave in ten minutes. Where are you? xx'

Shit. Supper with Patrick's oldest and best friend, the man we still call School Friend Sam, and Eloise the fiancée who will corner me and want to chat about the wildflower bombs she's chosen for her wedding favours. They will have done three courses of Nigella. School Friend Sam will have been sent to their local wine shop earlier with instructions to get a couple of reds from a small producer. Being late wasn't an option. I should have bought flowers, or some sort of succulent. Chocolates from that fancy chocolatier in Camden Passage, round the corner from their flat in a beautiful side street near the canal in Angel, the smell of spiced hot chocolate following me and my tiny, neat bag, swinging our way out of the door. That was how we did things, but today I had done none of them. I felt my heart pick up to a canter again. I was dropping the middle-class balls.

I started pedalling again. Faster. I looked around. It was helpful to get up some speed anyway, in case anyone on this quiet road was in the market for murdering me.

I had started cycling to and from work when it became obvious that I was never going to do the lunchtime runs I'd planned on when I started at the newspaper. I'd completed my first half-marathon the year before and had been hoping, then, to apply for the 2008 London Marathon.

'*And* they've got a gym in the building!' I'd told Patrick after my first day at the website as we sat on the sofa unwrapping burritos. I hadn't stopped talking since I had got in, hyped from my first day working at such a huge, buzzing company. Every time I went to take a bite, I would stop, as I remembered something else I needed to tell him.

'Did I mention they have a shower?'

'I would think so, if they have a gym. Pretty stinky place to work otherwise.' He had raised an eyebrow, and I laughed.

Patrick took a large bite of his burrito but I could still see his grin, and how happy he was that I liked the new job. My own dinner cooled, the chicken wrap fat in my hand.

'Seriously though,' I sighed. 'The place is incredible. And the job too. Finally I get to write something *real*.'

It had felt brilliant. Until then I had been working at a copywriting agency, producing content for brands. When I had graduated with a history degree, a family friend of Patrick's parents had got me in on work experience and my timing had been good – they were expanding and hiring and I was junior and cheap and somehow I had stayed there for four years.

Now though, now there was something to get my *teeth* into. Something to prove myself at. I could do my old job by then with my eyes closed. Sometimes I did, to be honest, for about twenty minutes after lunch if I'd had a late night. Working for a national newspaper though – that felt like a grown-up job. A real job. *My* job. I fizzed with it like shaken-up Coke.

'And, and . . . what a place to go running!' I could barely get my words out fast enough. 'Along the Thames every lunchtime! This is going to be amazing for my PB, I'll be out there every day.'

Ha, I thought, reliving that conversation now. The reality? *Once*, I've seen daylight on my lunch break, when I had a headache and was desperate for air. Other than that I go into the adjoining building to grab pre-packaged sandwiches, air-con, not air, necessity, not care, and then I race back as fast as I can, my heart thumping a little faster than it should and my jaw locked in position. The fear I have missed something. The fear of the chart. That's my lot, as far as lunch breaks go.

So, to make up for the lack of movement, the lack of non-recycled air, the fact that I stopped running and never came close to that marathon, I started cycling to and from work. It was more functional.

'I think that's where Will Frost's place is, too,' Douglas said to me once in a rare moment on the topic of my real life when I mentioned cycling and where I lived.

Something in me had instantly regretted that, like I was exposing too much of myself. Like he was someone I should seal myself off from. Protect myself from. After that though, I thought I saw Will everywhere in my local area. The pub, the book shop, the butcher's when I nipped in for a leg of lamb for Patrick and I to roast for friends at the weekend. I looked at flats wondering if they were Will's – the ex-council block opposite Clissold Park, the rows of converted Victorian terraces off Church Street. The one with the hanging baskets preening over the side of the balcony. The one that still hadn't taken their brown bin back in on *Tuesday*.

But really I couldn't picture Will in any of them, perhaps because it was hard – near impossible – to imagine our night editor having a real life. 'Dalston way,' continued Douglas, waving an arm in the direction of East London, like Southerners do to the North of England. 'Lucky buggers. The missus has me out in Kent these days. The schools, the schools, the bloody schools.' And off he went.

Because he was the kind of man who called his wife 'the missus'. The kind of man who didn't know that the ten-minute monologue on the school system he wheeled out often made the eyes of his child-free colleague glaze over.

I burst through the door, shouting the word sorry over and over and pulling off my helmet and then my clothes as I walked towards the shower. Patrick pushed the door open as I was soaping up my armpits.

'You know you've been in that office for twelve hours?' He sighed like that was news and not a standard issue day. I ran a razor quickly across my skin. Slice. Slice. Blunt. A little blood trickled down my side. Patrick didn't notice. He stood next to the loo and leaned back against the wall. He exhaled deeply and I looked up, noted it because Patrick was not a sigher. Weary was not his adjective. Patrick was a puppy and he bounded into rooms with bags of Haribo and a plan to go to a karaoke bar. 'I know it's your dream job . . .'

My stomach flipped as I remembered those thoughts I'd had earlier. I worked these hours, dreamt about the chart, scrolled news when I was getting physio because this was my Dream Job, capital letters, official narrative. So, no. No. Don't think it. I couldn't let myself think it.

But I *did* think. I thought of the way Douglas spoke to me and the way he exclaimed over people dying, and how last week the five strongest stories were all to do with women under twenty-two in various states of undress.

A wave roared over my head. What if I did all this, let everything else slide, and it *wasn't* my dream job anymore? But it had only been eight months since I was promoted from news writer. I *wanted* the long hours, the pressure, the highs, the lows, the adrenalin. I did. Didn't I? Or had I changed too much now? Was this a job for the old me?

I looked down at the floor of the shower; the water pooling around my toes, tinged red with my blood. Patrick left the bathroom and I turned the shower off. Stepped out. Grabbed a towel. And as I stemmed the blood from my armpit I wished I could speak to someone who might understand. I wanted to speak to Will. But I couldn't. Because I was about to go to School Friend Sam's house and eat truffle gnocchi and drink an ethical Rioja. And because by the time I had finished all of that, Will Frost would have disappeared, in the dead of night, from the chair we shared, the chair I would sit in, doing the same job, living the same life, just an hour later and I wouldn't cycle home again for a while. Because I would be absolutely terrified that I would disappear too.

Chapter 4

Thirty is perfect, thirty is hell, thirty is everything, the cusp, the precipice, grown-up child, all the contradictions, the beginning, the end. When you are thirty, you must be fun and stay up late, but you must remember the birthday card and the contents insurance. You must be top of your career, but you must also have a life beyond that, healthy eggs ready to turn into babies and a partner – an enthusiastic, committed one – to make that happen. You need a pension – do you not have a pension yet, wow – and you need an ISA but also you need a deposit for a three-bed with a small garden and original features in Leyton. You need hobbies too, of course, because you don't want to not be well rounded and you need a plethora of friendship groups, which by now should line up as follows: school friends, university friends, work friends, friends of your partner's who you have regular dinners with and count, really, as your own friends.

You need to stay late at work, get across town to the engagement drinks and have breakfast at 9 a.m. the next day with your friend who has the baby and has to get back for naptime. You are both. You are all. Don't drop a ball. Why would you want to drop a ball? All the balls are fun, see. You're lucky! You have everything. You're 30. Now, seriously, about that pension.

I thought about all that while Eloise told me about her bouquet and I smiled and then felt my breath come quickly, too quickly. That feeling again as well – a weighted blanket on my stomach.

We had money, my friends and I, bona fide salaries as opposed to the starting pocket money we existed on when we moved to London. School Friend Sam, like Patrick, works in banking but that's just an extension of their money because they don't just have money, they are the noun too, they *are moneyed* in the old sense. To be something is deeply rooted; to have something can always be transient.

If I am moderately middle-class, Patrick and School Friend Sam sit firmly in the old-school uppers. Their parents own art. There are wine cellars. School was boarding and private with a house dog named Coco and that was as everyday a teenage existence as crowded buses to local comps are to the rest of the world. When Patrick speaks of home, he will always, as long as he lives, refer to Foxlands, where he will head back for the annual family sports day and where a pigeon is as likely a supper – it's supper not dinner and it's only tea if it's a 5 p.m. sandwich – as a chicken. When he asks someone where they went to school, he will expect to know the name of it, even if it wasn't in his town. The same applies to most things: I've learned since being with Patrick that upper-class people use proper nouns more often than the

27

bog-standard kind. They don't tell you they're going to a hotel this weekend, they tell you they are going to Cliveden or Babington. They aren't going to a nice restaurant; they are going to Scott's or St. John. They expect you to know their reference points, because their reference points are, to them, the world. When we first met, and I told him I had never skied, Patrick looked genuinely confused.

'Prosecco?' asked Eloise, a commoner like me (in relative terms – my parents lived in a four-bedroomed house in a village in Hertfordshire and Eloise grew up riding horses in Somerset).

'Lovely!' Patrick boomed. He looked happy, despite my lateness, and it made me smile. I reached for his hand and squeezed, my thumb gently stroking his palm. We drank and toasted, before we sat down to pan-fried scallops.

I apologised, profusely, for my lack of succulents and Eloise pointed to the windowsill. 'We aren't short of succulents, Rose.' Her laugh zoomed straight to her eyes.

'Anyway, to your wedding!' she said, her cheeks pink and plump and happy. 'Only six weeks to go!'

'And to your wedding!' I echoed. 'Only . . .'

Oh God. I tried very hard to picture the invite on our bookshelf. I knew I had RSVPd to it because I remembered doing six wedding RSVPs and two hen dos in one week and mentioning it to Patrick. He looked gleeful, like that was good news, and I felt like something was pinching at my ribs. School Friend Sam cleared the plates.

'. . . six months to go!' filled in Patrick, charging his

glass into the air. He laughed lightly. 'I should know. Need to start collecting stories for that best man speech.'

I watched him masticate a scallop and I thought about speeches, and how I would arrange my face when it came to our turn and everything, everything blurred into that chewing jaw.

Eloise putting a plate of dumplings in front of me snapped me out of a trance. 'It's lovely seeing your natural curls, Rose,' she said, with affection. 'You never normally let them escape.' Her own hair fell into her eyes, poker straight and a muddy brown and parted down the middle like a sandwich. I needed to straighten mine into submission to get anything close to that effect, and tonight there hadn't been time.

I smiled at her, touched my curls self-consciously. 'This looks amazing. And those scallops!'

'Yes, don't let me leave without that recipe,' Patrick said, launching a fork into his own gnocchi. I ate and smiled and life felt good but sometime during that delicious bowl of gnocchi, things blurred and as they talked, I still managed to drift. Up and up like a kite, away from this chat and its age-appropriate themes of weddings and best man speeches and good wine to somewhere other, somewhere entirely removed, a whole world of its own. I pictured the homepage. I pictured the chart. I pictured data. My fingers twitched to read news, to do a quick scan, just to make sure. It owned you, that place, so that you longed to be anywhere but there all day long and then when you left, in the pit of your mind you realised you could be only there, you had lived and breathed it so deeply for twelve hours. The world was not the world if it wasn't accompanied by the ebbs and flows of the news agenda. If I wasn't clicking through fifteen or twenty other news sites to check I hadn't missed anything. The world was not the world if it didn't have floor-to-ceiling glass and a constantly moderated temperature. Switching off was laughable. Not knowing what was happening in the world for three whole hours was impossible. I was switched on, turned up bright, ready. Sleep was no longer deep, rest was pointless; I twitched for it like an addict but the drug didn't hit the spot anymore.

And yet, I used to love it. All of it. The buzz had been as sharp as coffee.

I looked down at my plate and put my fork down. I took a sip of wine. Three years, I had been at that place but it was only lately that I had felt like this. In the distance, I heard Eloise laugh, uproarious and real.

'Just nipping to the loo,' I said, and I sat in there scrolling, for as long as was not weird. I saw what Will was doing with the homepage and the stories that had been chosen and relaxed a little. Will did a good job. Even if it was done with the humour of a cyborg, it was a good job.

As I flushed the unused toilet, I checked something else. Facebook, where my request to be Will Frost's friend still sat there, unanswered, pending, alongside the suitably blank silhouette.

And pending – after what happened later that night – is where it would remain. People don't accept you as a friend on Facebook, see, when they're likely deep below the waters of the Thames. People don't accept you as a friend on Facebook when they are – everyone presumed when they talked about it in whispers in the kitchen, I heard them – as dead as the people in that bus crash. Funnily enough, no one live blogged that one.

Chapter 5

When I came out of the loo, I necked my wine to make up for lost time. I then necked a few more and barely touched the cheesecake they had made for dessert. I was back in the room, or I wasn't floating above it at least, or hiding in the bathroom. But I was very, very drunk.

'Rose, come with me, it's time to leave,' whispered Patrick into the frizz at my temples.

I looked at him. Grinned, I am sure in retrospect, the alarmingly stained grin of someone who had drunk at least six glasses of ethically produced red wine. Then I frowned at my fiancé, who had also drunk some red wine, if probably less than me. 'How are your teeth so WHITE?'

He ignored the question but we all knew the answer anyway, I thought, wise with wine: *breeding.*

'It's weird how you can tell posh faces, isn't it?' I mused with a slur. 'Like, you can just TELL if a person is posh? From their face. And teeth. Weird.'

Eloise snorted with laughter and I liked it and it made me snort too and then we were 15 in the back row in history class, and the giggles wouldn't stop.

'But it's true!' I shouted through our giggles. Breeding gives you white teeth and it gives you confidence and it gives you an ability to look down a 150-bottle strong wine list and say without dithering, without so much as a 'What do you recommend?', that you'll have the 2005 Roble, thanks, and when the waiter walks away you won't turn to your friend and go, 'Was that okay? Should we have just had the house? Are you sure you didn't want white? Do you even want a drink? Honestly, if you want to just can tonight I won't be offended.' You will be assured, and your smile will gleam.

No one knows why but those are the things breeding does. I try to replicate it. I send the thank you cards instead of the thank you texts. I put Aesop in the bathroom when people come round and hide the Carex. I iron tailored trousers and buy expensive ballet pumps. But you can't fake it in the end. Breeding knows.

'I have an 8 a.m. meeting and it's nearly midnight, Rose, I really need to go home.' Patrick was pleading with me by then but through my giggles, it was like he was issuing a dare. Eloise moved my glass slightly further away from my elbow. She had such a lovely face. I wanted to stroke her nose, squish her rosy cheeks between my thumb and index finger. 'Oh, she can stay!' she said, her own laughter subsiding. 'If she likes.'

Patrick took his phone out of his pocket, glanced at the time. That sigh again. 'She has to be in work early herself. She'll feel even worse than me. She starts at 6 a.m.!'

I looked at the floor.

'D'you know what, if you're going to be so stubborn about it, stay.' Half a smile. 'God you're going to regret this when that sadistic boss of yours sees you in the morning.' He shrugged. 'But I'm not your keeper.'

When Patrick had gone home, School Friend Sam went to bed and Eloise sauntered across their large open-plan flat to make me a coffee. I laughed when she put it in front of me, and then I chanted: 'Red wine, red wine, red wine.'

The next bottle was just from Waitrose. The small producers were clearly, at this juncture, wasted on me. When I finished the glass, Eloise brought me a pair of her pyjamas with tiny sheep all over them. 'They'll be massive on you but at least they'll be cosy,' she smiled. 'The spare bedroom is made up ready so it really is no bother.'

But suddenly, I needed air. The dare was up.

'It's okay,' I slurred, accepting. 'I need to go home. Own bed. He's right, I have work in the morning.'

'Do you remember much of last night?' asked an unusually po-faced Patrick when he woke me up for work with a black coffee. I shook my head, which throbbed.

'Go easy on me. I really do feel bad.'

Worse than bad. How could I keep doing this? I pictured that last red wine. Tasted it. But Patrick kissed me then pulled me into a tight hug. 'It's just . . .' I looked up, as he ducked his eyes. 'It's happening a lot lately. That's all.' He passed me my phone, which was on the duvet next to me. 'That's been beeping all night,' he said. He was getting frown lines around those big, enthusiastic blue eyes.

'Sorry, love.' I kissed him, and he walked out of the room as I clicked into my email. I would have to admit defeat: I couldn't be in work on time. But before I could type to Douglas, I saw them. Forty-eight emails to the group list, from our whole team, a lot even on a big news night. Last night had been the Golden Globes, precursors to the Oscars. Beautiful images; cleavage aplenty. It was us all over.

But our site – or more specifically Will – hadn't even mentioned it. Various members of the team had tried to message, some wondering if there was a tech issue and whether they could jump on laptops and help from home, but most just to rant. Emails flooding in. No one knowing why there was no reply. Berating and mocking, in full view of the whole team – Will would have been on the email list too. *Useless old night editor: probably fallen asleep.* The later messages said they had tried to call the office, but there was no answer.

And then, there was the most recent.

'We reported Will Frost missing this morning,' said Douglas, in an email to the team. I heard myself suck in my breath. 'This is now an ongoing police investigation.'

'Fuck!'

But still I had room to loathe Douglas. How he loved it: being inside the story for once. Real-life news! I could hear the faux solemnity. How he loved the gravitas, too, of his role as the deliverer of the information.

Did Will hate him, I wondered, like I did? Did he hound Will, like he had hounded me in the eight months since I started this job? Was it better when his interference came via email, on the phone, all night long, when at least he wasn't there in your face? Or without colleagues, without buffers, all alone in the quiet of the night, was it even worse?

I showered quickly, and didn't tell Patrick what had happened. There was no time and surely, anyway, it would remedy itself and there would be nothing to tell soon. Then I took a deep breath and headed into work, to find out what the hell was going on.

I had never met Will Frost. But there was an almost. One time when I got into the building early and caught a glimpse. A face staring straight ahead, not a flicker of emotion. And then gone, through the turnstile on the other side of the building. Before the mask came down though, there was a split second when Will did turn to face me. Recognition? I suspect so. Eyes half shut. Not tall, not small. If a label had promised that shirt was crease-free, it was lying. Classic journo, I thought. The dishevelled look just showed you cared, see. That you were serious about news. That you would never miss the chance to do one more news story by doing something so real-life-y as *ironing* or staying abreast of fashion. A true journalist lives hard and fast, you work twelve-hour shifts and you drink the bar dry. Clothes? Clothes are just a necessity. Now file your bloody copy.

Will fitted that bill, exactly. That creased shirt, then, with a grown-up version of boys' school trousers functioned as a work uniform, even though in the solitary hours of the night shift, no one would ever know if it was trackie bottoms and a football shirt.

Yes, I noticed the clothes. But the most noticeable thing that day, in that fleeting second of a sighting, was the paleness of Will Frost's skin. God, it was almost transparent. The lack of sleep, I imagine, not to mention never seeing daylight. That's the night shift for you. In the weeks after Will went missing, our night editor began to feel other-worldly. But you know what? Will Frost had already had the feel of a ghost, right from the very beginning.

Chapter 6

In my drunk sleep, I had been there again. And no matter how hard and fast I cycled – being late was an even bigger deal now I knew that Will had missed most of the night shift and how behind that had left us – the snapshots wouldn't leave my mind. One after the next. We had called it Chaos Night, the night of midsummer, when 10.30 p.m. felt like 7 p.m. and we drank into the early hours. Last June's had been the final sunny day before a week of rain would come, and we were waiting for the humidity to break. The sky was tense; the day in work – the summer news lull seeming to start early and Douglas stalking the place looking for somebody to blame – had been tense too. So we aimed for the opposite of tension; we aimed for release. We burst like rain clouds.

Release is most easily found, if you look around Canary Wharf, in bottles of average Pinot Grigio and equally average beer in chain bars. You can find it more easily if you shun the food menus, with their halloumi wraps and their chicken and chorizo burgers, and simply order another bottle of Pinot Grigio instead.

And we did.

Again.

Again.

Again.

Colleagues landed, one after the next. Ordered another bottle of wine, a few pints. Work disappeared. Top-ups splashed onto the table. No one counted.

The next morning, when I woke up in an unknown bedroom in an unknown flat, I remembered nothing. Drinking was nothing new to me, but this – a complete and total blackout – was. I had a deep sense that something was very wrong.

I looked around me. It was fancy, this flat, in a way that straight away said Canary Wharf not Hackney, Mayfair not Brixton. Chrome and a giant wall-mounted TV. Buttons for everything. Slick blinds that rose to order and behind them, like in work, floor-to-ceiling glass. On the floor was a plain grey rug that could have been Ikea but probably wasn't – this place would have turned its nose up at Ikea.

I checked my phone. Fifteen missed calls from Patrick. I pictured our bedroom. There was a spider plant next to our bed. A toppling pile of *Cosmopolitan* magazines I had amassed since I had started collecting them fifteen years earlier. I wasn't slovenly but there may well have been a teacup on my dressing table, left behind in a rush. A few tops, rejected before I settled on something yesterday morning, slung unironed on the bed.

Life, before. I would have done anything then to be there, safe and warm with Patrick. Instead, I looked down at myself, in that unknown bedroom. The lovely mint-green linen dress I had chosen in an attempt to stay cool was stained with vomit. With a smear of blood. On my hand was a large gash; I had no idea where I had got it.

I was so groggy. I tried to sit up, remembering where I was. A house party. Impromptu. Lizzie, a freelancer who does fashion content for the website, one of the only other women on 'our team' announcing as the pub closed that her husband was away for the week and we should all go back there. And God, by all, she meant all. There were thirty people on the website team. A few freelancers who dipped in and out, too.

I opened the bedroom door.

Life, after.

'There you are,' Lizzie smiled, holding out a coffee to me. 'I was just coming to wake you.' She touched her own forehead lightly. It was delicate, like her, and I looked again at the gash, the vomit, and I felt my fingers go numb and an urge to rush to the toilet.

I tried hard to smile. She kept her fingertips on her forehead as she carried on: 'Someone checked on you but said you were fine, just to let you sleep because you were out of it.'

I looked at the coffee and felt the bile in my stomach curdle.

'I'm sorry, I . . .' and then I ran to her loo and threw up. When I came out, I was shaking and apologising, and she pulled me into a hug.

'Are you okay?' she said, as she moved backwards, assessed me. 'I mean apart from the hangover, obviously, but are you . . .' She looked at the blood. 'Is that . . .'

I interrupted her.

'Who checked on me?' I said.

She ignored the question, noticing a fleck of red wine on a cream wall and rubbing it with her thumb. Pointless.

'Who?' I said again but I knew I was barely audible and she had moved on.

She shuddered. 'God, I'm an idiot. Nearly forty people back to my flat. Bloody good job I've got the week off and Matt's away. It'll take me a long time to clean this.' She groaned. Then she looked up at me. 'No idea who, sorry, I'm terrible with names.'

I looked down then. Took it in. The floor was like a bin, crisp packets, beer bottles, tissues, discarded clothes. She passed me my coffee.

'Forty people?' I said, still clinging to the mug that on a normal hangover would have been the love of my life.

I remembered little. Dancing, of a sort. The drinking. Finding a bed by accident on the way back from the toilet. Having a little rest to stop the room spinning. And then, what?

'At least forty,' she winced. Her eyes followed mine to the floor. 'You were out in force.'

'Everyone?'

She shrugged. 'I don't know names but there or thereabouts. And I can't remember much after 3 a.m. God knows who was running the website.'

Under my breath, I muttered, 'Will.'

She didn't hear me, shook out a bin bag and started sweeping things into it.

'Bloody Chaos Night,' she murmured, just loud enough to hear. 'I don't know why I can't get into yoga in a field or some sort of Pagan ritual and a weekend at

Stonehenge instead of turning it into my biggest drinking night of the year every bloody June.'

I made my excuses then. Called in sick for work that day, but I went in the next day, and the one after that, and the one after that. People teased me for having been so drunk. I bantered back, because that's what we did. That's what was expected. I was back in the pub, a few days later. I didn't mention that I had woken up that night at Lizzie's, blacked out, bleeding, covered in sick. That I had woken up with my dress around my waist. With my underwear on the other side of the bed.

I didn't mention it, even though I knew that one of those colleagues of mine already knew. Because no one else had been there. And so whatever had happened to me, one of them had done it.

'Rosie Rivers! She's alive!'

When I walked into work on the morning of Will's disappearance, it was 7.20 a.m., the latest I had ever been. I had been too distracted in the end, funnily enough, by the forty-eight emails about a missing colleague to let Douglas know I would be late. I murmured an apology, pulled out my chair and sat down.

I felt a wave of nausea rush over me. With it, irritation. Douglas was never normally here until 8.30. I should at least have had some time to get myself together. Drink some coffee. Of course, angry guy that he was, when he saw the emails about the Golden Globes he had changed out of his pyjamas and stormed – I mean, in reality he got taxis, didn't he, the fancy kind he has on account – to Canary Wharf where he had planned, he told us in his emails, to give Will what for. But he didn't get a chance to wield his macho power. Will had been there earlier, the posts and stories and work from the early part of the night left an indelible mark that said so. But by the time Douglas walked into our office, our night editor was gone.

My boss's voice made me jump. 'Thought we had a second missing person on our hands for a while there!'

I didn't make any attempt at laughing, and he wandered past. Instead, I tied my hair up in a bobble and changed my shoes. I tasted wine and gagged as I leaned down. The bike ride on a hangover might have been a bit much. The dream hadn't helped.

When I came back up to my desk, I looked automatically for the Post-its. But then I remembered. There would be no Post-its on my screen today. No handover in my email.

'Any news?' I asked Richie, the sports writer who sat next to me. Everyone had turned up early today.

'Lots of it!' said Douglas, before Richie had a chance to answer. He glanced pointedly towards the chart and laid his pudgy hand on the back of my chair. Long nails, a slight curl at the ends. 'That's why it would be helpful if you got to work on time, Rosie.'

Rose. He did it deliberately. I'd corrected him on my name a hundred, a thousand times. I flinched. When I looked up it was slow and deliberate. 'I meant about Will.'

I expected something mundane, that it had turned out to be a family emergency that Will had had to leave for or a bad stomach pain that was impossible to work through. I expected mundane because life's generally mundane. Everything reset. Will coming back (to a bollocking, of course) this evening. The biggest problem in the office was returning to a junior writer getting too many cabs on account, or who was going to do a tea run.

I was thinking about my hangover, and how much I needed to get downstairs and order a large coffee from Mo, and about when I could get out of this office to devour a giant sausage sandwich. I was thinking about staying too late last night. How much I had drunk.

I was thinking about the dream. I was thinking about that night, at Lizzie's.

But something flashed across Douglas's face that brought me back to the conversation. 'Will hasn't turned up yet. And related to that actually, Rosie, I need to talk you through some stuff that we missed overnight, and what to prioritise. Can you pop into the office?'

This was a bad time for me to realise I needed to throw up, and a second realisation: it was too late for me to get to the bathroom.

I knew Douglas hated me, but I don't think he ever hated me as much as when I was sick on his designer shoes. I had had a lot of ethically produced red wine.

Chapter 7

'Cops,' murmured our picture editor Pete, who had his back to Douglas's office on the desk opposite mine. He put two hands on the back of his shiny, bald head and looked up a second from what he was typing. 'In the office. This whole thing is *fucked up.*'

'Mmm hmm,' I muttered, glancing over the top of my screen as I headlined a story about a celebrity break-up and set it live. From my desk, I could see into the office, the two police officers sitting on his sofa.

'I see someone's put himself right in the thick of things,' murmured Keiran, one of the news writers. 'What a fucking surprise.'

I looked up to where his glance was headed. Our boss was perched on the edge of his desk, as usual.

'I guess they'll speak to us all at some point,' Keiran said without looking at any of us, as we did with most things as we talked and worked, talked and worked. I gulped my coffee, already on my third at 10 a.m. I had already accepted that it was a five cup kind of day.

'If Douglas will let them,' Pete murmured, with a rub of his ginger sandpaper stubble. It was an unlikely look, paired with the shininess of his head, but there was a confident swagger in Pete, and the whole thing worked. A lot of people across the company fancied him. 'News doesn't stop for missing people, *Rosie*.'

I grimace-smiled. Richie, Pete and Keiran were the people I was closest to in the office – literally as well, as we sat at the same bank of desks – and I appreciated the lack of ribbing over the fact I had been sick earlier. Luckily my hangover had come second in the gossip stakes to Will this morning, but still: a few of the others had poked a stick at me about it. Most of them love nothing more than the usual misogynist bollocks about me not being able to handle my drink.

The dream came back to me again.

Richie interrupted my rampaging thoughts. 'How well did you all know Will?'

I turned towards him but Richie was still staring at his screen, concentrating hard. I could see images of football players that he was cropping to save the always stretched picture department a job. To help out his mate. I did it often when I knew Pete was up against it too. I turned back to my own desktop. 'Barely at all,' I said.

'Same,' said Pete across the desk. He was leaning back in his chair. Didn't seem to be working, despite the busyness. To be fair to him, we were all struggling: it was pretty hard to concentrate in the midst of this.

'Me neither,' replied Keiran, with thought. 'Will was a bit of an enigma, right?'

'I think you can use the present tense,' I said, laughing. 'Will's gone AWOL during a shift, we're not dealing with a corpse.'

'Got an inside take on that, have you? Always said there was a news hound in there, waiting to come out.' I jumped at the voice, like I always jumped at that voice. Douglas, who somehow during this chat had come out of the office without me noticing and was standing behind me. I glanced over my shoulder. Those nails hooked over my chair like they were clinging to a ledge for dear life. I felt bile rise up in my throat. Not again. Not again. I swallowed it down.

Two police officers were with Douglas. I glanced above my screen at Pete, who made a V with his fingers on his chin and looked back at me with a slight frown. Was he worried? Perhaps I had underestimated how serious this was.

'Your turn, Rose,' my boss said then, his too-white teeth bared as I turned to face him. How different to Patrick's, I thought, even though my fiancé's look was clearly the one he'd paid a lot of money to try and emulate. 'Officers Parmar and Ford are keen to speak to you about Will. Think you can stop vomiting for long enough to do that?'

I felt my skin flush pink, and – I flinched – my stomach gurgle.

I nodded though, of course, the school child to his headteacher as always.

I saw Pete hop up and his gangly frame head for the door. He stopped. Tucked his slim shirt back into his skinny jeans and adjusted his tie. Then off he went, phone in his hand, towards the canteen. Getting the coffees in, for my return. I felt a pang of something. Gratitude. Friendship.

Douglas came into the office with me while I spoke to the officers, and it seemed incongruous but I didn't

47

question it. It was his territory, clearly marked. His office had some of the best views on the floor, so that any time he had a meeting with someone external, half of it was spent with him standing, arm slung around their shoulder, pointing out the high points of the London skyline and preening like a cat. Like this was his pad, his gaff, and he had invited them over for beers. I suspected he had done it with the officers already.

'Be quick with Rosie, would you guys?'

I was right. He was jovial with them. There was an old pals vibe.

I sat down in a chair opposite the officers, one that wasn't normally in there but had been brought in for this purpose. It wasn't a big office, and we were on top of each other. I put a hand self-consciously to my forehead; I knew it glistened with sweat.

'She's my day editor, see,' he said, same 'old mates' tone. 'I need her out there, getting the news up, keeping us at the top of our game.'

He placed a hand on my shoulder. 'We always say it, don't we Rosie, news doesn't stop for anything. Sadly, that's the case even when it involves one of our own.'

Surely they could hear how disingenuous he was? But Officer Ford, standing, nodded her head. Earnest. In total agreement. She moved slowly, her large middle curving outwards to make her into a circle. Thin legs in black tights stuck like skittles out of the bottom.

I gave a barely noticeable shake of my shoulder to remove my boss's pudgy hand.

'Go easy on her too,' he laughed as he got the hint and took the hand back. 'She's got something of an obscene hangover. Even threw up at her desk this morning! Whatever were you *doing* last night, Rosie?' But he didn't give me time to answer. 'Young people, eh . . .'

I was 30 but to them, straight out of school. Officer Ford was about the same age as my boss – mid-forties – and Officer Parmar in his fifties. I watched them now, all laughing, entering into Douglas's teasing and I felt tears threaten. But whatever I did now, I could not cry in this office.

'Would you like to talk to me about our missing colleague?' I interrupted. I sounded rude.

Officer Parmar leaned forward though, face recalibrated to serious. 'We would, yes.'

Douglas remained, perched on the desk and I thought: why can't *you* go out there and post some news so that the gnawing panic about numbers and the chart and leaving breaking stories to one junior member of staff could be relieved a bit for me to concentrate on this? But it was too menial a task for him.

My head pulsed and my wrist started to do the same. I could do with seeing Rania, I thought, as I massaged it like she taught me, but I knew there was not a chance of me being allowed down to her room for an hour today. Officer Ford glanced at what I was doing to my wrist. I stopped.

'I don't know Will very well,' I said. 'We've never met.'

'You don't know much about Will's personal life? Hobbies, weekend plans? Didn't confide in you about anything that was going on? Worries?'

49

I shook my head. 'Nothing. Will is . . . a bit of a closed book.' I remembered Keiran's term, and borrowed it. 'An enigma, I guess is the word you would use.'

I saw the officers exchange a glance. They'd heard this before. 'Never had a beer together?'

Something lurched in my insides. 'No. No beers.'

'Just work chat then . . . Douglas says you two are in contact quite a lot to pass the baton, as it were, day to night, night to day.'

I nodded.

'So how about last night then? Did you speak last night at all? Phone? Email? Messages?'

My phone was in my hand. I scrolled through. 'Couple of messages asking about stories that were up, pretty standard . . .' Some of which, I realised as I look at them, I didn't even remember reading.

'But you didn't reply?' said Officer Ford, reading over my shoulder.

Douglas raised an eyebrow at me. This job is twenty-four hours and the irony is that you're a journalist so you're expected to get blind drunk at every opportunity but you're also expected to be able to function as sober the second the job requires you to.

'No,' I said, quietly. 'I didn't reply.'

'Because . . . ?'

'It's a full-on job. Sometimes you have to switch off. The messages weren't urgent, Will would have figured it out. I was with friends last night.'

I avoided eye contact with Douglas, who I could guarantee would treat what I had just said with the 'Oh, it's

50

all right for some' response that would suggest I had left mid-shift for a two-week unplanned holiday in the Caribbean. But Officer Ford was nodding at me. Until my boss gave a giant belly laugh.

'I think what she's saying, officers, is that she was absolutely shitfaced and incapable of replying to a message.' He muttered the next part under his breath. 'Which might explain why she vomited on my £300 shoes this morning. Can you dry clean shoes? Anyone know?'

He wandered out of the room then, thinking I was done, most likely to call the missus and fill her in on his exciting morning with the police, or to bollock someone over some minor indiscretion, and he thought I was following closely behind but something stopped me, a mutter from one of the police officers.

'One second, Rose.'

Thanks to Douglas, they had built a picture of me as Will's drunk, useless, schoolgirl of a colleague, one to file away as no use to them. Inconsequential.

Or so I thought.

'One last thing,' said Officer Parmar as I turned back towards him in the doorway. Intinctively, I pushed the door closed. 'We have Will's phone log. The last call was at 2 a.m. this morning. To you.'

I felt my legs start to shake. I am a straight-A student from a Hertfordshire grammar who was never once sent to the headteacher's office. I try to tick all the boxes. Be everything everyone needs me to be. Do the right thing. I want people to like me. Sitting in front of police officers was a big deal. When they spoke to me like that, it was a bigger one.

'It must have been a follow-up to the messages,' I muttered, looking through my phone to catch up. But wait – there was no call from Will Frost listed.

Officer Parmar looked over my shoulder this time. Turned his head so he was facing the right way at my phone. Officer Ford was looking away from me so I couldn't see her face, staring out into the London morning.

'Huh. Looks like you deleted it. Any idea why that is?'

I sat back down. That good girl face was in flames. 'Absolutely none. I'm so sorry.' I felt like I was lying.

A thin smile in response. 'We'll let you go now,' said Officer Parmar. 'But one more thing. It wasn't a missed call. We have Will's phone records and you were speaking to each other for three minutes. At two o'clock in the morning. Right before your night editor went missing. What about that? Does that ring any bells?'

I felt my legs begin to tremble. Repeated myself. 'Absolutely none.' I tried a laugh but heard my voice crack. 'That's too much red wine for you.'

But no one offered a smile. We said our goodbyes and I promised to let them know if anything came up, or if I remembered anything about the call, and headed for the office door.

'Oh!' said Officer Parmar and when I turned, he had his palm clapped to his forehead like he was hamming it up in panto. I stood still. 'I lied. There wasn't only one more thing. There were two.' He motioned to me to keep the door closed. 'There was also the note.'

I stood still. Said nothing.

'You know. The one Will left, on your desk?'

I don't know if he saw the change in me but everything started to vibrate. 'I don't know about a note.' Hands, legs.

Officer Parmar raised a bushy eyebrow.

'I wasn't the first one here this morning, I was late. I didn't see any note.' Arms. I could feel it coming again.

'Only had two words in it so not a lot to go on, but still, we take what we have,' he said.

He was leading me and I knew it but still I asked, barely audible: 'What were the words?'

The officer leaned forward on the desk and propped his chin on his hand and I could tell he was loving it. Savouring every moment. I had thought they were the same at the beginning, jokes with Douglas, them versus me, but Officer Ford had more empathy, more compassion. Officer Parmar unsettled me.

I glanced out of the office. Saw Douglas sitting on Pete's desk and peering over his screen as poor old Pete tried to concentrate. Just then, my boss looked over his shoulder. Caught my eye. Frowned, as he realised I was still in there and hadn't left – as he had expected – shortly after him. He had thought we were done. He would be furious now that he didn't realise I had stayed behind. Unless, on the officers' part, that was deliberate. Did he already know? Was it Douglas who found the note? I was late and there was an emergency: quite a few people were in before me and I have no idea if he was first or if anyone beat him to it.

I repeated it. 'What were the words?' *Keep breathing, keep breathing.*

'Now this is an interesting one.'

Officer Parmar didn't take his eyes off mine, but one of those unruly eyebrows, flecked with grey, flew upwards. Then he spoke slowly. '*Ask Rose.*'

I only just made it to the bathroom before I threw up again, not sure this time if I could blame the hangover.

Chapter 8

'Chick, you do know it's not normal to be so drunk you can't remember whole events, don't you?' Rania said, her voice gentler than her hands as she kneaded hard.

I sighed. 'For you it's not normal, but I'm a journalist, Rania. Trust me. It's normal.' The number of times in my life I've explained this to people. You know what's not normal when you're a journalist? Having two glasses of wine and going home at 9.30.

But I had to admit, didn't I, that since Lizzie's party I had drunk more, way more than I used to. Even though drinking is what had put me in that situation in the first place – God, the irony – I couldn't help it. It was the only thing that chased it away for a while.

We carried on in silence for a few seconds, Rania pulsing at my arm as I tried to think clearly. Was she right? I wasn't a journalist the other night, when I was that drunk – I was Patrick's fiancée, Sam and Eloise's supper guest, someone in that sweet spot of life when you have no kids or a dog to get home for but you can afford alcohol you enjoy enough to sip, rather than guzzle. What had I been *doing*? I pictured myself chanting at

Eloise, red wine on my lips, my fiancé – my connection to these people – gone home. Her desperate to crawl between their John Lewis sheets for enough sleep that she would feel fresh in the morning. Sneaking glances at the clock over my head. *Why won't she leave?*

I pictured Patrick heading home, in good time to sleep before work tomorrow, like normal adults do. I cringed. Then I felt frustrated. Why could I remember up until then but not afterwards? Not talking to Will? Not *deleting* 'Will Frost' from my call log?

'Switch arms.'

Obedient, I put my other forearm out to Rania. She rolled up my sleeve. Kneaded me like dough. 'And there's still no sign of the night editor, I take it? What a nightmare.'

'I know. They got this freelance guy in to cover last night but it was a disaster. I've spent all morning clearing up his mess.' I looked up at Rania's face. 'Oh, you don't mean work-wise.'

A person had been missing for thirty-six hours and I was focusing on typos.

'They are focusing a lot on work but I wonder whether that's because there isn't much home life. Single, most people seem to think. Lives alone.'

Rania sighs. 'You'd have to, to do that job.'

Which makes what happened next ironic.

He called me Rose when he asked. That stood out. That finally, when he needed something, he called me by my name.

'It would mean a lot, Rose,' he said, and there is nothing to make your skin crawl like watching a cockroach try to be human. 'We can't keep getting freelancers to plug the gap. And no one junior can do this. Night editor is a *huge* responsibility. So many solo decisions to be taken when everyone else is asleep, or pissed, or shagging.'

He laughed. But it was pointed. It was Thursday now. Two nights of those freelancers plugging the gap and for once, Douglas was right: the site had been a mess when I came in in the mornings. It was hard for an outsider to get it spot on. The weekend night editor did other work during the week and wouldn't touch extra shifts with a barge-pole.

'You're the only one up to it, Rosie, the only one who knows how to run the whole site.'

Every comment, every line, every putdown about my lack of news sense and instinct came back to me, and I pictured them in speech bubbles dotted all around my hair. The only one up to it. Right. Now it suited, I was.

I wished I was brave enough to bring the comments up, but weirdly enough he did it first. 'Look, I know I can give you a hard time. I know you can be indecisive. But you make the right calls . . . in the end. I just like to . . . push people. And you're diligent, careful.'

Translation: I would never change the world but for the night shift, I could be trusted not to fuck it up until people came in to do the good stuff in the morning.

'Does that mean I would get no sleep, no booze . . .'

'No shagging?' he finished for me. Winked. 'I'm sure you'll find a way.' Pudgy hands on the table. He looked down at me, sitting in his office. 'It's temporary, remember, Rose – Will will hopefully walk through that door any time now. And if not, well . . . we'll be advertising for a replacement. A full-time night editor. In the meantime, though . . .'

He reached out to touch my arm, like that would make me more likely to say yes instead of thinking *get your disgusting hand off me*, and remembering how long his nails were and wanting to throw up, even though the hangover of yesterday was now – thankfully – gone.

I didn't want to acquire Will's pale, ghostly face. I knew Patrick would hate it and miss me.

'Would I get a pay rise?'

He looked aghast, then rallied. 'We could work something out,' he said. Then he perked up. 'And haven't you got a wedding coming up? I bet that would be handy for that . . . okay, let me speak to the money people and see what we can do, but there will be something.'

He clearly thought that was the biggest draw. In reality, it was just a bonus. Like the fact I could do my job without seeing Douglas's face across the office every day, and without him breathing down my neck, and without anyone calling me *Rosie*. They were bonuses. Added extras. But they weren't where the draw was. They weren't what was setting me alight.

What was doing that was wondering whether *this* was a way to know more about what had happened to Will. To get answers. To stop being so in the dark, when the police asked me about the note or the voicemail. When they looked at me like they didn't believe me – and who could blame them – when I had nothing, over and over again, to tell them.

Before I'd walked into my boss's office, another voicemail had popped up on my phone from the police. They had already called me twice this week since our conversation in the office. *Had anything come back to me yet, about that phone call?* They weren't calling anyone else, that I could tell. I noticed a constant slight shake in my hands. I *felt* guilty.

Could doing the night shift – living Will's reality – help me figure out what had happened to our colleague who had vanished into thin air, so that next time they called, I had answers for them? I believed it could. But it was more than that. I believed the night shift was key to unlocking something in my own mind too. *Ask Rose.* Key to understanding what it was that seemed to hook me to Will Frost. And to what that all meant.

But still, I thought of Patrick.

'I'll think about it,' I said.

'Thank you, Rose,' he said, and he almost sounded like he meant it, so I took the opportunity to ask something I had wanted to ask.

'Douglas.' I paused. 'What do you think happened? Why are the police here so much? Are they not focusing on home life, whatever was going on outside? Why here?'

But I remembered what I had said to Rania: because there was no home life? Again, my stomach lurched – but if I did the night shift, it would only be temporary, I reminded myself. I could keep my life out of work. The parts of it I wanted to, at least; it's not like I wouldn't relish being able to be more antisocial at the moment anyway.

'Maybe they think someone here holds the key to it, Rose.' He met my eye and for a second everything froze. But then he shrugged and stood up and walked around his desk and I knew we were done.

'We're journalists,' he said. 'We have a job to get on with that never stops, and we don't have time to sit around gossiping about Will. To be honest, I'm sick of all this speculating about it. So get out there, get on with it. Will will be back, I'm sure, but whether there's a job to come back to . . . Well, we'll see. The best thing you can do is leave the police to it. Get on with your job – hopefully your new one for a while – and forget about Will Frost.'

When I left his office, there was a coffee on my desk, lukewarm.

'Sorry,' said Pete from opposite me. 'I'll get you another one in a bit. Didn't realise you'd be that long. All okay?'

I shrugged. 'Who knows. But thanks for the coffee.' I drank it in one go standing up, even though the temperature took coffee that was always pretty bad over the line to disgusting. I chucked the cup in the bin.

'The police are in again later, apparently,' said Keiran, not taking his eyes off his screen, clicking his mouse, the same way we always talked, multitasking. At the thought of seeing the police officers, I felt my heartbeat quicken.

'It seems a lot, doesn't it?' Richie mused, without looking up. 'For one adult? How do they even know Will's gone missing, really, not just drunk somewhere, skiving?'

I kept my head down. Said nothing. But I knew, didn't I? It was the note. *That's* how they knew there was something to investigate. Because our night editor left a note, sending them in a certain direction. Mine. I looked at my work friends then and my mouth opened to tell them, but I didn't. Didn't want a flag against my name; a reason for everyone to look at me and wonder. *Ask*

Rose. I wondered if Douglas knew about the note. I looked around the office. Well, *someone* did. Someone had been the one to find it.

'You heard anything new about any of it?' I asked Richie, wiggling my mouse to bring my screen to life.

He kept his eyes trained on his screen.

'Nada,' he said quietly. 'Just going to try and forget about it now to be honest, mate, get on with work.'

I turned to him, but he kept his face straight ahead. Across from me, Pete had his head bent low in a story too. No follow-on questions, Keiran neither. In the toilet late that afternoon, I messaged Rania. *Everyone seems to be telling me to forget it, leave it, get on with work, but there are police crawling all over the office,* I tell her. *And we have to know what happened, don't we?*

Chick, don't give yourself any extra stress, she says. *This isn't on you.*

Except it was, wasn't it? The words chanted, rhythmic, in my head again, *Ask Rose, Ask Rose, Ask Rose.*

I'd spent the seven months since that night at Lizzie's losing the battle with this growing anxiety and with it, losing all of my past confidence. I was overwhelmed by even the smallest of decisions. It wasn't a surprise Douglas had lost confidence in me too. That he was starting to believe I had no news sense.

But this story, I couldn't bow out of. I was inside it.

Will was the other half of work-me. That water bottle in my drawer, that familiar handwriting dotted all around me. Push, pull. Will wasn't a robot or a ghost but a human being, living up in the sky in Canary Wharf in a world that was ruled by data, controlled air and sound-proofed glass. An inhuman world. An inhuman world that could sweep you up with it and render you inhuman too.

I don't think I could have stopped myself delving into what happened with Will, even if I knew how things would turn out. Even if I knew it would be far, far better to do what my colleagues were doing and look the other way, daydream out of those thirty-fourth-floor windows, and block out all thoughts of our former colleague and now official missing person.

Even by then, I don't think that was possible.

Chapter 9

The new stripy Selfridges tablecloth was on, and the candles were lit.

'Well, this is basically Claridge's,' said Patrick when he walked in from the gym, leaning in to kiss me as he threw a rucksack down on the wooden floor. When he pulled away, the musk of sweat was in the air and his huge white grin was directed at me like torchlight. 'Just going to jump in the shower and then I'm on the team to help.'

I smiled after him. It was Saturday, and we had his sister and her husband coming over for dinner in an hour. Tablescaping was not something I normally did, but I was making an effort. We hadn't seen them in a year since Eleanor got a job in New York, and I knew that most of their friends lived lives curated for Instagram.

Sweat meandered down my lower back. I was being casual to Patrick but I had been prepping for this supper for hours, to seem like a proper grown-up who could host people and do it right, when all I wanted to do was fling myself back into bed. It had been a long, exhausting week. Five days now, and our night editor was still missing.

As ever, though, I had been checking work emails

while I was doing everything else. I dipped in and out of news while the lamb marinated, and while I hoovered, and while I lit candles and sprayed air freshener masquerading as 'room fragrance' that cost me twenty-five bloody pounds and while I peeled potatoes and while I wrapped a present for Eleanor to pass on to her mum and dad, as she would see them before we would and it was their wedding anniversary next week.

I had cleaned our flat top to bottom. The meal should be passable, the nibbles were in the fridge, the drinks were cold. But something was gnawing at me. I knew what it was. It had been ten minutes since I'd last checked work email, and I had vowed that was the last one for the night. The plan was to go cold turkey. Eleanor and Gareth were only back for a week. I needed to give this my full attention for Patrick.

Patrick was pulling on a shirt as the doorbell rang. I took a deep breath and frowned, then caught myself. Since when did I find socialising with people I liked something that needed a deep inhale to prepare for? Not before. But it was another thing that had changed in me.

'Oh God, we missed you!'

'It's so so good to see your gorgeous faces!'

We were encased in joy, hugs and very detailed explanations of the wine they had brought.

'Cheers!' said Patrick as he poured champagne a few minutes later and I followed after him brandishing Gordal olives and boquerones. His smile was wide and catching.

'To having you home,' I added, mirroring it. 'Even if it isn't for long.' I put the food down and grabbed my glass, chinking Gareth's.

I saw Eleanor go to open her lovely rosebud lips on a face that had always seemed birdlike to me, pointy this, pointy that, but Patrick didn't notice. 'Shall we clamber out onto the roof terrace?' he said, heading for the door that lead to our tiny outdoor bolthole. 'I know it's January but it's so mild out there.'

'Ah, that perfect marriage of climate change and city smog. Coats back on, everyone!' said Eleanor. Out we went, past the dead plants and the unused herbs. Gareth bumped his large, muscular shoulder on the doorframe on the way out, and I pictured him on beautiful roof terraces in the States, in converted warehouses envisioned and brought to life by interior designers.

Outside, at our tiny heavy metal round table, donated to us by Patrick's parents and the kind that is so robust it would survive the apocalypse, Eleanor's bouncy blonde curls were touching mine and I felt her tense as she set down her glass.

'It is for long.'

Patrick set down his own glass. Flicked through Spotify on his phone to get his speaker to play some nineties indie. 'Pardon?'

'I left my job,' she said, pulling her coat right around her. 'It is for long – that we're back. It's for good.'

My fiancé leaned back against his chair. Popped an olive, whole, into his mouth. Chewed it fully before he spoke. 'Go on.'

He saw her put the drink down too. A hand gravitate to her middle. We knew. Patrick's grin was wider than ever.

'Due in June,' smiled Gareth, to my left. 'The maternity leave at US companies is ridiculous. We'd have to hand our child over to a stranger when they were tiny, when what we want is horses and fields and time together. So Kent it'll be, probably. Or Surrey, near your parents.' He looked at Patrick.

Then he shook his head, to get out of his internal chatter. 'Whatever, we'll work out the specifics later, but yes, that's the rough plan. It's a little earlier than planned but we're moving that picture forward. Shipping out of the work work work crowd.'

Patrick was out of his seat hugging his sister and I followed closely behind, pulling her in close as Patrick headed round to do some manly back slaps with the lovely Gareth. But still, I was a little wounded: *I* was the work work work crowd. Their choices being right rendered mine wrong, didn't they?

Still, I thought, for me it was different. I was doing my dream job. So why did something chew on my insides again? *Don't think it.*

'And you're back for good!' I smiled. That was the best part to focus on. That part I was pleased about. 'How lovely.'

Mostly I was happy for Patrick, who would be delighted to have them home. Delighted to get a niece or nephew. He would babysit, take them to the park, tickle them until they shrieked. I looked at him, and he was radiating pure joy. I was happy too, though, until two drinks later when we were back inside eating and I had had time to process things and I realised I was happy for them and simultaneously discombobulated with an unsettled stomach and yes, that was it, the emotion that was difficult to pin down: *terrified* for me.

I looked down at the roast I had made to welcome them back to England and realised I had barely touched it. It was edging closer, the next phase with its horses and its fields and its knowledge of maternity packages. An expectation that I would be fully formed and ready for that when actually, I felt like I was going backwards lately, and unravelling, and less formed than ever.

My chest pulled tight. I knew they were thinking it, even if everyone there was too well-mannered to bring it up directly: *Will you try straight after the wedding? Do you want children? How many?* Decisions. Big decisions. Choices.

'Anyway, that's enough about us. Rose, how are things with you?' Gareth said, spearing some lamb. A little red wine jus dropped off the end of it. 'Patrick mentioned something odd happening at work, with your night editor?'

How could I describe this feeling? Of disloyalty, somehow. To be talking about Will, who was this huge part of one of my worlds, in my other world, as though it were gossip. It felt wrong. But when I looked up, everyone was looking at me expectantly, even Patrick. Eventually, when I didn't speak, he did.

'Terrible thing,' he said, taking ownership of the story as he saw my eyes dart downwards. 'Their night editor just *disappeared* from the shift in the middle of the night.'

Eleanor looked at me and put down her knife and fork. 'Did you know each other well, Rose?' she asked gently.

I shook my head. Kept it simple. 'Not at all. Few emails, but we work different shifts so we've never met.'

Gareth chewed his roast potato and shook his head, the universal sign for 'a terrible business, this'.

'Any family?' he said when he finished eating.

'I don't think so,' I said, hesitant. 'Always been quite a private person. No one knows too much.' I pushed a roasted carrot from one side of my plate to the other.

No one knows too much. Didn't mean we knew nothing. I sipped my champagne and longed for a change of subject. But this was far too juicy for anyone to want to pivot away from it.

'Are they treating it as suspicious?' asked Gareth, head on his knuckles now as he leaned forward towards me on the table, his plate cleared.

I shrugged. 'Difficult to say. The police are in the office a lot.'

I thought of the message I'd had earlier from the police. 'Any more thoughts on that note, Rose?' They weren't letting it go. And I still had no more idea why Will had written it than I did before.

Eleanor raised her eyebrows. 'I guess when you're in a job like yours – like all of ours – you spend more hours at work than you do at home. So perhaps they think that's where the answers are.'

I had no idea what their plans were now but in New York, Gareth had been a senior PR exec and Eleanor had worked for an investment bank. I nodded. Tried to eat a little more lamb.

Gareth followed up. 'That was our point about the baby, about work/life balance. So especially if there wasn't a family at home, maybe work *was* real life. It is, for a lot of people. Maybe that's why they're in so much, the police.'

Thinking of the note, of the message from the police, had made my jaw tighten. Patrick took a big swig of champagne. Topped everyone up. He put on a gruff cockney accent, emulating every TV cop show we've binge-watched together into the early hours of the morning. 'Which begs the question,' he growled. 'What were *you* doing the evening this night editor went missing?'

Gareth laughed. Eleanor not so much. I delivered my fiancé a reedy smile. Patrick looked at his sister and her husband as he served up his punchline. 'Well, don't tell the police but she was shitfaced on red wine and refused to leave our friends' house with me and came home alone and can't remember a bloody thing.'

He hugged me tight, pulled me into the joke with him but I felt my body stiffen.

'Case closed!' exclaimed Gareth, laughing along, with a big gulp of champagne. 'It's the tiny day editor wot did it. Bring her in. Lock her up.'

Eleanor, still eating in small, birdlike mouthfuls, caught my eye and knew I didn't find it funny.

'Patrick,' she said, brandishing her champagne glass. 'Now you know I can't drink this, can you fetch me something else? An elderflower cordial or something?'

I flashed her a look of gratitude.

'Oh, nonsense, the baby will love a little glass of champagne,' said Patrick, a little tipsy now, still sitting down. A mischievous smile. 'It's related to you, after all, Eleanor.'

'The baby has had a few sips to celebrate, and a pretty potent red wine jus for that matter, and that is all the baby wants,' she said, with a smile but firmly. 'Elderflower, if you have it. Or a San Pellegrino? Any sort of soft drink if not. Thanks.' She set her knife and fork down. 'Thanks both of you. That was delicious.'

As Patrick went to the kitchen for his sister's drink, I shouted after him. 'There's San Pellegrino in the fridge, Patrick, and grab the chocolate torte and some bowls.' Then, another thought. 'Actually, bring the tequila too!'

Patrick, Gareth and I did a shot with dessert to celebrate Eleanor's pregnancy, and then Patrick put the lid back on but I took it off and topped up, and topped up, and topped up and only when I was at the point where I couldn't remember why I cared about Will Frost and what had happened that night, and when I needed help from my fiancé to take my clothes off, and when I wanted to cry with joy or fear or something unknown, did I head to our bedroom, and pass out.

Chapter 10

The next morning, I woke, sat bolt upright, body drenched in sweat. The clock on our bedroom wall said 9 a.m. I had been dreaming of the office, empty, late at night, seeing myself circling it, unable to get out, even though there were doors on top of every desk; miniature wardrobes with their own separate Narnias. I couldn't open them, though. My reflection in those floor-to-ceiling windows loomed. Warped. I had been dreaming, too, of our night editor. Patrick stirred when my whole body jumped awake. 'You okay?' he asked, rolling towards me. It was all relative. I could handle a mild hangover and a nightmare.

'Was I annoying last night?'

'No,' he said like a reflex. 'You just talked *a lot* about the night editor thing.' He yawned widely. 'I think you were planning to put the police out of a job and solve it.' He slipped an arm around me. Said it sleepily, on the croak of a laugh. 'Happy Sunday, Miss Marple.'

I stiffened in the crook of his armpit. I had dim memories of saying I didn't want to *leave it* like Douglas had told me to, didn't want to keep my head down, get on with it.

That I wanted to *know*. Wanted to figure it out. Declaring it very loudly, at times. Of Patrick, laughing: 'Look at you, news hound!' Like that wasn't my job. Like I didn't work at a newspaper. I suspected he thought me spending more time copy and pasting and chasing clicks than beating my shorthand rate in a courtroom negated my job title. I remembered us bickering. Oh God, Eleanor – pregnant and sober. I did so hate it when someone was sober.

Now, drunk bickering forgotten, Patrick stroked my head. 'Take some wisdom from my sister,' he said softly. 'Don't put everything on work.' He held his hand up, a defence, and it floated above us as we lay in bed. 'I'm not saying don't love it, don't be passionate about it. I'm not, I promise. But don't make it everything. Let's live a life. Travel. Eat amazing food. And we'll want to . . . you know, it was interesting, talking to Eleanor and Gareth last night. We'll want to ship out soon too, won't we? After the wedding.'

I pulled back from him.

'How will we *ship out*? Your office is in Canary Wharf too! We're tied to London forever, as far as I can see.'

He stood up to walk across the room and open the window. With tequila fumes all around us, we needed the London air desperately, however questionable its quality.

When he got back into bed, Patrick lay on his back and pulled my head back into his armpit. His skin was warm. Soft.

'Exactly,' he picked up. 'We'll want to move somewhere nice with some fields out in Kent, Surrey . . . and we can't both commute every day.'

I stared at him blankly. 'Why not?' My head was suddenly pounding.

'Well in a few years there will be nursery pick-ups and then school . . .' he said, hesitant. 'And like Gareth says, who wants strangers being with your kids all day? One of us will need to be around.'

We had never firmed up our thoughts on kids. Never planned beyond the wedding in terms of where we would live, or if we would procreate. I knew which one of us he meant.

'So in the meantime, I should just tread water?'

He frowned at me then shook his head firmly. 'Don't make me that guy, Rose. You know that's not what I'm saying and it isn't fair. You do a brilliant job and you earn decent money. That's not treading water.'

Decent money. It's a good salary, for a journalist. For an industry that's struggled in the last ten years or so to find its feet – print sales plummeting, the phone reading that replaced it not nearly so ripe for the beautiful, large imagery that the advertising industry loves and needs. I'd done well to find somewhere to fit within it to be honest. A proper job. Holiday pay. A pension.

But it's not city money, is what he means. It's not the money you expect to get, your whole life, when you go to a school like Patrick's. So now I was supposed to figure that out. How to segue away from my life, my career, and forge a new one and this was all the more annoying because part of me was screaming no way, it's your dream job and the other part was reminding me that most days, I hate it. This is what I meant about decisions. How could I make them at the moment, when I was unsure and fearful of just about everything?

I said nothing but Patrick sighed then as he felt me bristle. 'You're misunderstanding me. Let me start again. All I'm saying is don't get obsessed with it. Stop checking your emails twenty-four hours a day. Don't fixate on someone you don't even know who's had a bit of a breakdown and done a runner. Just treat it as work. Take the money. And then when we're ready to ship out, we go, with a massive deposit from selling this place and enough to buy a five-bed with a few outhouses.'

Imagine being so sure of the future. So certain of it all. I felt a sting in my eyes. But I used to be sure.

'I'm going to take a shower,' I told him.

When I came out, he was googling brunch menus. I stood next to him, hooking the back of my bra. We were due to head out in five minutes or so with Eleanor and Gareth, who were getting ready in our spare bedroom.

'Just so you know,' I said, adjusting my strap a little, 'I'm not going to be around much for the next few weeks. I'm going to be covering another role in work, different hours.' I glanced in the mirror, and caught a glimpse of Patrick's face in it as I said the words. 'I'm going to be the new night editor.'

Of course we didn't discuss what I had said when we had five minutes to get ready, and there were two people staying in our spare room.

Of course we didn't discuss it during the meal, either. Instead, we discussed whether pregnant Eleanor could have runny eggs in her shakshuka and huddled around Gareth's phone to click through images of £2 million houses that they might buy in Cobham.

Eleanor was talking about knocking through something, somewhere, and everyone was wading in with ideas for what they could do with the old barn. I saw my future flash in front of me: hosting the PTA meeting on the lawn and an enthusiastic interior designer waving swatches at me. Patrick caught my eye, down on the table instead of on Eleanor's phone. He reached for my hand and he looked worried. Like I was slipping away. And I *felt* slippery.

If that's not what you want then what is, Rose? Working through the night in a job that makes you cringe at times, making sure 'nip slip' is in the keywords, adding twenty-four pictures of Lauren Goodger's bum from different angles? Taking on the night shift, so you can get closer to a ghost? It was like meeting the friend you know signals danger, having the tequila shot you know will mean the night will go on three hours longer than it should and mean you spend all of the next day paranoid and hazy.

But I wanted to know what had happened to Will. I *needed* to know what had happened to Will.

When Eleanor and Gareth headed off to Waterloo to travel to Patrick's parents' house, we waved them off at the bus stop and walked home via Clissold Park. Patrick and I didn't let go of each other's hands, mine gloved as they would be until spring was well and truly under way, his warm whatever the weather of their own accord.

'Why did you say yes?' he asked and he was gentle with it, as we finally got to the topic that had waited patiently through double glazing and how would you like your eggs and a particularly chintzy but promising four-bed. 'To the job?'

We kept walking, past Clissold House, a few brave souls huddled up outside with hot chocolate and slabs of cake. Past the kids' play area – and someone I recognised from a BBC sitcom telling his child to be *gentle, Albie* – and the tennis courts where a slight redhead walloped an impressive backhand. I contemplated his question all the while.

Why did I say yes? I didn't tell the truth. 'I thought it might be a break from the treadmill.'

'The treadmill of having a normal life?' asked Patrick. He looked aghast. Stopped in the middle of the path, a woman with a pram tsking at us for making her swerve. He held a hand up in apology. I grabbed it and tugged, kept him moving. How did I explain this?

'In a way, yeah.' I squeezed his hand. 'Everything is so *much, all the time*.' And that was true, whatever I was omitting.

'But we like it that way!' he laughed, incredulous. 'We get to do so many fabulous things, Rose. We always say it!'

I smiled. We did. We did say it. The holidays, the nights out, the dinner parties, the soirees, the weddings, the hens and stags, the family gatherings, the theatre tickets. All of it. We said it.

We used to say it.

As I stared at him, I wondered how he could have missed how fundamentally I had changed since last summer. Yes, he had commented on the fact that my drinking had increased – he thought it was part of having a more stressful job – but that was about it. Perhaps he didn't notice that I had been shedding my friends one by one because we were so constantly surrounded by his.

Patrick went to open his mouth again, to remind me that life was great, that I was self-sabotaging. I held a hand up. 'I wondered if working overnight, being off when everyone else is, maybe it might mean things calm down a bit. Break the pace.' We locked eyes then. I ploughed ahead. 'And how else will I do it? You can't just start saying no to every lunch or dinner invite that comes your way, and you don't *want* to either. But maybe if I had to, if people knew I just wasn't available, that might be kind of *freeing*?'

I watched his face in that second and saw genuine confusion. It wasn't just the friends he hadn't noticed. He hadn't noticed how much I had started to detest socialising and being around other people, the majority of the time. The anxiousness. My inability to make a decision. Anything he did see, he credited to the drinking, to the stressful job. He didn't realise that I had been falling apart. I felt my stomach sink. Douglas noticed more of this than Patrick did – and what did that say about us?

'Would you be available for *me*?' he asked. And it was then that I realised something. Patrick *had* noticed. He couldn't not. But he'd ignored it and looked the other way – and I had been very happy to gloss over everything and not talk about what was really happening too, most of the time – because he didn't want anything to change. He loved his life how it was.

I had that slippery feeling again, and I held on tight to his big, warm hand. 'Of course I would. In a way, maybe I'd be available more. Less pulled in every social direction. At home more.'

But I knew he was picturing dinner parties without me, work events he'd have to attend alone, organising his parents' anniversary dinner without my exhaustive knowledge of fine-dining restaurants in the Surrey Hills area.

'I can't help feeling this is a lot to do with you being fixated on what happened to the old night editor too, Rose,' he mumbled, as we tucked into the side of the path to make way for a toddler on her scooter.

I swivelled round. 'This is *nothing* to do with that,' I told him. 'I was just drunk last night. Being ridiculous.'

I was lying to Patrick, of course. Taking this role had everything to do with wanting to know what had happened. I thought of those officers, telling me I spoke to Will that night. About the note. Patrick couldn't notice the flush that burned across my cheeks, then, could he? It was cold. My face stung with that already.

Somehow, stepping into the night editor's shoes felt like the start of figuring out what really happened that night. And somehow, I *did* believe I could do that. I also believed that I had to. Because it wasn't just about Will, was it? Perhaps I had a newsier instinct than anyone – Patrick, my colleagues – gave me credit for. Or perhaps I was just waiting for the right story. Not just Will's story when it came down to it.

But mine, too.

Chapter 11

Douglas's eyebrows met in the middle and, if I was not mistaken, his teeth were two shades whiter than they had been before the weekend. What an odd combination it made, with his sallow, peaky skin. That would be the regular takeaways he ate so he could talk about how he'd eaten dinner at his desk every night, thus winning the hours in the office-off performed by a lot of my colleagues. Okay fine, and occasionally me. But it was difficult not to get caught up in it.

I stared at my boss, mute but for the odd affirmative uh-huh as he talked at me – we must have been entering the twentieth minute – about all the things he would expect from me as the night editor.

Halfway through I caught Richie's eye as he walked past, and he pulled a face: *Well, you only have yourself to blame.* Keiran, Pete and Richie thought I was crazy when I told them I was taking the night editor role and that I was on my way in here to tell Douglas.

Now, through the glass, Richie drank an invisible cup of coffee. I nodded at him. Then I was back in the room. Douglas paced his office as he talked, while I stood awkwardly. Heels didn't help. I switched my weight from one ankle boot to the other and stared resentfully at his flat brogues.

'You do remember it's not my permanent role, though?' I said, when he finally paused to suck air. He ran a tongue over the snow-white teeth. A laugh too loud to be natural was followed by a sweaty hand on my shoulder. I felt myself tense. 'I remember, Rosie, don't worry,' he said, I'm-a-good-guy-on-your-team grin. 'Just until we recruit. Then we'll get you back to that fella of yours and you can get back in sync with your sleeping, your drinking and your shagging.' A loud guffaw.

He walked back to his desk and smoothed down his monobrow. Then he looked up for a moment, and I thought I saw a human being. 'I appreciate this. You've got me out of a hole.' But then, 'For a minute there Rosie, I'll be honest, I thought I was going to have to come in every fucking night *myself*.' He did a hammy shudder. All thoughts of humanity were banished.

'Any word on Will?' I didn't know the words were coming out, but there they were, floating around the office.

He tapped a pen on his desk. Tap, tap, tap. Suddenly he was transfixed by his screen. 'Zilch.'

I was about to leave the office when I thought, fuck it: he'd never feel more grateful to me than he did at that moment. I should use it. 'What do *you* think happened?'

He looked up. The tap continued, though sped up, tap tap tap tap. When he spoke to me he was staring out of our thirty-fourth-floor windows, to London beyond, to a sky that always felt close; to a drop that would break your bones and kill you instantly. It had the air of a film set sometimes. We couldn't see the detail down there on the ground – the Pret wrapper floating in the breeze or the couple having a row. We just saw the skyline and that image was so ubiquitous, so static that it was hard to remember that ours was the walking talking version. The real deal. I stared, then. Trying to make it come to life. Meanwhile, my boss stayed silent. I don't know how much time passed. But I stood still and waited.

When he looked up, he seemed surprised to see me. There was even the hint of a jump, like he was coming out of a trance.

'I think sometimes it just gets too much,' he said, and I was surprised he remembered the question that I had asked. 'For all of us. Some days, you can't handle it.'

I didn't know whether he meant that place, or life, or something in between. But if he was suggesting that Will had jumped, I thought, then that was impossible. I frowned. There was no body. We all knew that. Didn't we? When I went to clarify, he spoke over me. 'Some days, you snap.'

And something in his voice told me that that was the end of the conversation. I left. Five minutes later when I glanced over at his office, he was still staring out of the window. I frowned. The word trance came back to mind. *Some days, you snap.*

'What about meeeeee?' asked Rania, dramatic hand to forehead when I headed into my last appointment before

I switched to the night shift. Most of her wild dark curls were pushed back with a headband; a few tried to escape at the crown. I swung my legs up onto her couch. I laughed at first, at the thought of telling Douglas I'd changed my mind because I would miss my mate, but then I realised she wasn't just my mate, she was the woman who made my hand work enough for me to be able to function in my job.

'Oh shit Rania, I won't be able to have appointments with you.'

She raised one of her thick, natural power brows. 'Yes chick, that's what I'm getting at.'

My physio, and my unofficial work therapist. Though maybe I wouldn't need a work therapist when I didn't have to deal with that crew. When I was in the peace of the night-time, dealing with everything that came my way *in my way* quietly, efficiently. But I definitely would need a working hand. Now, Rania's fingers kneaded into it. Little letters on her nails today: PEACE. LOVE X.

'Do you do appointments outside of work time?' I asked her. 'If I paid you?'

'Oh shush, chick, you can't pay me,' she said. Then she paused. 'What am I talking about, I had to buy own-brand chocolate buttons the other day and I'm going raving in Berlin with my lo-ver in April. So yes, you can pay me. When? Where?'

I told her I would message her, and felt the relief charge through me. Partly for my hand. Partly for my sanity.

'Lover?' I asked. Rania pushed at a knot in my forearm. She stopped to wave her arm in the air, dismissive.

'We can talk about that later,' she said. 'What I want

to know is why the hell you, a young, sociable girl who *glows*, for God's sake, would want to do the night shift, and end up with that night editor spook's pallor?'

'How do you know about the spook's pallor?'

She didn't need to smile: whatever the opposite of Resting Bitch Face is, Rania had it. 'You talk about that night editor *a lot*, chick.'

I waved my other arm dismissively, mirroring her, while wincing in pain at the one she was working on. Went back to her original question. 'Anyway, it's only for a few weeks.'

She pressed and pushed in silence then for a minute or so, which was unlike us, before she spoke. 'Just make sure it is,' she said, and her voice had lost its playfulness. 'I know what they're like up there.'

The rhythm of her kneading soothed and it took me by surprise when she spoke again, even though she was far quieter than before. 'And the last thing in the world we want is for you to end up like the other night editor.'

When I left her room half an hour later, it occurred to me that I didn't know if she was worried I'd end up with Will's pale complexion. Or if she was worried that I too would disappear without trace in the middle of the night.

Chapter 12

I was clutching my KeepCup of coffee to me when I walked into the office at 10 p.m. for my first night shift, just over a week after Will had gone missing. Seven hours stretched ahead of me. I had tried to sleep during the day. Failed. Hopefully the shift would exhaust me. Hopefully I would slip into the pattern.

'Rosie Rivers!' he boomed. He had to be kidding me.

'Hi Douglas.' *Why are you here?*

'Wanted to stay and settle you into the new gig.' Wait for it. 'Not that I wouldn't have been here anyway.' A sigh. 'Clearing up everyone's shit, as usual. Barely seen the missus this week. She'll be at it with the tennis coach if I don't get home a bit more often.'

Trademark guffaw. The teeth couldn't be *even* whiter today, could they?

'I'm sure she understands how hard you're working,' I mumbled, setting my coffee down on my desk. Taking off my gloves.

I pulled out my chair and sat down, then clicked on my emails and scanned. Mass-deleted 99 per cent of them. Flagged the others to reply to later. 'No one's done me a handover?' I spun round to him.

He was shrugging on the long leather coat that he somehow hadn't realised screamed MURDERER at people. 'Have they not?' he mumbled, head in his phone. 'The buggers. I'll have a word tomorrow. You'll figure it out though. Will always did.' *Because I did a thorough daily sodding handover.* But my boss was gone, across the office, to peel his missus away from the strong and toned arms of the tennis coach.

'Good luck, Rosie! Call me if any problems.' I heard him calling a company account taxi. To *Kent*.

'And that there is why we have no budget for pictures,' I muttered quietly as he pressed the green button to leave the office and headed for the lift. Or maybe I just thought it. I'm not sure I would have braved it out loud – he was not a man you wanted to piss off. I of course would be getting the tube home when I left in the early morning. I had been planning to cycle, to get over the fear that had taken over since Will had gone missing, but with no sleep, the thought of making it through an eight-hour shift then exercising instead of falling into bed at the first possible second was unbearable. *And this is how it gets you*, said a voice in my head. You wonder why Will Frost looked like a shell of a human? No vitamin D. No exercise. See, I thought, my decision to take on the night shift vindicated. I was already getting insights. I was already understanding. Will probably existed on junk from the vending machine. And does that make you more likely to snap, too?

'Shit!' I realised in that second that I was so used to running downstairs to the in-built 'this is a whole world, why would you leave it' shopping centre and buying takeaway salads that I had brought no food with me and now I couldn't leave the desk because there was no one else there.

By the time things were calm enough that I could risk braving a ten-minute dart down to Pret, it was 11 p.m. Not 11 p.m. in Soho. 11 p.m. in Canary Wharf. Everything except the bars had closed. Was Will more organised? Or did this happen a lot? No exercise. No vitamin D. No vegetables. *Eight years*, Will had been doing this job. What does that do to a person, in the end? I was halfway through a Lion bar from the vending machine when my phone rang, and I leapt like it was a gunshot.

'Rosie! There's a fucking TYPO on the top story headline on the homepage! Sort it out. Makes us look like a student fucking newspaper!' And my charming boss slammed the phone down on me before I could even attempt to speak through half a mouthful of chocolate and caramel.

No exercise. No vitamin D. No vegetables. A heart, racing; palms, sweating. That *silence*. Not to mention your only human contact all night long being a voice on the other end of the phone, speaking to you like you are no one.

I fixed the typo, swigged the last of my coffee, then headed straight into the kitchen for another. At least that was available to me, all night long. I spooned in the granules, then thought of how many times Will must have done this, over eight years in the job. I watched the kettle. *Good God, Will. If it weren't for the problematic lack of a body, I'd think you had just keeled over. I would think you died of night shift.*

As the kettle boiled, I loitered at the corner, so I could still hear my phone ring. Still dart for it if Douglas had a bollocking ready for me. I thought about emails *I* sent in the evening to Will. It would only seem like odd things, little favours I needed, tiny mistakes that had been made. But if everyone did that, and it was a drip-feed of where you went wrong, from a gaggle of colleagues you never interacted with to humanise them . . . How would that feel? I pictured that ghostly face.

11.30 p.m.

My heart thumped, thanks to the juxtaposition of utter silence and screaming phone calls and more coffee than any human being should drink.

The day shift was long but moved quickly between meetings and a screaming boss and a dash to Pret and fast-moving news. I spoke to Mo in the canteen about his weekend plans when he served my drink; chatted all day long to colleagues; knew about the football match Richie was going to and how Pete's kids were getting on at their new school and about the terrible date Keiran had been on last weekend. Here, it was busy, yes, but there were also hours and hours of nothing. Quiet. I glugged my coffee. I was panicking over nothing. Tonight was my first night; I was just getting used to things. It would normalise, and then it would be over. The new night editor would start and I would slip back into existing alongside the rest of humankind, having figured out what had happened to Will.

I headed back to the desk and clicked Heart on the radio, humming to some Girls Aloud. I checked the wires again and posted a couple of stories. When my latest cup of coffee – fourth? Fifth? – was finished, it was half past midnight. I still had six hours left.

I checked my email. There were a tonne of requests from colleagues to amend their stories or sling something up for them but hopefully it would slow down now, as they went to bed or got too drunk to care. I had hoped I would get access to Will's email, so that we didn't lose out on stories from the PRs, sources and freelancers who had stuff to share overnight but didn't know about Will going missing. That didn't happen. It would have hampered the investigation, apparently. It's the main way communication with the world would have happened for Will, out of kilter with everyone else's time zones.

Like I was now.

I looked around. One o'clock in the morning. I'd been in the office until around now before, on awards ceremony nights, huge news days that had run on and on on a wave of adrenalin. But that had been with a team of people; an event, pizza ordered in, even a few beers. Will – or the freelance weekend night editors – came in later than usual those nights, after we left. The relay race of shift work. Now, though, was later than I had ever been there. Heading into the real dead of night. Suddenly the radio felt intrusive and too much with the silence of this huge open-plan empty space. I switched it off. Tidied up some headlines. Boosted some SEO. Glanced at the chart above me and felt despondent at the numbers until I realised: of course they're low, everyone is asleep. My expectations needed recalibrating.

I closed my eyes for a second and woke with a jolt a few minutes later. *Marvellous work, Rose: your first night shift and you've fallen asleep at the desk.* But I was exhausted. It wasn't surprising. Perhaps the only surprise was that I woke up so fast and didn't end up flat out in my chair for an hour until my boss called, furious at the static homepage.

Why did I wake up? It must have been that dream I had, about the lift coming up and the door opening. About a shadow, over on the other side of the silent, empty floor.

Spooked, I went for a walk around the floor. Nothing. *Calm down, Rose. And stay awake, for God's sake.*

Back at my desk I yawned and stretched out and under the desk I felt my boot hit something. A rustle. I leaned down. Just a plastic bag. It wasn't mine, so most likely it was Will's.

I pulled it out.

When I opened it, the reaction hit straight away. Bam. Bam. Bam. When I looked at what was in that bag, the feeling that painted itself across me was like nothing I had ever experienced.

A pair of Clarks shoes. That's all. Bland, black, sensible work shoes that someone would change into when they'd worn comfy trainers for a commute. And yet for me, they sparked something. The hint of a memory. Me, looking at those shoes from above. And then, those shoes retreating. Another snapshot. Hearing my own sobs. The terror that came next.

I shook my head. Because how could I think this? How could I picture Will's shoes in that bedroom at Lizzie's party? It wasn't possible. Will had been on the night shift.

But didn't this make sense? A connection. Will's story. My story. I shook my head, hard. Tried desperately to make sense of this. I had taken on the night shift to find out what had happened to a colleague. But hadn't there been another reason? I thought of that note: *Ask Rose*. Of the missed call, deleted.

I couldn't explain any of it, that part was true. And yet . . . Somehow I had known when I took on the night shift that something fundamental linked Will and me. And that doing this job – living Will's life – might eventually help me figure out what it was.

I looked down at my lap.

And now, there was my reaction to these shoes.

I put them back in the bag and kicked them as far as possible under the desk. Away and out of sight. But they didn't leave my mind. Will's story. My story.

Ask Rose.

Chapter 13

Tonight would be better. For starters, I had a feta and beetroot salad in my bag so no need to eat Lion bars at midnight, and I had slept – albeit only for five hours. But people function on five hours' sleep, don't they? I thought of my little sister Annie, the only one of my siblings to have had a baby. Our little Robin was ten months old and Annie told me a good night was if she cobbled together six hours and got more than two in a row. And she was alive! She functioned. She did look quite alarmingly exhausted most of the time but still, she existed.

I also knew now what was needed from me. Tidy up everything, boost SEO, keywords, focus on the US, do a few India bits in the early hours ready for when they wake up over there. Pick and choose the requests from the demanding team but keep the news flowing. I could function. Hopefully on less coffee than last night.

The main thing I needed to do tonight was block out the row I'd had with Patrick when I'd got in from last night's shift because I was 'rude' (otherwise known as robotic with tiredness) when he tried to speak to me about a fancy-dress party at the weekend. I had suggested that after my first week on nights I might want to wait to see how I felt before I committed to weekend plans.

'It's the only time we can do stuff together, Rose,' he said, pulling on his trousers for work as I took mine off and pulled the duvet he had just thrown off, back up. 'If you don't feel okay at the weekend, this night editor thing will have to stop. We need *some* time together. Jesus.'

'Will "have to stop"?' I had repeated, incredulous as I climbed into bed. I hadn't even eaten or got a glass of water. Nothing could beat sleep for my attention. I used my last energies on sarcasm. 'Oh, hi Dad.'

It wasn't fair. It was a throwaway comment, and Patrick was worried about me. It wasn't fair on my dad either. Father to five daughters – the Mitfords, we call ourselves – and us having a mother who absolutely would, and does, tell us what to do, my dad bows out of all instruction. Sits in the garden to admire his vegetable patch with a cup of tea. Keeps his head down while my mum marches about the place, booming orders and judgements.

'Do what you want,' my fiancé said, glowering at me from our bedroom door as I lay on my side and faced away from him. 'But just know that we have a nice life right now, Rose. A brilliant social life, good friends, money.'

'Money's not everything, Patrick,' I murmured, knowing I was being deliberately awkward, feeling sleep coming, fighting it to win the row.

He ignored that. 'We have a *lovely* life. And you, *choosing* to upend it, choosing to spend every night away from me, choosing to cut your social life dead . . . it's weird, Rose. I get it if you were looking for a foot in the door to management, but you have that already! You got made day editor eight months ago.

'It's weird to volunteer for this. Look at you now, coming in as I leave, getting into bed when I get out of it.' He waited for me to respond. I pretended to be asleep. When he spoke again, I think he believed I was flat out. 'It's so sad, Rose. I hate it.' His voice was softer then and I very nearly turned round to him but in seconds, I really was asleep. Even all of those overnight cups of coffee couldn't stop that.

The next night, I swore to limit the caffeine and stop at 2 a.m. I made some other rules too:

1. Take deep breaths to stop your heart racing when Douglas screams at you down the phone. Remember his solo eyebrow and his Arctic teeth. Laugh (inside).

2. Stop panicking about the bloody chart.

3. Do not go near the vending machine (especially of note re: Lion bars).

4. Try not to fall asleep at desk.

At 2 a.m. when there was a lull, I picked up my phone. Replied to messages from Eleanor and Eloise sent when I'd been asleep between shifts. I stared at the screen. Nothing in return, of course. This would be life for a while, twelve-hour gaps between our messages. No real-time chat. I was essentially living in Sydney, without the weather and the beach and fresh juice at an outdoor table for breakfast.

I thought about the police, sitting opposite me in the office. 'How about friends?' they had asked. 'Did Will seem to have many friends?' No one could say for sure. But certainly no one knew of any. Well of course, I thought: how often would there be a chance to see them, when you did the night shift? But I get now that it goes further than that. It's not only the face-to-face meet-ups. You exist on different time zones. By the time you reply to a message, the moment is gone or the problem is solved or the place has been taken.

Back to work it was then. But when I checked the wires, all was quiet. I needed a screen break to wake my eyes up but if I was going to stick to my four-cup limit and vending-machine ban, it was best I didn't stray near the kitchen. The cafés in the shopping centre below the building were closed and venturing outside the Walt Disney bubble would mean I'd be away from my desk for too long. I was in charge after all. Me, all me. I was chained to this desk.

Herbal tea bags, I thought. That's what I will bring tomorrow. I clung desperately to a belief that I could do this job and still be some semblance of a healthy, balanced person. I spun backwards in my chair. Looked around this huge open-plan office. Thirty-fourth floor. East London. Centre of the world. The buzzing heart of the city's work life. And here I was, just me. Does anyone ever have this much space to themselves in East London, whether indoor or outdoor? I thought about square footage. I should have been basking in this. How many people got to experience it? That's what I should do for a screen break. Bask. I stood up. Walked around. Tried to bask. A sigh. *What did you look at, Will, every night, all night?*

What did you look at on that final night?

When I wandered back over to the desk, I stretched and felt my toe touch the bag again. Those shoes. My stomach flipped. Unable to concentrate on work now, I opened Will's top drawer. The drawer below was the one I used, and I would tuck myself – the part of myself that was made of notebooks, dry shampoo and some of Patrick's mother's cookies – away in it when I left for the day so that the desk became Will's for the duration of the night shift. Will did the same. If I felt bad opening the other drawer now, I reasoned that they were allocated to each of us wordlessly. Nothing was officially mine; nothing was officially Will's. It wasn't a locked cupboard or a locker with our names on. Just an unofficial space to shove a notebook in when you were sharing a desk. How could that be an invasion?

Still, I glanced over my shoulder. This was not my territory, officially or not. I wasn't showing the respect I usually did. But Will was missing. Surely the rules were out of the window now? Did the police look in here, I wondered, as I opened it? Who knew, but it was mostly empty with only a few Post-its, notebooks and a chewed-down biro. I sighed. No other territory belonged to Will. Unless . . . I crawled under the desk and pulled the Tesco bag from deep among a sea of wires. I stuck my hand in. One work shoe, then the other. That sensation, again in my gut. Bam. Bam. Bam.

But inside one of the shoes, there was something else too. I whacked my head on the desk and swore, just before my hand folded around this tiny blue box. I took it out and opened it slowly. Inside, there it was: a small but bright diamond ring.

Jesus. I glanced behind me again. Looked at it more closely. An engagement ring? Right before disappearing into the night? That's pretty unlucky timing, unless the two things were related. I leaned back in my chair. Felt it settle back with me. Will wouldn't have left that ring here in the long term; anyone could have found it. Hundreds of people work on this floor alone and could have gone digging around under that desk for myriad reasons. It would have been madness to keep that ring there. But one night, knowing no one else worked these hours and needing somewhere to stow it? Sure. That would make sense.

I jumped at the shrillness of the phone. I stared at the ring as Douglas shouted at me about a lack of sport on the homepage, some big football story being too far down. *It's basic news instinct Rosie, for fuck's sake. How did you even get into this industry?*

I was distracted by Will as I told him that I'd move the football story up and willed him to *please now for the love of God go to bed*. My hands shook at the sneer in his voice. They always did that, and I hated how tangible it was. How clearly his effect on me showed even if, on the night shift, it was only to me. I put the phone down at 2.30 a.m., carried out the orders my boss had screamed at me with those shaking hands and then sat, looking down at the ring.

Why would someone on the verge of plans, of a future that marriage signals – that is surely the point of marriage, to plan, to make a statement of intent about where you will be in ten, twenty, fifty years – leave of their own accord? Why would they run? Something in my stomach moved in recognition. Why, indeed. I opened the box, tipped the ring into my palm and looked at it again. Nothing special, but pretty. Then I put it back in and looked at my own. Bigger, yes, with an emerald; a family heirloom of Patrick's. I loved it, and I was unable to be cool about that fact: that rich green bulb with all its stories that he'd slipped onto my finger late that night in the Highlands. I was also, though, utterly terrified of it. Falling off my finger. Losing the emerald after one too many vodka tonics. Of breaking his heart in twenty years' time and letting the ring down. Every time I looked at it, I was scared.

I opened up the box again. The oddest thing about it was trying to imagine the near-dead pallour of Will being alive enough for love, passion, the pure, optimistic romance of an engagement. I pictured Patrick and me in the Highlands. Tried again to imagine my isolated colleague surrounded by the things proposals involve: raised glasses of champagne, tight squeezes from friends and family. But I couldn't do it.

Which was a reminder that we only shared a desk. I didn't know Will. We worked different hours, had different lives, there was barely a word spoken. *I thought I knew you, Will, because I knew your habits with the home-page and how you would structure the handover email, but what did those things mean?* They were not real things; not the ones that make a person.

Why did those shoes make me respond like that then? And what was that note about? *Ask Rose.*

But deep down I knew, didn't I? I did not know Will Frost. I did not know Will Frost at all.

But that didn't mean that Will Frost didn't know me.

Chapter 14

I groaned as Patrick came in to wake me from my day sleep for my shift; he was working from home for the day. 'At least it's the weekend soon,' he said, kissing my head.

'That'll probably make it even harder on Monday though,' I said, groggy. 'Perhaps I should stick to the same hours then, make sure my body clock gets the memo.'

He stared at me. 'Are you kidding?'

I held my hands up, sitting up in bed. 'Of course I'm kidding. What would I do with my weekends? Go raving with eighteen-year-olds? That's about all that's on offer if I want to stay up until 6 a.m. and please God don't wish that on me. I'm supposed to be retiring to Kent soon, aren't I? I'm certainly not up for reclaiming my teenage years.'

Patrick didn't laugh. 'No one mentioned retirement.'

I said it mostly under my breath, as I headed to the shower: 'I think they pretty much did.' I knew I was taking out my tiredness on him and being unfair, again. I knew I was picking a fight, again. And I knew all of that was related to the job that Patrick hated me doing.

And yet later, there I was again, alone in the world, firing off emails that weren't being picked up, tweaking copy that was hardly read, existing in the ether.

It's not real life, I reminded myself. It's not real life. It's just about figuring out what happened to Will, then getting out. There was so much more to this story, and it all still eluded me.

Security was so tight in our building, and yet I always looked over my shoulder.

2.15 a.m.

I made more coffee. My limit was proving difficult to stick to, despite the fact it was disgusting. I thought of the Americanos I picked up from Mo. Did he wonder where I was? Or did people just accept it when you disappeared, and move on? I swore I heard a noise as I walked back to my desk but this kept happening and I knew it was in my head. It was too quiet here. The paradox of seeing the whole of London alight but its noise trapped behind glass. This giant open-plan behemoth of an office with its dead silence was unsettling. It was enough to make you imagine noises. It was enough to make you imagine the sound of a lift travelling the thirty-four floors up to you. To make you imagine heavy footsteps. To make you imagine a door opening, and a voice.

'Rose. Good to see you again.'

I screamed, loudly. This time though, I was not imagining any of it.

When they heard my scream, they were apologetic.

'It's the middle of the night.' I sat down. My fingers

gripped onto my mug. I felt my heart race. Adrenalin. Fear. Panic. An absolute shitload of caffeine. 'You didn't tell me you were coming. I already dropped the ring off at the station. What are you doing here?'

Officer Ford pulled Richie's chair over and sat a little too close to me. I glanced at my screen. Did I get special dispensation if I missed something because I was speaking to the police? Unlikely. The idea of Douglas giving me special dispensation for anything was inconceivable.

'Officer Parmar was keen to visit the office at the time Will would have been here,' she said, in the voice that was so incongruous with the solidity of her appearance. Oddly high-pitched, it surprised me every time. 'And we'll talk about that ring while we're here, if you don't mind.'

I glanced over her shoulder at Officer Parmar, who had disappeared over to the other side of the office, past the newspaper section and to the supplement desks, which were distinguishable from everywhere else in the building because of the eyeliners piled high, the wobbly stacks of fiction ready for review on the ends of desks, the fashion rails ready for a shoot with Holly Willoughby next Tuesday.

'So you didn't know Will was in a relationship?' she said, as she took the ring out of her pocket and opened the box.

She glanced over at her colleague, who was wandering back over, reading the back of the new Lindsey Kelk. I sighed. 'How many times . . . I did not know Will. I had no idea about anything.

I felt my chest pull and my breath shorten. I glanced nervously at my screen again. Officer Ford looked around. Nodded. 'We came now to get a taste of how it would have been for Will on a normal night shift,' she added. 'And to speak to the people the night editor would have been working with.'

'Not that there seem to be many of them,' said Officer Parmar then, too close. 'Sorry, didn't mean to make you jump.'

I hadn't realised he was behind me. His voice boomed and it was unnatural. It was supposed to be silent here, in the night-time. Officer Ford crossed her legs. Sensible slacks, I noted. An efficient brown slip-on shoe, a little sag to a popsock beneath. It reminded me of my mum. 'You never mentioned that you do the night shift.'

'I don't!' I felt like they had caught me out somehow and I needed to correct them quickly. Whether it was the phone call, the note, my reputation on the team as someone who drank too much and forgot everything . . . I felt wary around them. Judged. Hunted.

'I mean, I do, now.' I sighed. 'It's to cover. For Will. It's not permanent.'

'Ah. I see.' Officer Parmar looked around. 'And no one else is here, that's right? Just one of you?'

I nodded. 'That's website budgets in 2010 for you. But not a lot happens overnight really, and it's such a small percentage of our traffic. One person is enough to be here to keep it ticking over. And then, you know, if the Queen died or something then people could come in, or work from home, or whatever . . .'

I could tell he was getting bored about the minutiae of our working life and I trailed off from the detail.

'Shit gig though,' he said. 'Mates heading out drinking after work and you're just rocking up for your shift?'

I shrugged. 'I'm kind of past the boozing-after-work stage of life. Being here is helpful in a way. Gets me out of stuff.' Sheepish smile, but of course it was true. For all of its downsides, the night shift is a bona fide unbendable excuse not to be around people. After what happened, I had distanced myself from friends, ghosted people who asked too many questions about why. This made all of that a lot easier. 'Gives me a bit of alone time.'

I didn't know how to say no, except to say I don't want to, *I don't want to.* I want to lock the door and have a bath, and be quiet. And the one who it was hardest to say it to? Patrick. A man with unmatchable energy who never wanted to say no, thought that was a missed life, a missed chance. A man who didn't know what had happened to me. Who didn't have the context. And who didn't want our life to change. So I went with him, to the brunch or the work drinks on the roof terrace or the fancy-dress party with his mates, and I drank too much and I felt exhausted and it was *endless.*

I tried to explain, but I couldn't really – not without telling them what had happened to me at Lizzie's party. And I couldn't tell anybody that. Ever. I never had.

'It's sort of . . . a life pause.'

Officer Parmar was having none of it. 'Oh come on!' He nodded at my left hand. 'You're in a relationship, planning a wedding. I've seen you with colleagues, you have mates at work.'

Had he been *watching* me?

His eyes scanned around the office. 'This cannot be fun.'

'I never said *fun.*'

Silence fell for a few seconds. Then Officer Ford looked down at the ring box that was in her lap.

'Where was it again?' she asked. 'When you found the ring, where was it?'

I felt the dampness in my armpits. I had told them this already.

'Just in a bag with some of Will's . . . shoes.'

Those shoes. I stared at the carpet and tried to breathe slowly. When I looked up, Officer Ford was frowning. 'Everything okay, Rose? It's just that you didn't respond to our last couple of messages either, and you look . . .'

Pulling my head upwards felt like it needed the effort of a puppet string. 'You asked if I had remembered anything and I didn't have anything to tell you,' I murmured and I could feel my face redden. 'And the night shift, the times I sleep . . . it's hard to call back sometimes.'

Her eyes bored into me like a drill. 'Okay,' she said slowly. 'But don't forget to keep in touch. We do still have a lot of unanswered questions, Rose.'

The subliminal message: that because of the note and the weird phone history, I was the one to answer them.

We sat in more quiet. I checked the wires. 'Sorry. It's only me here. If news breaks . . .'

Officer Ford swivelled round on her chair and then stood up from the momentum, a little hop as she landed. She walked around our desks. 'A lot of pressure, that. On one person.'

A minute later, Officer Parmar was across the room, looking over the London skyline. 'Impressive though, eh?' he shouted, as he bounced back over, large belly hanging casually over trousers that sat low. 'What a place to work.'

I downed the last of my coffee and did the shrug that appeared, with those two, to be my trademark. 'Sometimes you barely look up enough to notice it all day. You could be on a trading estate in Rotherham. It makes no odds.'

'What a shame,' said Officer Ford, and she sounded genuine. 'Not to be able to get the kick of that view every day. What a waste.'

She sounded like Patrick. He'd said something very similar to me recently. Patrick liked to maximise everything. He tried to achieve the best use of time, the best life, eat the best meal, see the best exhibition. It was a good quality. It's one we shared. Except that lately, I didn't have the energy. Lately I wanted to be complacent. I wanted to watch TV, do something average. Even better, I wanted to do nothing.

A pause. Loaded.

I twitched to get back to work. My missing colleague, fine. But I didn't have time to talk about the view.

Why don't you get to it? I thought. *Ask Rose.*

My eyes landed on Officer Ford's. Something occurred to me. 'Do you know for definite that that note was even written by Will? It's the kind of thing that Douglas would have done for a wind-up, for a joke, to set me up and make me panic. Are you sure that's not what happened? Was he the first here, that morning?

'We'll check that out,' she said, brow furrowed. 'One question though: why would he forge it? Do you have any reason to think Douglas would do that?'

I shrugged again, petulant teenager. 'No. I don't have any reason to think that he would forge the note, but I'm just raising it. As a possibility.'

My hand moved to my mouse. I'd seen a typo in a headline about the earlier Manchester derby. Delete. Amend. Save. 'Sorry, he'll be on otherwise.' They knew who I meant.

'At 3 a.m.? He doesn't sleep?' Long grey wisps came out of Officer Parmar's dark eyebrows and I couldn't take my eyes off them.

'You wouldn't think so.' My email pinged and I turned back to my screen. Remembered to add some extra images to a football story that Richie had asked me for earlier.

I looked up and saw them exchange a glance.

'That seems to segue nicely,' said Officer Ford. 'We did want to ask you some questions about your boss.'

All I could think was: How did you know what you wanted to ask me? I thought you didn't know I would be here. And I had that feeling again, of being hunted.

Chapter 15

Rania came on a Saturday. It had only been five days since I had seen her, but my RSI was bad at the moment. It had been the bane of my life since Cambridge days of writing 3,000-word European history essays, but it was compounded when I started at the website. There was no let-up. No downtime. Speed and volume is key, it's clicks, it's ad revenue, it's our jobs; our very existence. No one else was affected though, apparently. There were no bad backs. No carpal tunnel. No chronic anxiety. No migraines from the eye strain. Just me and my useless wrist and a roomful of stoic, unbreakable journalists in their shirts. That's the impression Douglas gave me anyway. It made it harder to think what could have happened that night sometimes, too, because I always pictured Will as one of them. Absolutely, resolutely 'fine'.

Rania kneaded hard, her brow furrowed.

'Guess what happened on my shift the other night,' I told her, as we sat next to each other on my sofa. Patrick had gone out to buy an outfit for the fancy-dress party we were going to later. He had been planning his look for weeks. I, so far, had nothing. 'The police came in.'

She stopped. Pushed that hair that was made for bouncing around a shampoo advert from her face. 'In the middle of the night?'

'That is when the night shift takes place.' I paused. This was okay, wasn't it? To tell her? I couldn't remember anyone telling me not to, and it was only Rania. 'They took a while to get to it but I think what they had come for was to ask a lot of questions about *Douglas*. What he's like to work for, how he and Will got along.'

'And?' She moved down to my palm, moved her fingers in circles.

'Well I could tell them what he's like to work for – a slightly tempered version maybe – but in terms of their relationship I told them I had no idea. He doesn't give me the impression they were close but beyond that, who knows? Maybe they settled into something a bit more pleasant than we have at the moment, a mutual understanding?'

Her fingers stopped for a minute and she bit her lip, thinking.

'Anything else interesting?' she asked, as she started moving up my forearm again.

I shook my head. 'To be honest, half the time they were staring out of the window, harping on about the view. I was panicking about getting on with work, checking the wires and there they were, pacing around by the windows, from one to the other, all around the floor.'

Rania paused. 'Oh!' she suddenly exclaimed. 'I know why that will be.'

I looked up. How could Rania know anything about this? All her information on our night editor's disappearance came from me.

'Someone from one of the other companies came in to see me this week,' she said, conspiratorial suddenly. 'That's why they can justify having a physio on site: the news guys might be too tough to need her but there are a whole host of other departments – marketing, HR, sales – plus the other businesses in the building who appreciate her as much as I do. 'Got chatting about "the missing editor". Turns out he – Marcus, he's called – knew Will a bit at school. Nothing major, not best friends or anything, but he remembered one specific thing: Will screaming the place down on the bus and demanding to be let off it and walk when they went on a school trip to the Welsh mountains.

Rania stopped massaging me. 'Marcus said he laughed when he found out his old school mate worked on the thirty-fourth floor. Because Will Frost had a lifelong, pretty debilitating phobia of heights.'

Something was sitting oddly. 'Why would that matter though?' I said. 'Will wasn't cleaning the windows. In that building you don't feel as though you're up high, you're just in an office. Especially for Will – it's dark on the night shift.'

She frowned at me. 'You haven't heard the rumour?'

And I thought, *of course*, Rania spoke to so many people in this company, how had I never realised she probably knows more than anyone?

'I haven't heard anything, Rania. I go into work after everyone heads home and leave before everyone arrives. People only speak to me to scream at me or get me to clear up the mistakes they realise they've left when they can't sleep at midnight.' I heard myself sound a little snippy – another side effect of the night shift. Patrick was bearing the brunt of it but one of my sisters had commented on it on the phone the other day. It was now spreading its net wider.

Rania started pushing her fingers into my forearms, hard, and dragging them across my skin. 'Ah, right.'

She realised I was waiting. 'It's probably nothing,' she said then, hesitant. 'But a lot of people are saying someone was spotted on the roof that night.'

I scoffed. 'No body. If Will jumped from our building, there's a body.' But, macabre, I pictured it. Our night editor. Dead. Broken into pieces.

Rania nodded. 'You're right. Probably just gossip.'

I was barely listening though because I knew this place, I knew my colleagues, I knew news people. We – yes Douglas, I included myself in this – liked facts. We liked germs of facts that could spread themselves out into the real thing, with digging. We liked the story, but only if the story was true. It made no sense, Will going up onto the roof, but what does, until you pick it apart?

I thought. Imagine being terrified of heights and thinking, 'I know what I'll do in the middle of the night, I'll head for the roof.' How bad would things have to be for you to do that? How dark a place would you have to be in?

And so, there it was, underlined in black. My reason to be in Canary Wharf alone at night while my beautiful, smiley fiancé slept alone in our bed. To be young and in love and alone in the office. To have taken this awful job.

Yes, the quiet time was a bonus but the real reason I

was here was clear: because this mystery was getting more and more odd, and I wanted to solve it.

I would find out why our night editor left a ring behind. And if, after leaving it, my nearly-colleague fell 250 metres and smashed into a thousand pieces.

Chapter 16

Before I could do that, though, there was the rest of the weekend and a Sunday date night with my fiancé.

The date night was to make up for the fancy-dress party I had bailed on the night before, after Rania left, citing exhaustion, omitting the part about the fact that every time I thought about it, the idea of being that on show, people pulling at my costume and shrieking at my make-up, made every part of my body tremble.

Patrick had been disappointed. 'This is the kind of thing I meant, though. About the night shift. It means we can't do fun stuff together.'

And I thought: this is the kind of thing *I* meant though. About the night shift. It gets me out of fancy-dress parties. Patrick went to the party with School Friend Sam and Eloise, dressed as Tom Cruise's character in *Top Gun*. I sat down to watch some TV; something inane, where someone was baking a torte. I drank a glass of wine, fast. I drifted off from what the presenters talked about often, thinking about that night, that roof. And then out of nowhere, my vision started to blur. I felt hot. Before I knew it I was dripping with sweat and I couldn't see and a voice was telling me quietly, matter-of-factly, that I was dying. Here, now, alone. That was why my heart was beating so hard. It was a heart attack, and for me, life was over.

Afterwards, I slept for twelve hours. I woke up, despite the long sleep, only an hour before Patrick. My life wasn't over.

I made my fiancé breakfast and tried to make the picture look normal. When Patrick stirred, I came into the bedroom from the living room. I stepped over his discarded all-in-one and aviators, leaned over the bed and kissed him. 'Sorry I bailed last night.' I smiled at him, he was blurry-eyed and cute. 'Was it fun?'

It passed through my mind to tell him what had happened to me while he was on a dance floor with a Spice Girl and Ali G. About how I had known – felt like I had known – that I was dying. How I had been so *sure*. But I felt stupid, and I didn't. Instead, I handed him a bacon sandwich and kissed him again.

'Well. I missed you.'

I climbed in next to him and slipped into his side, handing him my phone with a booking on its home screen. 'To make it up to you.'

'SushiSamba!' Patrick grinned wide through a mouthful of bacon. 'Tonight? Awesome. Thanks for that.' He yawned, and the smell of ketchup hit my nostrils.

Cuddled into his side, I smiled back, glad to make him happy.

I felt tired but I had to rally. To make sure what had happened last night – whatever that was – didn't happen again. Didn't happen, next time, in front of people. Because that would be more than I could bear.

★   ★   ★

113

Later, Patrick wore a shirt and I wore a long-sleeved black dress and heels and we clutched hands on the tube and grinned at each other. And I almost felt relaxed.

'You look nice,' he whispered into my neck as we wobbled and lurched our way down the central line to Liverpool Street.

'You look nice too, my love.'

A teenager next to me looked away, appalled. That dichotomy of thirty again: old to the teenagers, the fountain of youth to the middle-aged.

At our table on the thirty-eighth floor of the Heron tower, the view was impossible to ignore, which meant other things were too. Thoughts of the night editor, out there on the roof. The darker ones, again. I looked out and down. I pictured that teenager, on a bus in South Wales in the nineties. Shivered. Rain sleeted, angry, at the windows. Under the table, I squeezed my own hands together.

Was what I had last night a panic attack? I had looked it up, briefly. It could easily have been. Is that how Will would have felt, up there on the roof? Because surely you would have a panic attack, wouldn't you, if you were scared of heights and you went onto the roof of a fifty-floor building?

'What are you thinking?' asked Patrick and I jumped, guilty, *the night editor again, sorry*, before I realised he meant what was I thinking I would eat and I laughed and picked up the menu.

We ordered tuna ceviche. Samba rolls. Sashimi and edamame. We ordered bellinis, then sambatinis. We chatted with the waiters, and with each other. An hour and a half passed, and I stopped looking so often out of that window.

'Shall we get a bottle of Chablis?' I asked Patrick, as I skewered a nigiri with my chopsticks. He hesitated just long enough. I was just tipsy enough. 'Do you think I have a problem with drink?'

He had said a few things lately.

'Do you?' he said it softly, head down as he speared some sashimi.

When I answered he was chewing, eyes on mine. I attempted a smile. 'Maybe that's a positive of the night shift. Stops me drinking so much.'

Before I started at the newspaper, I could go for days without alcohol. Patrick and I, actually, unlike a lot of our friends, could take it or leave it. Instead, we wolfed spontaneous mutton curries at our local Indian Rasa on Sunday nights; we sat with our limbs wrapped around each other in Clissold Park. I walked down Essex Road eating overpriced frozen yoghurt that dripped onto my forearm because I didn't want to let go of his hand to mop it up. We ice-skated in a real-life postcard at Somerset House and rode bikes in Hyde Park. We were sated, with each other.

I drank, sure. Prosecco on date nights, a glass of wine in the bath. When I went out, a little more. But that was about it. When I started at the newspaper, it increased a little. Journalists drink like medical students, like people who don't want to go home. It's as much a part of their culture as morally dubious senses of humour.

That's how I ended up blacking out at Lizzie's. I wasn't used to it like they were and I matched them drink for drink for more than eight hours. My insides must have been in shock. Poisoned like I had taken Class As.

After that happened, I drank more, and regularly. Despite, and because of, what it had led to last time. I alternated between hiding away in my baths with a bottle of wine or – if I had to go out – throwing alcohol down my neck to get through it until suddenly it was 3 a.m. and I was blacking out in a bar. If Patrick or a friend were there to get me home safe I was lucky; if they weren't, and I made it . . . Then yeah. I was luckier still.

I didn't tell anybody about the night I had been unlucky.

At SushiSamba, I dipped a chopstick in some soy sauce and looked at it, thinking about Patrick's question. 'It's the same how I am with food. Things get too much and my appetite drops and I just . . . eat a lot less. That's not an eating disorder. And the wine isn't a drink problem. They're just sort of . . . symptoms. When things aren't good.'

'What's not good?' Patrick asked. Calm. Eyes on mine.

I felt caught out. 'I didn't mean not good. Sorry. That's not what I meant.' Because how could things not be good? A beautiful wedding coming up that would be paid for by my much-loved nearly parents-in-law; a ceremony in the village church then over to a marquee which was a stately home by any other name for 200 people in their giant garden. All the champagne you could want. And then, a life with a good man who loved me.

'I just mean stressful. A lot on. You know.'

But he stared at me and I knew that, no. He didn't know.

I tried again, feeling my cheeks burn. 'With work

116

and the night shift, and planning a wedding at the same time. It's . . . a lot.'

I put my chopsticks down. Stared out of the window. Smoothed my hair down again, though it was straight and smooth as a ruler. And then Patrick spoke.

'I worry when you drink too much that something will happen to you.'

I stared at him. There. Wasn't that confirmation of what I had already thought? That Patrick would draw a direct line between me getting drunk that night and what had happened to me. And wasn't that tantamount to blame?

I opened my mouth and willed the words to come out, finally, all these months later because maybe that would help us, maybe that was what we needed, but I couldn't, I couldn't. It wasn't just the fear of blame. I couldn't bear to see my pain mirrored back at me. I felt like seeing him hear that news would be doubling the horror.

He didn't want anything to change. And I had.

So that night at SushiSamba, I drank down sobs. We ordered the wine. We always ordered the wine, once a thought had crossed my mind that I might order the wine. I think that was his point. I drank that down too.

When we had finished the wine and our meal, Patrick and I went to a bar for a nightcap. I linked his arm as we walked through Shoreditch but something was off. I could hear a slur in my voice, yes, but I didn't feel as drunk as I should. No, I didn't feel as *relaxed* as I should. That talk about my drinking had thrown me. I tried to battle it, in a loud bar via a negroni. It didn't work.

'Patrick!' said a voice that was relaxed, or drunk, or a combination of the two. She flung her arms round him and then stood back to survey me. A large man with a neat beard stood next to her and Patrick snapped into public school mode. Even Cambridge hadn't taught me this stuff.

'You must be Cooper,' he said, pumping his hand hard. He turned to me, put a light hand on my lower back. I wondered if he noticed that it was clammy now. 'Rose, this is Daisy, from work. And her husband Cooper.'

I nodded, but said nothing. Daisy was wearing a large hat, even larger earrings, an oversized dress that swamped her and clompy, stomping boots that had her inching above Patrick. I smiled at her, and felt myself shrink. She was *magnificent*. I stared at her and tugged, embarrassed, at the plain black dress I had bought five years ago that now seemed dated and maternal.

'Awesome to meet you, Rose!' enthused Daisy, a large mouth coated in red beaming at me.

'Good to meet you too,' I said quietly, my smile barely turning up.

The music seemed to get louder. The people seemed to loom larger; confident and outgoing where I was shrinking away. They oozed the life of people who bump into each other in Shoreditch at 11 p.m.; they danced together where there were no dance floors, toasted to everything, shrieked with joy at every song, every anecdote.

They got larger again. I shrank further. The neon signs were brighter, like curtains thrown open on a hangover. I blinked away from them. And the music! God, the music. Faster. Faster. Faster. The beat was hard and it felt like my heart pumped alongside it, like I could be sped up by a DJ, like I was that malleable. That out of control.

Patrick was nodding. Had a smile on his face. Cooper whirled Daisy – who hadn't bothered to stick around and chat to me when she got so little back – round in a circle.

'I have to get out of here,' I said in Patrick's ear. My armpits stung with sweat.

'No worries, just let me finish this pint.' Some sort of craft ale he'd been excited to see they had on draught. His foot was tapping. 'Love this one.' The song. Was it really music? It was designed to drive you crazy, I swear. Make you feel panic you had never felt before. My brain whirred, to the past and back. Faster. Faster. I tugged on his arm, that toddler again. I couldn't contain it.

'No. Now.'

My breath was catching like a pin in my throat. My heart couldn't keep going at this pace, with this ferocity, surely. It would give up. This time it was definitely true. I was going to die.

Patrick looked down at my palm, sliding across his forearm, before he looked at my face. He didn't say anything, just put his drink down, grabbed hold of my arm and pretty much dragged me outside, where the music faded to dullness and I felt my breath start to slow. I leaned up against a wall and he stood behind me, a human shield.

'Breathe,' he said. 'Just breathe.'

And I did, eventually. But as I did, I pictured him back there, with those people. Sparkling. Alive. Loving it. And I knew that that's what Patrick wanted from life. He wanted to bump into people and host people and see people and he wanted people, people, people. He wanted that fast music and those bright lights. And when I was there with him, the only thing I could think about, sharp, clear, in focus, was that if I didn't leave, if I didn't find an empty box to hide in, then I was going to die.

I felt his chest on my back, his arms tight around me, our whole bodies touching, and I thought: *I have drifted so, so far away from you.*

How bad would things have to be to climb up to the roof, when you were scared of heights? I held on to that wall in Shoreditch, graffiti emblazoned across it. I looked at my fiancé, brought down now, and knew that I – and my desperate need to be alone and retreat – would suck the lifeblood out of him, in the end. How bad would things have to be?

This bad, perhaps?

Chapter 17

The Monday night shift. I had ten minutes, I figured, before I was risking missing breaking news, being away from my desk for longer than I could feasibly blame on a toilet break or the need for a drink. It would be tight getting to where I needed to go in ten minutes. But I had to try.

I took the lift to the top floor. When the doors opened, I jumped at the sound of my own black Chelsea boots clipping with every step. Each one echoed. Doors. One of which led, I presumed, to the roof. I tried to picture Will here, but it was hard to muster, so incongruous was the idea. Our night editor had a set place in the images in my mind and there they were: at our desk watching the wires with a coffee, writing, editing, copying, pasting. Cropping images – no picture desk in at that hour – and picking headlines to fit.

Will did those things. Will did not take the lift to the top floor roof and . . . And what?

Then I realised I was standing still. What a waste of minutes. I could think at my desk. I went to open the first door I saw but it was locked. I moved on to the next door.

Three.

Four.

Five.

All were locked, of course. Triple, quadruple. They would be. There were a lot of overworked staff in our building, people living life on the edge. They drank too much, they worked too much. Do not, whatever you do, give them easy access to the roof. Jesus, think of the insurance pay-outs.

I stood still. Tried to muster the image again, Will Frost up here in the middle of the night, as I was now. The air smelt unused. Not like newness, but like it was stagnant. Everything up there had that feeling, actually. Me too, I thought, looking round with a sigh, knowing this was no use. *Stagnant*. Me too.

A sound; a sharp click. My head swivelled. Adrenalin flooded my body like I was being attacked on a dark road but there was nothing and no one there. Just the unused top floor of a large news building and a lift door closing behind me, heading off to another floor.

'*Fuck!*'

With a shout and a lurch of my stomach, I realised: the stairs don't come this high up. I fell into the lift button and pressed it over and over, hard. No, I was ready to leave. Now. No. What if it wouldn't come back? I talked to myself. Off the ledge. Come on. Of course it will come back. No one else is here.

But it didn't come back. Instead, I waited while it was called to another floor, went about its business. Something gnawed at my insides. Who else gets lifts here at 2 a.m.? I hit it again. Come on. I looked around. I *thought* this was an unused floor, but was it? There were doors. Locked doors. Doors that wouldn't show me their wares; not the shiny, modern doors of our floors below but thick, mean jail doors that shut me out and turned their key. I slammed the lift door again. Push, push, push. I'd left my phone on my desk.

Bile made its way up from my stomach and bubbled at the lower part of my throat. When would anyone find me here? How long would it take? Who came up here, if anyone? *Will?* I felt a line of sweat drip down into the small of my back. Slam, slam, slam on the button. 'Come *on*.'

But the lift continued, like the perfect employee, to do its job, calmly, efficiently. Unlike the rest of us, it couldn't be rushed. Slam, slam, slam. A weird noise, like a squeak. Shit. What if I was breaking the lift? I stopped banging it. Stood obediently still. How long had it been since I left my desk? More than my self-allocated ten minutes, that was for certain.

Again, it niggled me. Who calls a lift at 2 a.m.?

But there were other companies in this building: banks, businesses I had no knowledge of. There were myriad reasons someone could have been there then, needing the lift to go home, to get some air while they pulled an all-nighter. I tried to slow my breathing. To remember that. *Come on.*

And then, suddenly, the lift lurched and announced with a bang and a guttural moan that it was coming back, and I should have felt better but I didn't because all I could think was: what if someone was in it? When the doors opened, what if I stared into a face I didn't want to? A face of nightmares.

Ding.

And what if somehow, that person knew that I was up here? I knew who I was thinking of, didn't I. Finally, the lift landed. Paused. And I paused with it, held my breath. Up here, if I was alone with someone who wanted to hurt me, I stood no chance and had no hope. And then there was no time to think anymore. Because the lift was opening.

Empty.

I exhaled. Rushed in, like the lift was home after a long night. I slammed the button for my floor and leaned up against the side while my body recovered, and switched my attentions back to my day – well, night – job, praying that no one important had died or revealed their nipple while I was up on the top floor of our building.

The other lift-goer, whoever they were, was forgotten. Our night editor was forgotten. All there was then was a bog standard fear of my boss and that terror he placed in my gut.

I heard his voice then, sneering. I saw him bringing it up when I was back as day editor, my disappearing act on the night shift just at the time that news broke. Reminding me, over and over, in front of my colleagues. Encouraging them to mock me, to poke their sticks at me.

'Just likes to go for a wander sometimes, our Rosie, doesn't she? Never mind that she's in the middle of a shift! Probably meeting that fella of hers for a roll-around.'

The bile rose higher. My hands were wet to the touch. I knew my armpits under my thin black polo-neck jumper were the same. But when I fell back to my desk, I appeared to have got away with it. There were no messages, no breaking news. Nothing. It was as eerie, for a few seconds, as it had felt up there on the top floor.

I leaned forward, ribs pushing into my keyboard. I double-checked the wires. Started writing. Fast. Making up for the time I'd taken off. Trying to paper over my missed minutes, rendering them non-existent if anyone looked back over that night.

I swore to the universe: *I won't do it again.* I had used up my chance. I couldn't make myself feel like that again. From now on, I would be chained to my desk.

This is what it was like for Will, said a voice in my head. Trapped and tethered, night after night, despite being a journalist and naturally – I presume, like the rest of us – curious. A lion in a zoo. *For eight years.*

'Argh!'

When my phone rang, I dropped my mouse. The sound, in this silence, at this time, was as shocking as a fire alarm. I got ready to take the bollocking. It must be a bad one for Douglas to ring at this time. It was 3 a.m. now. But it was a number I didn't know.

'Can you talk?' said Officer Parmar, voice bright. 'I'll be as quick as I can.'

'It's the middle of the night,' I protested. Déjà bloody vu.

'Yes,' he said, and I could hear him smiling. 'That's your bag isn't it? Thought you liked to keep things nocturnal.'

I sighed. Checked the homepage. There was lots going on tonight: a plane crash, a storm forecast, and I was still playing catch-up. 'I'm busy,' I said. 'What is it?'

There was a beat then, which made me sure this was no casual call. That there was some news.

'This engagement ring,' he said eventually, with thought, like he was rolling this around his brain even though I knew he would have done that before he spoke to me, formulated his thoughts. He was, then, just pretending to roll it round, like I was on his team, could help him figure something out here maybe. Why? 'Before you found it, did you know anything about Will's love life?'

'No,' I said on an exhale. 'I told you before. I told you over and over again. I don't know much about Will's life at all. We are — were — *just colleagues*.'

'Mmm hmm, mmm hmm,' said Officer Parmar, thoughtfully. 'Yeah. That's what I thought. The problem here is that I've done a lot of digging about this engagement. There aren't many people out there close to Will Frost. Parents dead, no siblings, an adult orphan, bless.'

He couldn't have sounded less sympathetic.

I stopped moving my mouse then, phone trapped between my chin and neck. 'That's sad,' I said carefully, thinking of my dad pottering around his garden and watering the tomatoes, my mum just getting home from work, popsocks in her slippers. The solidity of that, in place; the ground certain beneath my feet.

'But the ones who are close?' said Officer Parmar. 'They would swear blind that Will was not in a relationship at all. So why was that ring there, Rose?'

I thought of last Thursday, when the police had pretended they didn't know I was there overnight, but clearly did. How many times I had spoken to them now. Four? Five?

And today I noticed something odd about this question, too. Officer Parmar asked it like he was certain I knew the answer.

Chapter 18

Patrick placed his knife and fork down and they were not together, and that was how I knew he was feeling genuine shock. He stared at me.

'You can't cancel it,' he said.

'Why can't I?' I cut into a poached egg. Watched the yolk run, and felt it turn my stomach. I put my own knife and fork down. Braved a grin.

Patrick brushed his blond back off his head, where he normally kept it covered – I'd once found the hair transplant research in our Google history so I knew he was self-conscious about it receding. I smiled at him, with more authenticity this time. At his lovely hair and his lovely teeth.

'Why can't I?' I said again. 'Hen dos are not compulsory. No vicar will make me show my cock straws before he can go ahead with the ceremony.'

A tiny drip of sweat started to make its way down from Patrick's forehead to the frown between his thick, dark eyebrows.

He smiled at me, though it was a smile that didn't make the frown lift. Patrick had got back from his own stag do late the night before. It was a month before our wedding, a Friday. I had got in from work just before 6 a.m., headed straight for bed and had six hours' sleep. Now it was 1 p.m. and Patrick had the day off work for hangover recovery. We were out for breakfast, finally on the same schedule, – ish; I could have done with a couple more hours but it was important, as Patrick said over and over, to make an effort.

He didn't rush to answer me. Swigged from his pint glass of water and chased it with coffee. I sucked green juice through a straw and he ate a hash brown. Patrick speared a sausage and I picked up a piece of avocado on toast. We chewed, in the comfortable quiet of people who have been in a relationship for eleven years.

'Do you want to talk about why?' he said, gently. 'Or not now?'

I pictured that dance floor, last week. Heard the music in my mind and remembered how my heart had emulated its beat. I thought about how much Patrick was buzzing from his stag do, and how that was my worst nightmare now. I shrugged. 'It's just a lot at the moment. With work.'

It hit me then what completely different paths we were on. But how could I be having these thoughts? It was *Patrick*.

As he looked at me, it felt as if he had read my face like a newspaper and my cheeks stung.

He wiped his hungover brow with the back of his hand. 'Nothing to do with what happened in that bar after SushiSamba?'

I shook my head.

'Nothing to do with that chat we had about booze?'

I put my toast down and leaned back to the comfy surrounds of our booth. I shrugged. 'Maybe.'

He put his head in his hands as he finished chewing his sausage, and when he came up, the food had gone but he had a tiny bit of brown sauce on the side of his mouth. I reached across the table to wipe it away. Kept my hand there for a second against his cheek.

'It's not a bad thing, is it?' I said, quiet. 'To avoid a situation that would end up being a massive booze fest?'

This night, unlike a lot of the others lately, I didn't have to 'get out of'. I could control it. Cancel it. Done. It was my hen do I was bailing on and it was in London, so there was no hotel to battle with over a deposit, no flights to lose.

'It doesn't have to be boozy though,' said Patrick, and I looked at him, Polish vodka coming out of his pores after his three nights in Warsaw, and laughed. These things were boozy enough but for me there was no sense of moderation. I didn't step in, out, like a hokey-cokey. I threw myself into the circle and didn't come up for air. My smile was sad. 'It does though, Patrick. I don't know how to do it any other way.' Not anymore.

'A spa trip, an afternoon tea?'

I laughed. 'Yeah. Maybe.'

Then I shook my head, firm again. 'No, it's the social-ising I need a break from as well as the booze. The plans. The Google calendar entries.'

Patrick looked confused. 'But you've barely been out lately,' he pushed. 'You haven't seen your friends in ages, and then with the night shift . . .'

And finally, he acknowledged it and we edged closer to the truth. For the hundredth time, perhaps the thousandth, I opened my mouth and ordered myself: *Just tell him*. But the shame I felt, as ever, won out. The thought of what his face would do. Making it real. Imagining that conversation.

I felt my stomach flip like I had been on the Warsaw trip too, as though I had necked the shots and got the three hours' sleep. But that's not what had happened to me. Instead, I was in the grip of what I was starting to recognise as anxiety. Patrick saw something happening and reached over for my hand.

'Are we done here?' asked a waiter.

'Yes great, just the bill,' said my fiancé, tightening his grip. Holding me together.

'Please will you think about talking to somebody,' he said, coming round to join me in my side of the booth, putting an arm around my shoulder. We had been down this path many times. Patrick thought I needed to see a therapist to discuss my drinking but I didn't have to analyse it. I knew why I drank.

'There's no need,' I sighed.

'You're cancelling your hen do so that you can't drink.' He slipped an arm around me.

'No, I'm cancelling my hen do because life is too much sometimes, Patrick.'

But I knew he wouldn't get that. And that he didn't want to hear that. Didn't want to know that while there were still some parts of it I hated, I liked how the night shift was distancing me from normal life. That something about it was settling in my bones and it had crept up on me: I no longer wanted to chase Douglas down to ask when this would be over. Actually I sometimes thought of when it was over and returning to my normal life and *that* was when I felt the panic set in again.

The card machine wasn't working so Patrick went to the bar to pay the bill and as I sat, waiting for him, I thought to myself: *is that why you would stay, tethered, for eight long years, to the night shift? Was a need to retreat the key to unlocking what happened?*

We walked the ten minutes home up the bustle of Church Street. Patrick, still hungover, gagged at the smell drifting out of the butcher's. We put our hoods up as it started to sleet. I noticed a new Brazilian place had opened where the pub we'd gone to for our last anniversary used to be. We bemoaned time passing. Things changing. But mostly, we walked fast against the weather and we were silent. I was glad. Silence was something I was growing to appreciate more. Perhaps, from the night shift, that was settling into my bones too.

As we got home and I shut the door behind us, my phone beeped. Keiran. 'Divers in the water at the docks,' it said. 'Looking for a body.'

Chapter 19

Nearly two weeks in and I felt it more and more: we'd found a groove, the night shift and I. Douglas was on my case less now I knew how this worked and could do a decent job.

'Helping my marriage, having you in this gig,' he said the other day. 'I make it to the marital bed a little earlier these days.'

I will never know if he winked as he was on the phone but I would bet a year's salary that he did.

'Glad to be a . . . help,' I muttered, then hung up and got on with the news agenda.

The divers hadn't found anything. It was still business as usual. My hen do was now officially cancelled. It was helpful that my friendships had become distant over the last seven months anyway. None of them were close enough to object strongly. The biggest issue was the Mitfords: my sisters Flo, Annie, Sophia and Squidge (now twenty-two and no longer keen on her nickname as the youngest and squidgiest but she gets what she gets; that's families for you). Uproar in our email chat, an emergency call from eldest sister Flo to check there wasn't a problem with Patrick and the wedding wasn't off. When I told her that wasn't the case – I was just a bit . . . tired – there was silence.

'You're cancelling your hen do because you're . . . *tired*?' said Flo, plummier vowels than the rest of us despite the same schooling, most likely down to her beautifully spoken wife Nell and the kids she teaches at her sweet village school in North Devon. 'Rose, this is not normal behaviour! Is this anything to do with what's been happening at work?'

'Nothing to do with that. I'm fine, Flo, I promise, and will you tell the girls that too?' I paused. 'But speaking of work . . .' I glanced at our living room clock, which had landed exactly on 8 p.m.

'Of course. The night shift begins soon.' She sighed.

I sighed back and made an 'ugh' sound, because that was what I was meant to do but something in me relaxed. I would go to work, silence would fill the space where the bustle of London streets and the constant chat of life lived and I would exhale, deeply. No one – especially now I knew how to do the job – would ask much from me.

And now, I was back here. I relaxed into my chair, glanced at the homepage. On the chart above, the traffic was looking quite decent for 11 p.m., helped by a celebrity engagement and a couple of big football games earlier. Or I was getting better at the job, at knowing what worked at night.

I sipped my coffee. Took out my notebook and checked the list of requests I had from the team: amends to stories, pictures and video to drop in. Methodically, I started working through them. Save. Sip. I turned quickly every now and again with a noise, a jolt, a shift in air pressure. I thought about that top floor. The roof. The shadow in my dream. Copy. Paste. I thought about the ring, which was still with the police. Typo in a sell on a football story. I fixed it. My stomach growled with hunger and I realised I hadn't eaten since lunchtime. Should fix that too. I went to reach for my bag, and the sandwich that was inside it, but my landline rang before my fingers found the tupperware.

'News,' I answered.

'Douglas,' he said because he didn't believe in wasting words on such pointlessness as 'hello'.

My body reacted and I was primed. To defend. To take the vitriol.

'I know it's late, but I thought you should know. Would want to know. Get ready to be excited, Rosie Rivers, and drum roll and all that because . . . we have found a new night editor!'

And somehow, that was worse than the vitriol.

'How long until they start?' I shifted in my seat.

'Five weeks,' he said. Then he sounded nervous suddenly, and I realised he needed something. 'Will that be okay? To cover until then?'

Five weeks. Five weeks to work out who, if anyone, could open those doors on the top floor. Who had a key, access. Who might have helped Will get out onto that roof, or *taken* Will up onto that roof, and why. It's all I could think about. Even though what I should have been thinking about had completely slipped my mind: that my wedding was in four weeks, on a Friday. That I had time booked off. So no, five weeks wouldn't be okay.

I remembered just before we hung up. 'Shit! No. I mean my wedding is in four weeks, then I'm off straight afterwards on honeymoon. I have it booked off. I can't do the five weeks. But until then, no problem.'

I heard him rub scratchy stubble hard. 'Well that fucks me over.' Like I had planned my wedding deliberately to this end. 'Fucking *honeymoon*. All right for some. What is it, Maldives?'

'Safari.'

A grunt.

I stayed silent.

'Fuccccccckkkkkkk!'

Not one to hide his feelings, Douglas. Professional demeanour wasn't his thing. He went off to see if the new starter could move her dates forward and I opened up my calendar. Now there was a finish line. A deadline. I had just under four weeks until I had to re-enter my life. Just under four weeks to figure out what the hell happens to a person when they fall off the face of the planet.

When my phone pinged I was deep in thought and my body jolted like it had been shocked. He had got back to me. Marcus, that friend of Will's from school.

'They didn't keep in touch,' Rania had told me.

Marcus, now, told me differently.

Chapter 20

'Argh, that hurts.'

She laughed.

'Is it funny, my pain?'

'Your low pain threshold is quite funny to me, yes,' Rania admitted as she pushed my skin like she was trying to remove it. I pictured my arm, bare like a skeleton. 'Sorry chick.'

It was after work for her, before a shift for me, 7 p.m., and she was at my flat again, working on my wrist and arm after a flare-up of my RSI.

'So where's that dishy fiancé of yours tonight?' she asked. They had met, Rania and Patrick, a few times before, in my old life, at after-work drinks. 'It's like he's avoiding me. Not another fancy-dress party he's prepping for?'

'Patrick is at a fitting for his wedding suit,' I murmured, still wincing as she swapped to my other arm. He had gone with School Friend Sam, who would be his best man.

'Wit woo!' she said. 'Traditional? Bit chill? Whatever, that will be one mighty fine groom.'

'Traditional, *of course*. Patrick loves an occasion and will give it the gravitas it deserves.' I smiled.

As ever, she skipped topics quickly and before long we were back over in work, with the night shift.

'Tell me everything,' she said, still kneading. 'All the updates.'

I shrugged, lying on my low sage green sofa as she kneeled next to me. She stopped and took a swig of the mint tea I had made her before we started. I sat up and sipped my own.

'There isn't a lot to tell. Do you want to sit up here?' I offered, as she crossed her legs on our large grey rug.

She shook her head. 'Happy down here, chicky.'

I puffed out some air. 'Well, there was one interesting thing.'

She looked up, kneeling like she was in prayer. 'Oh?'

'I spoke to that old school friend. Turns out, they did keep in touch a little. Not much face to face – though there was the odd weekend lunch – but messages fairly regularly.'

I watched her face.

'Huh. I'm sure he said they weren't in contact.'

I carried on. 'Well, he confirmed what you said about the heights thing. That if Will was spotted up on that roof then something was seriously wrong. And . . .'

Rania was looking at me, intent, and for some reason I flushed.

'And . . . I mean it's nothing huge. It's nothing that tells us anyth . . .'

She raised an impatient eyebrow at me.

'He just said that Will had been . . . off lately. Not

replying to messages. When he did get a reply, he said the messages were angry. About work especially. He said Will had never been resentful about this place but was suddenly, "fuck them", "fuck these hours". To the point that when Marcus heard Will was gone, he wasn't massively surprised. He was surprised later, obviously. But at first he just thought it was a storm-out on the job and they'd meet up for a beer and talk about it soon.'

I sighed. 'It was just a relief to talk about it to someone who seemed to give a shit to be honest. It's only two weeks since Will went missing, but most other people have stopped mentioning it. I know I'm not with the team in person but on emails, social media . . . It's so odd.'

She looked thoughtful. 'And what about Marcus, then? He didn't have any idea? What it was that had caused this shift in Will?'

I shook my head. 'None. They hadn't seen each other for a bit, he said Will was never free and it was tricky with the night shift. It was just on messages and he said if Will hadn't gone missing, he wouldn't have thought much of it. I guess everyone gets resentful about work sometimes.'

'True enough.'

'Everyone else though . . . they are a team of people who thrive on mysteries and missing people and misery in their work,' I carried on. 'Especially the *news* guys . . .'

'They like news.'

'You'd think.'

'Does that include you?' she smiled, mug touched to her lips.

I hugged my own drink close. Smiled. 'Nah. Everyone knows I'm a charlatan. When I was a writer I did the soft stuff. Never the meaty stories, or the misery. Not my bag. I did the TV reviews, the Christmas gift guide, where to go for a Bank Holiday day out under twenty quid.'

'And yet this time . . .'

I tucked my legs up beneath me, hugged my mug tighter. 'Yeah, the irony. This time I'm the only one who seems to give a shit. The only one who seems to want to know what happened.'

She frowned. 'The only one who wants the story.'

Suddenly her face did something odd, an expression I had never seen it do before. Guilt?

'In that case,' she said, with a slight cough. 'There's something I should tell you. I am breaking patient confidentiality but the police have never even asked me, and surely it's . . . I don't know.'

I was staring at her now. Holding my breath.

'It's probably not relevant,' she said, rummaging in her bag. She took out her appointment book. Moved her finger through the pages, then landed on what she wanted. 20th January, 7 a.m. 'There. The day after that night. We had an appointment booked. It wouldn't work in the office with the night shift hours but I was going to go to Will's, after work. Since Billington Place is right where I get on the bus anyway.'

Billington Place. I recognised that name. 'That's good of you, Rania. So was it RSI? Or something else that needed treating?'

And what? This wasn't exactly breaking news. Rania

said nothing. But she pointed to the book. Next to Will's appointment was a small cross.

'When was it cancelled?' I asked, heart hammering as I realised the implication.

'It was cancelled at *1.30 a.m.* on the 19th,' she said. 'About an hour before Will went missing.'

'By Will?' I asked.

'I presume so,' she said. 'The voicemail was brief, from an unknown number that I presumed was the office.'

'So what do you think?'

She shrugged. 'Tying up loose ends? Knew a disappearing act was on the cards? Went up to the roof maybe, thought about it . . . but then decided against it? Then left, to travel round Laos or something. Will is probably having the best time, and there's us, in London with sleet running down our necks, panicking.'

'Did you not tell the police?' I was shocked. Not to mention a bit confused that she was telling me all of this suddenly. 'About the cancelled appointment?'

'I didn't think it really . . . what could it have . . .' But she trailed off and blushed. 'Now we talk about it, you're probably right. I will.'

Then something else occurred to me. 'Had Will been to see you before?' I asked Rania, still staring at her appointment book, that tiny x in the corner next to the name. She looked pained.

'Like I said, patient confidentiality, chick . . . I've told you too much already.'

I laughed. 'Oh as if, Rania. You're my friend. You know what this means to me.'

Her lips fastened like a button.

'Why start telling me then?' I said. 'What was the point if you're clamming up now?'

She sat up straighter. Eyeballed me. 'It's not nothing, Rose, patient confidentiality.'

I frowned. 'So why tell me anything then? You wanted to give me a snippet and now I go and run with that, or what? Are you telling me there is something here, or not?'

She would tell me, surely. I waited for her to exhale and sag, break open.

'I once heard someone compare patient confidentiality to protecting sources for a journalist,' she said then. 'Think of it like that. You would do that, wouldn't you, no matter what. It's a big fucking deal. So I've already gone above and beyond telling you this.'

My eyebrows shot up. She was serious. 'Well that was your choice!' Still, silence.

'We have talked so many times before about this,' I said, incredulous. 'And you have never once mentioned anything. That's weird, Rania. That's *weird*. You're mentioning just enough to make my mind go into overdrive but not enough to be in any way useful.' I pulled my cardigan back on. Physio over for now, the atmosphere – so filled with warmth as she kneaded my forearm a few minutes ago – too strained. 'And not telling the police . . .' I shook my head. 'I'll transfer the money tonight,' I said, as Rania shrugged her arms into a coat.

She nodded.

'Hey,' I said. She turned back then, just before she opened my front door. 'Who compared patient confidentiality to protecting a source?'

142

And before she answered – refusing to tell me, of course – a flush ran from the tattoo in Sanskrit on her shoulder all the way up to the couple of greys that sprouted out of the beautiful dark hair at her temples and stayed there, a flashing light of warning. I had no way of knowing, of course. And yet I did. Will Frost. Will Frost. Will Frost. Will Frost, to Rania, was a person with thoughts and views and theories. Will Frost, to Rania, was nothing like a ghost.

And what did that mean?

Chapter 21

There was just time before my shift to get there. I pulled on my cycle helmet. I only had twenty minutes to spare.

I glanced at the time on my phone as I pulled up in front of the sign, breathing hard. BILLINGTON PLACE. I would need to be quick, and I would need some luck. But this was doable.

I chained my bike to a railing, my breath still coming quickly. Rania either didn't realise she had said the name of where Will lived, or thought I already knew. But finally, *finally* I had something.

At the first three doors no one answered – not a surprise, it was 8 p.m. in London, and a lot of people weren't back from work, or were just settling into a booth at a restaurant in Soho.

Door four though was opened by a small child in his pyjamas. 'Yeah?' And then a voice, loud and fearful from behind. 'Sebastian SEBASTIAN do NOT ANSWER THE DOOR, how many times?' A woman in her late thirties in a beautiful green Zara shirt I recognised was looking at me like it was my fault her son had answered the door. She was holding a saucepan like a weapon. 'Yes?' she barked.

I backed away. 'Apologies, wrong flat.'

Door five was opened by a woman clutching a theatre ticket and a handbag and opening the door to leave, rather than for me. We nearly slammed into each other. 'Oh!'

'I'm so sorry! Sorry!'

She stepped backwards.

'Apologies for bothering you as well but I've forgotten the number of my friend's flat. I thought it was five, but clearly I've misremembered . . .' I whacked the side of my head to illustrate my own stupidity, and told her the name.

She stared at me. Then she literally ignored me and as I stepped backwards, she slammed the door behind her and ran past, answering her taxi driver as she went.

Flat six were friendlier: an Asian couple who both had a glass of wine in hand and seemed quite excited to see me and did think hard if they'd ever met anyone with that name but ultimately had nothing for me. Seven and eight were in the work/Soho restaurant camp. I pulled my phone out of my pocket. One more, and I would have to go. I sighed. But as I stood in front of number 9 Billington Place, I had a gut instinct. This was Will's flat.

And then the door opened.

He looked at me.

'Well well well,' said Officer Parmar. 'Fancy seeing you here.'

And so there I was suddenly, propelled into the night editor's real world that I had wondered about and imagined so often. Sitting on Will Frost's sofa, looking at Will Frost's bookshelves.

'Very eclectic taste, right?' said Officer Parmar, glancing at the books a few minutes later. 'But then, maybe you already knew that?'

I looked down at my feet. My bright blue trainers were mud-splattered from the cycle. 'I didn't have a clue about Will's taste.' I sighed. 'I have told you *over and over again*, we did not know each other.'

He exchanged a glance with Officer Ford. *They don't believe me. They don't believe anything I say. They think I am guilty.*

Of *what* though?

I wondered what they were doing here. Whether they were collecting evidence or whether this was more about people. Were they waiting for a flatmate or a partner or whoever that ring was intended for? Though there didn't seem to be anyone else here now. Perhaps they had been talking to Will's neighbours?

Officer Ford wandered over to the bookshelves and thumbed a Stephen King. Officer Parmar followed my eyes watching her.

'Can we get back to the question I asked you when you knocked at the door, Rose, and which you *still* for some inexplicable reason haven't answered?' he said. 'What are you doing here, if – as you insist – you didn't know your colleague outside work? How do you even know this address?'

Officer Ford put the book down on the coffee table and looked at me with interest. 'Everything I said was true,' I said quietly, chastened. 'But I'm desperate to know what happened. Isn't that normal? To be curious? When another colleague mentioned the address, I just . . . I thought I would come.'

'Expecting *what* though, Rose?' laughed Officer Parmar, incredulous. *They don't believe you, Rose, they don't believe you*, and that thought plus how stupid he made me feel when he laughed at me made my face flush scarlet. 'That Will would answer the door, cup of tea in hand? That the whole thing had just been an excuse for a Netflix binge and some time off work? Genuinely, I'm interested – when you knocked on this door today, what did you think you were going to get?'

Out of nowhere, tears threatened. Something sat in my gut shaped like dread because I knew what coming here had done now. It had made me even more interesting to the police. It had made their distrust for me greater. 'I don't know,' I said, shaking my head. 'I don't know. Perhaps I thought I would speak to a flatmate who would know something . . .'

The laughter had stopped now and the reply was sharp. 'We might have thought of that, Rose.'

I nodded. Put in my place. 'Of course. I'm sorry.'

And then for a few seconds we sat in silence and I looked around. Here I was, in Will Frost's home. So what was it like? The room was neat and minimal, the walls were off white. Rented, I presumed. There were barely any pictures on the walls; the ones that were there were generic. No pretentious art books on the coffee table though those bookshelves – I'd seen them in Ikea – were well stocked with everything from footballers' biographies to Ian McEwan to J.K. Rowling, spilling out and stacked on top of each other and not – as far as I could tell – in any sort of order.

'*Is* there a flatmate?' I asked it quietly. 'Or a partner?'

The glance that the officers gave each other couldn't have lasted longer than half a second but I knew what it meant: they wouldn't be telling me whether there was a bloody flatmate or a partner or not. They wouldn't be telling me anything because it was an ongoing investigation but also because they *did not trust me.*

In fact, as far as people for them to trust with information on this case went, I was languishing at the bottom of the list. They suspected I knew more than I was letting on. And they'd be shipping me out of here before I had the chance to look around and find anything more revealing than the two complete sets of Harry Potter books I had clocked on the shelf.

'I really didn't come here for any other reason than to try and make some sense of it,' I tried again. 'I know that probably sounds unlikely. But it is true.'

No one said a word. Officer Parmar looked at the large chrome clock on Will's wall. 'Ding! You need to be getting off for the night shift, I would have thought Rose. Time's up.'

I was desperate to stay there to persuade them that I didn't know what had happened to Will. But I followed the glance to the clock and saw they were right: I really did need to leave. I was pulling my rucksack onto my shoulders the next time either of them spoke.

'See you soon, Cinderella.'

I was escorted out, past the four other doors in the flat. Every one of them firmly shut.

Chapter 22

A strong gin and tonic sat in a bulbous glass in front of me, sprig of rosemary from the sprawling garden perched on the side.

My request for the Tanqueray had been met with a slight but notable wince from Patrick's father, who likes things to be in order, and believes a G&T after a meal rather than before is very much not in order, but is also a very polite man and would never have said that out loud to me. As I took a sip, he sat next to me in the sitting room in a large, wing-backed, navy chair, sipping a strong whisky. *That* was the way to do things in the correct order. He played with his phone.

'How about this one next . . .' he muttered to no one but himself as another interchangeable jazz track came on.

'Lovely, Henry,' I muttered with a smile, settling back into plump sofa cushions. 'Just lovely.' And I meant it. It was interchangeable but interchangeably soothing, and I was as relaxed as I had been in a long time. I leaned forward and picked up my glass again, took another long sip of my gin and tonic. 'Mmm.' I heard the contented sigh come out of me and noted Henry smile kindly in my direction.

Patrick and I were at his parents' home, Foxlands, a sprawling estate buried deep in the Surrey countryside where Patrick had grown up playing cricket on the village green and helping his mother shake the apples loose in the orchard. It was the definition of English gentility: soft, comforting, privileged. I felt my eyes droop. I was blocking out the voicemail Officer Parmar had left me, asking for a catch-up when I was free and reminding me to make sure I didn't go paying any more visits to Billington Place.

I knew Patrick's parents had been worried about me and my stress levels. I knew they wanted to look after me that weekend, after what had happened at work. While Henry and I had been shooed into the sitting room to relax, Patrick and his mother were cleaning away our plates, smeared with the remnants of the pan-fried guinea fowl we had polished off an hour earlier. I couldn't hear their conversation, out there in the large kitchen, but a giggle would make its way out at moments; some convivial chat as they walked past the room we were in.

'No point eating anything else in February,' said Henry, putting his phone down. 'Game all the way for me.'

I nodded. 'Consider me converted. It was delicious. And that plum pudding . . .'

'She's a wonder,' affirmed Henry, but I had no idea if he meant his wife, Alice, or someone behind the scenes. They had 'help', I knew. But how involved they were, I wasn't quite sure. It felt uncouth to ask, even if Alice and Henry were second parents to me, even as I had my feet tucked under me on their sofa, a good-sized double of their gin in my hand.

Henry put his own head back too, onto the deep mustard velvet cushions. One of their cats, Anastasia, walked across the back of the sofa and made me jump, and Henry smiled. 'Jumping at old Anastasia,' he said. 'It must have been a while since you've been here.'

His tone was light, but I was aware of it – it *had* been a while. Work had been busy, even before what had happened, but since the night shift . . . We normally headed over here every few weeks for a break from the city, but a break now involved sleeping in my own bed in the night-time and eating the kind of normal meals most human beings did at normal hours. A trek out to Surrey wasn't high on my agenda. This weekend, though, Patrick had pushed me on it. Alice had followed him with a phone call.

'Please come, my darling,' she'd said, that lovely voice pronouncing all its syllables so calmly, like she was taking part in a diction test. 'We'll look after you and spoil you. We miss you!' A pause, loaded. 'And we are worried about you too. All this stuff at work . . .'

If she had been there I think she would have shuddered. It had been nearly three weeks then since Will had disappeared without trace from the same seat I sat in every night. I could see her point. Sometimes I forgot how crazy it all was. So I agreed to come, and Alice and Henry were true to their word: from the moment Patrick and I arrived at lunchtime Saturday, me having had only a few hours' sleep, his mother was at my beck and call. There was mint tea – the real kind, in a pot – and the good red wine from the cellar. Toast spread thick with Henry's homemade strawberry jam, and that guinea fowl: gamey, with rich buttery roast potatoes.

I was to relax, I was told, soft expensive blankets placed next to me, a hot-water bottle tucked into my side. Anastasia and the Harts' other cat, Freddy, sensed the cosiness and nestled in close.

'All this, with a wedding coming up,' said Henry now, swilling his whisky round his glass. 'It's a lot for you. Patrick said you cancelled your hen?'

Ah. I opened my eyes, only realising as I did so that they had been closed. 'Yes. Not my thing these days anyway, all that mayhem.'

Alice walked into the room carrying port in a beautiful crystal glass. 'I don't know,' she said, winking at me. 'I remember you didn't mind a bit of mayhem when we went on El's.'

Oh God. Eleanor's hen do last summer existed as a blur, snippets of memory in amongst hours and hours of nothing. It had only been a few weeks since that night at Lizzie's and remembering it – even the small parts I could recall – was traumatic. I forced a smile. 'Yes. Maybe that's why I should stay away from the mayhem.'

'Pshhhhtttt,' said Henry, crossing his legs. One slipper dangled loosely off the end of his foot, threatened to drop. 'What's life for if not a little mayhem?'

He and Alice exchanged a glance then and it was intimate and lovely. They had lived through some mayhem in their time, I suspected. Were remembering it fondly.

Patrick walked in, holding the same glass as his mother. He smiled. 'What's all this about mayhem?'

And here is a funny thing: while Patrick had concerns about my drinking, Patrick's parents would have been more concerned if I wasn't drinking. I knew that because of the look on their faces then, when I put my empty gin glass down and conceded defeat to the exhaustion that was making me feel ill.

'I'm sorry,' I told them. 'I have to go to bed.'

Alice was aghast. 'It's only nine thirty, darling, and we haven't seen you in so long!' She looked down at Anastasia and Freddy, next to her. 'Even the cats are sad!'

Henry simply ignored me and fetched me another gin. I lasted until ten. Tried again. Was met with a similar response.

'Let her go,' said Patrick, sadly. 'It's the night shift. It wipes her out.'

'But I wanted to show you some options for my wedding outfit,' said Alice, her youthful face with that soft blonde bob pleading with me. 'And chat favours. The Roberts-Ruperts had little bottles of gin for Susannah's and I thought that was terribly sweet?'

I nodded, barely awake. I assured her that we could talk about it tomorrow. I took my hot-water bottle with me and climbed into a bed with cool sheets that were ironed and tucked like I was at a five-star hotel. I was asleep in seconds. I had no idea what time Patrick came up but I didn't hear him and we slept late, until 10. When I woke up there was a glass of water next to me that I hadn't brought up myself. Some brand-new slippers, not mine, sat at the end of the bed waiting for me. On the back of the door was a dressing gown that looked new and I slipped it on, tied it tight around my waist and pushed my feet into the slippers. The comfort made me want to cry.

'Shall we?' said Patrick, looking similarly decked out. He offered me his arm. 'Happy Valentine's Day, by the way.' He smiled and we laughed at ourselves, as we shuffled downstairs like octogenarians, to spend the year's official day of romance with his parents.

Breakfast was sprawled across the table. Large bulbs of strawberries, fresh pain aux raisins that had been delivered this morning. We sat in the kitchen this time, not the more formal dining room of last night and Henry stood up at the hob poaching eggs while Alice brewed some coffee. Patrick sat straight down and dived into the sausages.

'Are they Wilfred's?' he asked, referring to the pig farmer up the road who was also his godfather, without looking up at his dad.

'Of course, darling,' Alice answered for Henry. 'Wouldn't eat any other sausage!' She managed to sound always just a little filthy, as only truly posh people can. I laughed. *I love you*, I thought, looking at Alice, and then around at this beautiful place that felt like home, and I had no idea why, even as I thought it, I felt so sad. I speared a piece of perfectly cooked bacon on my fork. Added a tomato. Some hot, buttery toast appeared by my side, along with a strong coffee.

When breakfast had settled and we had all read the *Daily Telegraph* – me grabbing *Stella* magazine for the least right-wing option – Henry looked at me across the kitchen table. Gave his glasses a quick clean on his sleeve. 'You bring your wellies, Rose?' Without his glasses on, he seemed to peer at me more closely. 'I feel like we could do with getting you out for a ramble. How much fresh air are you getting, with these night shifts?'

When I looked up, Alice was standing there too, brow furrowed and staring at me. She nodded. 'We worry about you, you know.' She glanced over her shoulder. Patrick had nipped to the bathroom. She lowered her voice. 'And my boy worries. He worries it's going to impact this wedding day of yours, too.'

I thought about them, and the money they had given us for the wedding. How invested – both monetarily and emotionally – they were. I shook my head, firm, tried to convince myself too. 'No no, it'll be done by then. Normal service will resume.'

She brightened. 'Oh! That is good news. Just a few weeks then?'

'Just a few weeks. And then everything will be back to normal.'

I forced a wide smile. Realised I had repeated the word normal like I was trying too hard to make it the reality. But what would normal look like when I went back to the day shift anyway, as I sat in that chair wondering where Will had gone? I pictured that empty living room at Will's flat.

And what would it feel like to dance at my wedding and to pick out my favours and go on the honeymoon we had planned to Kenya, and then to come back? Back to waiting for someone who could be dead and decayed at worst, lost at best, with a new permanent night editor in the chair.

Could I do that? Move on. Forget it. Cut the giant

white cake and reapply my lipstick? Ignore it all, as though Will's narrative were entirely other to mine when I knew really that that wasn't true.

Ask Rose.

Living, in the absence of Will, with the absence of answers about my own life too?

Henry, Alice, Patrick and I put our wellies on and headed out into countryside so beautiful it almost stilled my swirling thoughts. It was one of those rare perfect days: cold, yes, but with a bright blue sky and a calmness. Still, it couldn't quite do it. I could feel my phone vibrating repeatedly in my pocket too, though I was trying to ignore it. To be in the moment. To be properly here, with my family – future family – and present. But when we stopped at The White Horse for half a cider and some truffle chips and the noise in my mind got louder, the temptation was too much and I nipped into the toilet and checked my phone. Eight messages, from Rania.

I'm sorry.

You're right, telling you half a story wasn't fair.

This has to be totally confidential.

I mean it. Promise?

This is probably better on the phone, will call you.

Ah, I remember now, you're at the in-laws. Call me, if you can?

That wasn't the first appointment. Carpal tunnel. One of the worst cases I've seen. We had them regularly. We talked.

I knew things.

When I had called her back and returned from the toilet to the table, there was an odd atmosphere. Alice and Henry were silent, and Patrick was staring at me.

The only thing I could hear was the crackle of the fire; we had got the best table in the house, right in front of it. We had appreciated it when we first came in, but now I was sweating. I rolled up the sleeves of my sweat-shirt.

'Is everything okay?' I asked Patrick.

He looked down. In front of him was an empty pint glass; next to that my half, full. I looked at Alice and Henry, whose drinks were also finished.

'I'm sorry, was I . . .?'

He glanced pointedly at my phone, still lit up, in my hand. I shoved it into the pocket of my gilet. I had only had a quick chat to Rania. Surely no one had been bothered by that? 'You were thirty minutes, Rose,' he said.

'No, I can't have been, it's only . . .' I took my phone back out, glanced at it. Shit. He was right. I looked at Alice and Patrick, who deal in napkins and plush cushions and looked like they would rather be anywhere than in this conversation. I directed my apology to them. 'I'm sorry.'

Alice waved her arm around in a motion that said 'no bother' and Henry muttered, 'No no, not a problem to us' under his breath but the atmosphere said otherwise, and I knew Patrick must have been complaining about it while I was in the toilet: how I always do this, how my mind is elsewhere, how our wedding, our life comes second to work and that is how it is. Manners were everything in that house, and I thought about how rude I must have seemed. Tears welled in my eyes but I blinked them away.

We walked back to the house and Patrick and I got our train back to London a few hours later and the goodbyes were tactile and effusive but something sad sat between us all. It was like something was unreachable – even though we all wanted to reach it, all wanted to move past it – and it was unavailable to us for now, a contentment and a togetherness. A weird thought passed through my mind as we waved at Alice and Henry on the train platform and their figures shrunk back towards their car. That I would never see them again. But I knew that was ridiculous and I pushed the idea away.

The train journey took an hour and Patrick didn't speak to me. Which, though unpleasant, gave me quite a lot of time to think properly about what Rania had just told me. What I had found out in the end toilet cubicle at The White Horse had made me want to be sick. But what I had found out in the end toilet cubicle at The White Horse had to be the key to finding out what had happened to Will, didn't it?

My chest pulled tight. Tighter. I heard my inhale as a gasp.

I looked at Patrick, who was pretending to sleep. I considered wedding favours and the food tasting we had coming up this week and I thought how I couldn't find it in me to care about those things and how I was consumed instead by Will, by the thread that tied us together, by the night shift, and how that was weird and wrong. But how I couldn't change it. And how that wasn't fair on Patrick. And what that meant. I pretended to be asleep then too. So much pretending.

Ask Rose.

Chapter 23

It was Monday evening and the atmosphere between Patrick and me was still strained. I had been relieved to leave for work.

In the office now though, I had drunk too much coffee already and I was jittery with a pent-up rage that swelled within me. I slammed my fist down on the desk. The sound echoed, like everything echoed when you were alone in that giant box.

Only four weeks until my replacement would start on the night shift and nothing was giving. I was in regular contact with Will's old school friend Marcus, but he had heard nothing.

Another brick wall.

I sent another email to IT. 'Really could do with access to the above email account please,' I typed. 'Lots of overnight stuff that I need background for. PLEASE SORT IMMEDIATELY.' I marked it urgent.

But I knew it was no use. I'd had this request rejected over and over. I checked the wires. All was quiet, and I switched to Google. On the internet, just like in real life, Will was a ghost. A blank LinkedIn page with little more than a list of jobs. A few links to stories. Not a hint of social media. I sipped more coffee. Something crashed at the other side of the room, and my whole body jerked in shock. I looked over and saw that it was just a precariously balanced pile of books. No bother. But even then it took me five minutes to stop shaking.

I didn't see my colleagues now I did the night shift, of course, but when they messaged me, people mentioned Will less and less. Even Richie, Keiran and Pete. There was a subliminal message and I got it: I was supposed to stop mentioning the whole thing too. No one wanted us to be tied to police investigations and missing people. They wanted to move on. Run a website. Have a pint. Live without shadows. Except sometimes it's not so easy to move on. Especially for me.

Now that I knew what I knew.

Now that I had started to connect the dots.

I thought about the phone call with Rania. About what I'd heard while my cider sat undrunk with Patrick and his parents.

'We talked a lot, Will and I,' she had said. 'You know how it is, in those sessions. But then it spilled over and we talked about something else. Something that had . . . happened.'

I hadn't asked, just held my breath. Patrick and his parents, out there in the pub, had ceased to exist. All there was in my mind's eye was Rania, saying those words.

As she spoke, I had felt my hands curl into fists. And then she had told me what Will had said to her. What Will had told her. They wondered why I was in that toilet cubicle so long? When I got off the phone to Rania, I needed time to decompress. Time to process what she had said to me. Time to calm down, to unball my fists, to not wear my rage when I walked out there to them, all over my face.

There had been no one else at the party. Just the team from the website. So why did I stay in that job, after I was assaulted by one of my colleagues? That's the question, isn't it?

For a start, I couldn't make my brain accept that I wasn't the one in the wrong. I berated myself for drinking until I couldn't remember. At the very least, I hadn't said the no you know you should say. Never mind that I had been passed out; all I focused on was that.

So why should I get the easy way out? I had to get on with it and accept the shame that sat just below my throat every day, in morning conference, when someone brought me a tea, when the banter went on and on and on and I had to go to the toilet to sit alone for a few minutes and breathe and *I still didn't remember.*

Secondly . . . Secondly is harder to explain. If I had left the website then, after that night at Lizzie's flat, I would – even if only to me and one other person – forever be the woman who had been attacked by one of her colleagues and then left, shamed. If I stayed, it was one drunken work night in a sea of drunken work nights, some Pinot Grigio in an ocean of Pinot Grigio. I wouldn't be the victim but the colleague, the mate, the girl with the banter who was in on the joke and didn't take things too seriously. Perhaps too, I hoped that it would come to me, who and what happened, if I stayed in its epicentre.

It never did though, and many times I was in meetings with those men, staring at their faces, in another place entirely. Wondering *who, who, who.*

'Rose!' they would say. 'Earth to Rose.'

Then I would stand up, big grin, and I would say: 'Right guys, who fancies a tea?'

Chapter 24

More coffee.

I still hadn't been sleeping well during the day; there was no fighting it any longer, caffeine and sugar were what I needed, herbal tea and midnight salads weren't cutting it.

It was 4 a.m. now. Only an hour left. And then something on the screen caught my eye. A story about a woman who'd been sexually assaulted in a London park. And there it was, my heart off at a canter, reminded of how it used to work.

Overnight, when Will was there, stories like this appeared regularly. Sexual assault after sexual assault after sexual assault. A reminder, how many women, every day. Assaulted by partners. Strangers. Colleagues. Only I would notice them – they were listed on my handover – because they were buried deep on the site. If I mentioned one of them faux casually to Keiran or Richie or Pete, they had never seen them. If it didn't make the top ten on the chart, then who cared? And they never did: more often than not, those stories weren't big enough to be on the site at all. Why run them then?

For me, I always thought. Will put those stories up *for me*. To goad? To taunt? To remind me? To warn me? To send me a message?

What do you know? I thought every time one of those stories went up. *How do you know?* Because Will *couldn't* have known anything. Will wasn't even there that night. Will didn't socialise, Will did the night shift.

And yet, there must have been a link, mustn't there?

And then, Will went missing and left that note and I was even more sure I had been right. There was a link between us, even if it was formed of invisible chains.

Wired now, I ransacked the drawer again. Work notebooks, pens, staples, but nothing that told a story. No receipt from a favourite restaurant and a seafood paella for two. No shopping list for the way home. No photos of someone Will loved in the sea on the Norfolk coast, or the two of them eating spaghetti in Rome. Nothing.

I thought about Patrick and I and felt nostalgic for how we used to be. We did all of those things, and a thousand more, and I had snapshots running through my mind of all of it.

Lately, it was different. Our bodies grazed past each other and our messages were brief and perfunctory, hello, goodbye, I'm tired, I'm awake, I'm home, I'm gone. Things had been awkward since we'd got back from Surrey. We hadn't spoken about it as there was nothing to say. I was rude, he was embarrassed; my priorities were in one place, his were somewhere else. Where do you go from there?

I thought about Rania again, and what she had said. I thought about my story, and Will's story, and converging stories and dichotomies. As I slammed the drawer shut, I thought about going back to Will's flat, checking to see if there *was* a flatmate or a partner there, but I knew that if there was, they would have been warned against me now anyway. If I turned up, there would be a call straight to the police and the last thing I needed was to make them suspect me even more. So instead I stuck to my own territory.

I looked around. Sighed. What now? I had exhausted this desk but something had to *give*. The next thing I knew I was there, at Douglas's desk, trying to guess his computer password. His real birthday? Or the one Pete told me he makes up that puts him two years younger? I tried both. Nothing.

'What the fuck do you think you are doing?'

I leapt up. The coffee had had my heart racing. Then though, when I heard that voice, quiet, menacing, just through the door across this empty box of an office, it felt like it stopped. Douglas was a joke to me until he wasn't. Until he made me feel pure, tangible fear.

'I . . . don't know.' And that was the truth. Why was I snooping round Douglas's desk? What *was* I looking for? I only knew that I had ran out of avenues, and that the police seemed to think the answers lay in this office, and if anyone on our team would be involved in something bad, something worrying, surely it would be him.

'Is this to do with Will?' Douglas said. 'You snooping around?'

I shook my head. Scrunched my hands up so he didn't see them shake. 'No. I just needed a pen.'

'Pens live on desks, not inside screens, Rosie. Don't treat me like a fucking idiot.'

When he walked in, I had been hunched over his keyboard. I stayed silent. Eventually he sat down. I retreated back to my desk. But he was over, in seconds. 'You wondering what I'm doing here putting a shift in so early?'

I shrugged. 'A bit, yeah.' *Just leave me alone. I don't care why you're here.* Except I did care, didn't I? Because the picture I had of Will's existence was solitary, it was of Will in total isolation every night until the door of this building was exited at five in the morning. But now it was 4.30 a.m., half an hour before that, and Douglas was here. So was this the first time this had happened or did Will Frost, at the most exhausted, spent part of the shift, often acquire a colleague?

I waited for him to speak.

'Get a little jump on the day,' he said. 'Big meeting with the bosses upstairs later.' He narrowed his tiny eyes at me. I stared at him. A jump on the day at *four thirty in the morning*? 'I meant to warn you. Perhaps I should have, then you might not have leapt five feet in the air when I walked in and found you snooping at my computer.'

'I wasn't—'

He held up one of his hands. 'Whatever. You clearly couldn't get in anyway, so whatever the fuck you were doing, just don't do it again.'

I locked eyes with him. They were odd, Douglas's eyes, not brown, not hazel, not green, but the colour of paints so muddled by kids, the shade didn't have a name.

'Hello. Earth to Rosie.'

I snapped to attention.

'You look nice,' he said, taking in my monochrome maxi, black tights and boots slowly, head to toe in a way that made me want to fold in on myself. He nodded. 'Good for you, making an effort when there's no one else here.'

What was he talking about? I felt the impact of the countless cups of coffee again. 'What?' My voice was louder. Douglas was heading back to his desk, designer shoes clacking. Half an hour later, I went to leave.

At the last second, I stopped at his office door. 'Did you ever come in early when Will was here?' The words were out without me knowing they were coming.

His face suggested I had cracked a joke. He ran a tongue over those too-white teeth. 'Is that your idea of investigative reporting, Rosie?' We were eye to eye again. Mud, mud, glorious mud. 'Must. Try. Harder.'

Chapter 25

When I finally slept that morning, I kept going right through the 3 p.m. final food tasting for our wedding that Patrick had booked a half-day off work for and when I finally woke and called him, tripping over my apologies, he was as angry as Patrick ever gets. Actually, that's not true. He was angry briefly, then he was sad. Which was worse, of course.

'You are into this, aren't you Rose?' he said eventually, when I had said a hundred sorrys. I heard a tube announcement playing out in the background. 'Sorry, just got to Bond Street.'

'Into what?' I said, rubbing my eye, thinking about what Douglas had said this morning and how long I had before my next shift.

And then there *was* a note of irritation. 'Our wedding. You are into our wedding? Because in Surrey, what happened in the pub, just your whole vibe was off, you were . . .'

I went to open my mouth to tell him of course I was into our wedding. That it was top and bottom and both sides of my world. But then I remembered how it looked to him: I had cancelled my hen do, slept through our final meal tasting and had gone from a fiancée who messaged him about the minutiae of our big day continually to one who could go days without mentioning it when we were only weeks away. How his parents had seemed more excited about it last weekend than I did. His voice came back before I found mine. The tube announcer passed on some more information about delays on the Northern Line, people bustled past. A busker played Ed Sheeran.

'Rose?'

'I am into it,' I said. 'I am into it.' I realised I was crying. Too quietly for Patrick to notice.

'But?'

I swallowed a sob. But? But I am more into what happened to the night editor. But I am not as into this wedding as I should be. But we are diverging. *But* I have the night shift, and the night shift consumes me. But I want to crawl into a quiet space. But the wedding has been rendered ridiculous somehow and I wish that wasn't true but it is; the squid starter, Eloise wanting to chat to me about place settings when my colleague is missing and everything – the shoes, the note, *everything* – is telling me that that is linked to what happened to me.

But, but, but something happened to me.

But I am unravelling, at a time when I feel like I need to be fully formed, as I charge ahead into a future.

'But not as much as you deserve me to be,' I said eventually.

Chapter 26

A day later, I told Patrick I wanted to press pause. Not stop. Just pause. The wedding was being treated badly, squeezing itself into a brain that was elsewhere, that wasn't loving it like it should be loved. I needed to remove something from a head that was overloaded. I needed to halt that process of unravelling.

'Clear the decks, of plans, of thoughts . . .' I told him, heart beating fast. I was having panic attacks daily by then and knew another one was imminent. Twice, even during that conversation, I had had to run to the toilet.

'Bullshit,' he said quietly, sitting up in bed with a cushion in his arms and the duvet around him, like he was trying to cover as much of himself as he could. My heart hurt. He was crying, profusely. 'You're breaking up with your fiancé and cancelling our wedding. Don't sugar coat it. People do it. It's what you're doing. But don't give me bullshit about breaks and pauses.'

I tried to firm up an explanation I thought might help, might simplify things, about how I had changed, about how we didn't want the same things at the moment. But

God, every formation of that sentence sounded like such a *cliché* and I couldn't make myself utter it.

So instead, like most people who have ever called off a wedding and been told they are a liar and watched someone's pain, and not been able to handle what they are doing, I ducked my head, avoided his eyes and took it. Another cliché that was true: perhaps it would be easier if he did hate me.

'Where will you go?' he asked an hour later, as I packed a bag.

It was Patrick's flat that we lived in and I was the one in the wrong, so off I went.

'I'll call a friend,' I said but I was lying because for the last seven months I hadn't trusted myself to see any of my closest friends. They knew me too well. I didn't want them to ask questions. I didn't want to risk answering them.

I pictured my bedroom in my old shared house, where I had lived with friends before I moved in with Patrick. The photos that had covered my wall, of women I loved and who loved me. They would still let me stay, most likely, but how could I ask when I had been so distant, so rude? Plus nothing had shifted: I still couldn't bear for them to see the change in me.

I reassured Patrick though. Yes, my friends and I had drifted apart – that was life sometimes, wasn't it? – but I would go to them now. 'Honestly, it'll be fine.' I avoided his eyes.

Leaving was a mess, the whole thing, and thwacked me in the middle with its pure devastation. It took until

I was standing on Church Street inhaling the scent of a posh burger and being calf-barged by some toddlers on scooters that I realised that in the absence of those good friends I was pretending I still had in my life, I had no clue where I was going. I stood still. That didn't help the calf-barging. Or the panic attack that surged through me and took over. My fingers tingled with numbness. *I will die, I will die, I will die.*

Ten minutes later I sat in the Rose and Crown beer garden, serving as the polar opposite to the joyous drinkers wrapped up in their cardigans and coats and bobble hats, dipping chips in ketchup and overflowing with laughter that felt to me at that moment like an affront. In front of me sat half a cider. I clutched my rucksack close to me. It barely contained anything, fragments of an existence, but right now it was the whole of it, and it felt like my only life raft. With the other hand, I scrolled through my phone for someone to go and stay with. The As brought up Annie, my sister. She lived in Edinburgh with her husband and their baby. But how would that work? Sorry Douglas, it's tricky to get to work when I'm commuting from Scotland. That was the problem with all the Mitfords. Squidge was travelling around Europe with a pack of friends. Sophia was twenty-four and cabin crew, and possibly flying over the Atlantic Ocean at this very second, if she wasn't sleeping at home in her shared flat which happened to be in Manchester. Which left Florence, my big sister – the only one older than me – and the one who was constantly trying to persuade me to come and stay with her, her wife Nell and their dog Bella for a while. But the night shift doesn't lend itself to a commute from Devon, whatever Flo might say.

I thought of my parents, in our family house in Hertfordshire. Just about commutable, as a one-off, if I did a normal 9-5. But I didn't do a normal 9-5, did I, not at the best of times and certainly not when I was the night editor. Which led me back to central London. Who could I stay with, in central London?

'Not a soul,' I muttered to myself. Not now I had shed my friends like peeling skin. I put my phone down, reached for my cider and took a long swig.

The irony is that when most Londoners in their twenties and thirties can barely afford the rent on precisely the minimal space they need, Patrick and I had multiple friends with spare rooms. They were our circles. Oxbridge, rich parents, banker jobs, flats snapped up when people first moved to London, no mortgages. And yet none of *them*, the dawning realisation came, felt like people I could call, now I had ended things with Patrick. They were his people. His team. I scanned through my phone further. Alice. Eleanor. Eloise. All Patrick's. Now it came to it, I was alone.

But then a name jumped out. She wasn't Patrick's. The woman who massaged my arms and listened to my woes and who had told me more, much more, than she should have about Will Frost but who had been quiet since then, off radar. Waiting for me, perhaps, now, to tell my part? She was perceptive, Rania, and I had a gut instinct: she knew there was my part too. She always had.

'Rania. It's me. Please pick up, it's not about Will this time – it's about me having nowhere to sleep tonight.'

But she didn't reply. Which is how I ended up asleep in the fashion cupboard of *Be*, the magazine that came free with our newspaper arm, while the freelance weekend night editor did his job at the other end of the floor with no idea I was there. I knew, of course, as my head rested on a pile of thin spring knits, that I would not be disturbed, that he would never wander in there. I knew, as I covered myself with one of this season's key look coats and closed my tired eyes, that he would never meander over here in a quiet moment. Because I knew how the night shift worked. I knew that he was tethered.

Why didn't I just book a hotel? A wool coat is not a duvet and a spring knit is not a pillow. I woke up with bones that were in their sixties and a neck stiffer than iron. I had barely slept; my skin crawled with tiredness.

I wasn't great at saving, but I hadn't been paying rent for the last four years living in Patrick's flat and I earned a decent salary. I had enough for a bloody hotel. The next day I walked straight to one and booked myself in for the night.

'If I need to stay longer, do you have availability?' She wasn't sure what they would have going forward. I booked a second night, to be sure. Ignored the question of: And after that, then what? I showered, slept and charged my phone, which had died. And then, before I went into work for the night shift, I phoned Patrick, who had left countless messages checking on me.

His voice was soft when he answered, and kind. Mostly it was relieved. 'How have you been? Are you at a friend's?

I didn't know where you were and I was kicking myself for not asking and I was so worried, Rose.'

My eyes filled with tears. I was loved. Why couldn't that be enough? I looked around. A Premier Inn. Sparse. Between it and my spartan backpack, we had very little of the stuff, this room and I, that it takes to make us human.

I pictured our bedroom, Patrick's and mine, eleven years' worth of being human and being together. Not a surface unaccounted for. Our life, everywhere, in the photos, in the foods we stocked the cupboards with, in the pictures we had chosen together for the wall. In the joint bills on the coffee table and the muddy shoes by the door and the shampoo in the shower and in the calendar up on the wall with the birthday parties we would go to. With our own wedding, scheduled on there for three weeks' time.

'Yeah,' I lied, swallowing it all whole. 'At Lou's.'

We exhaled down the phone at each other, settling.

'Can I come over before my shift?' I asked.

Patrick worked from home on Thursdays. 'Yeah,' he said. 'It would be good to talk.'

I leaned back on pillows that crunched. Thought of my own lilac pillowcases, as familiar as the rest of my flat, that settled with me like skin as I lazed. 'I'll make a list before I come,' I said. 'Of stuff to cancel, who to contact.'

A noise came from Patrick that I had never heard before and sounded like something being snuffed out. 'I thought we would talk first,' he said. 'Before we got that far.'

But we were that far in my head. The wedding at

least was off. Patrick and I could, perhaps, be salvaged sometime later down the line, but not the wedding. I thought of everything it would entail. People staring at me and seeing me whole. Being 'on' all day. An attempt at perfection, to create the most self-enclosed neat day. I pictured myself, smoothing my hair down if it frizzed, pressing down my dress if it wrinkled, avoiding red wine, sweat, tears. All day, swatting the problems, trying to stop anyone knowing there was reality behind it all. It swirled and whooshed and took over me.

No. No. No.

I was saying it out loud, I realised eventually, when Patrick broke it off with a shout and I found my hand clamped tight to the base of my neck.

'Stop! You're okay, Rose. Stop.' His voice dropped a note. 'Come over. Just come over now. We'll sort it all out when you get here. But just get here.'

Chapter 27

And then it hit me – why it was worth giving up my silk pillowcases and the roll-top bath I sink into when it all gets too much.

It was worth giving up all of those things because there was no option, with Patrick, to elope or live a small, quiet life. Patrick wanted a big life and since what had happened, all I wanted was to shrink. He would be found at the centre of a dance floor, he would host the New Year's cocktail party. When children came – a crew of them because he would thrive in the noise and the chaos – he would host his friends for weekends, toddlers roaming in the big garden he would inevitably have out, of course, in Surrey. Friends would camp in the garden or get cosy under Egyptian cotton in the spare room.

They would remember everybody's birthday, the Harts, and they would send you flowers when it was your first day in a new job. They would be members at the tennis club and fundraisers for the local hospital. He was reared for it, all of it. Patrick was reared to be public facing. But I no longer fitted in the picture.

I crossed the road, approached our building. An old Victorian terrace, converted into two flats. Imposing, with its big white windows, coming out to greet you, close to the street. Never backing away. Something stalked across my stomach. It was only when someone walked into me and muttered that I realised I was on the kerb outside our flat, standing still. Delaying going into the home that had been a sanctuary, now, for so many years. In the end though wasn't it bricks and mortar, walls that would be repainted and baths that would be replumbed. It didn't pump blood.

I put my key in the door of our ground-floor flat.

'Hi.'

'Hi.'

And like that, you are awkward with each other when only a week ago you would shave your legs in the bath while he had a wee.

He kissed me on the cheek. 'Are you okay? Are you feeling better?' He looked worried.

I nodded. 'Yeah. Just.'

We walked into our living room and I noticed everything like I was an estate agent and would be writing it all down later. Registering it for a time I knew would come when it wouldn't be part of my life anymore. The yukka limping on in the corner, both of us useless at watering it.

Photos everywhere that told stories. At Foxlands for his parents' wedding anniversary, on a boat on the Thames for Eleanor's thirtieth, her ringlets stroking the edge of my face. I looked at that one closely. My face was plumper than it had ever been: Patrick earnt quite a lot of money by then and liked to spend it on food. Those perfectly runny yolks, the shared crisps, the bagels he brought home from Brick Lane. Alice had grabbed a cheek with her hands and squeezed.

'Bit more meat on you than normal, Rose,' she had said, glass of wine in the other hand. She leaned in to kiss that cheek. 'It suits you.'

It did.

But then came the shift. It was the ones from our engagement party – held in a pub on the river in Barnes, champagne raised high – that I looked at next. Only taken in July. Thinner cheeks. But mostly, the difference was in my eyes.

I stared at her, this haunted woman, who stood there still in shock from what had happened to her a month earlier, only weeks after we had got engaged. Our uni friends were squeezed in next to us in most of the pictures, glossy hair, barefoot on grass, for champagne toast after champagne toast. Light.

Patrick's parents had paid for a free bar and everyone was too drunk to notice that night that I had spent twenty minutes in the toilet cubicle and when I came out I drank three glasses of champagne back to back before I spoke to anyone. I stared at the picture.

'We look happy,' Patrick said, following my eyes.

'Yes,' I said, the tears starting to fall at how much he didn't know. How much I kept from him. 'We do.'

'We *are* happy.' Fierce determination. He could will it true.

'We aren't.'

'I am.'

I looked up at him then. Patrick knew where he stood on things.

I remembered when I used to know that, before I was knocked off my axis. I looked at Patrick. Opened my mouth to tell him everything. Lizzie's spare room. The underwear, crumpled up, on the other side of the bed. That feeling, smarting. Blood. Snapshots. And the other feeling, afterwards, that I couldn't trust just being me anymore.

I was not sure I had had courage in a single one of my convictions in the last six months. I didn't know what I liked. I didn't know what I was sure of. I lay awake at night tortured by choices I should have made. If someone voiced a hint of disagreement with me, I presumed that they were right. Instantly. My default was that I was wrong, had done wrong, was in the wrong.

I sat down on our sofa. Put my head in my hands. I knew I owed Patrick an explanation but exhaustion was superseding honour and respect. I simply sat there and wept and let him comfort me.

'Eleanor saw a therapist for a while. What if we speak to her and contact them? Would that help?'

I shook my head.

'Then let's postpone,' he said, on a sigh. 'It'll be logistically . . . there will be stuff to sort but it's not important compared to . . . and at least we were having the reception at home anyway so that won't be a . . .'

I didn't know my head was shaking side to side until he stopped speaking. The shaking stopped. The weeping stopped. Even the buses, which hurtled their way down to Newington Green and then Angel past our window constantly, seemed to stop for us. Life was still. I breathed out. More slowly. Almost normal.

'Do you not want to marry me?' He was sitting close to me, and it felt like he was holding his breath.

I tried to explain. I remembered that afterwards when I wept in horror at what I had done to him. I tried.

'We can have a quieter wedding.'

I shook my head. 'That's not it.'

But it is hard for someone to listen when you are cracking open their heart. It's hard for someone to listen when you're not telling them the whole story. Patrick had begged me to come home that night, he had offered to pick me up or come and get me, but I had been in my new role for a month and the pressure was immense, the wine had gone down fast. I was more drunk than I had been in my life. I had shouted at him that he was being possessive. Controlling. That I was *fine*.

I had drunk more.

More.

I had put myself in that position, despite having a kind, loving fiancé who would have turned up in a taxi and scooped me up and taken me home, even at four o'clock in the morning.

More.

How could I tell him what had happened to me, then?

So without that knowledge of what had changed me, all he said was 'Is it the night shift?' and *you know what*, I thought, as I took off that ring with its big, bold emerald shining bright, and passed it to him as he wept. *You know what, you know what, in a way, maybe it sort of is.*

Chapter 28

An unexpected benefit of the night shift: my cycle to work, now I had started to brave it, was beautifully still. Not quiet like ambling through a bucolic Yorkshire village on a vintage bike with a basket on the front. But quiet for London.

It was only the second time I had done it since Will had gone missing, since the night shift, but I was running late from being with Patrick and anyway, cycling fast was a good distraction. No time for self-pity when a red-faced man in a Peugeot is screaming at you to fuck off the fucking road. I stuck two fingers up at him and kept going. Not today. The rage was the only thing that stopped the tears.

When I got to work, I was panting like a dog. I looked at my phone while I waited for the lift: two minutes late, which even Douglas – unless he had stayed late, which he was doing less, either because he trusted me or couldn't be bothered – wouldn't notice. Surely.

I pressed the lift button again. Peeled my parka off. Took out the clips that had kept my dark bob back from my face. Smoothed down my hair. The lift arrived and I checked my face in the mirror and wiped away a smudge of mascara under my eye. Sweat or tears or both. I had left him there forty minutes ago. We had broken up. But that was all there was time to think before the lift opened on floor thirty-four and I walked out to the night shift.

My phone beeped as I was reading my handover, which was fairly comprehensive; Alex on the news team was always one of the more thorough journalists. While I covered the night editor role, numerous people were stepping in to be day editor. It was ad hoc and higgledy-piggledy; not the order and symbiosis of the see-saw I was on with Will.

I glanced at the message, expecting Patrick, and steeling myself. I couldn't get emotional here. Not alone, with work to do. But the message was from Rania.

'Thank God,' I muttered. I scanned it. She was apologising for missing my messages – she was always bad with her phone – and then a reply: yes, of course, come and stay. Her flatmate was away for a couple of weeks actually. The room was mine if I wanted it.

That would be appreciated, I typed. *Currently in a hotel. Running out of ££££££.*

She phoned me then. 'Oh chick, I'm so sorry!'

I didn't know if she meant about the end of my relationship and my aborted wedding or not replying to me.

'Come over after your shift? We should have an hour or so before I need to leave. I can make you a tea, show you where stuff is. Does that work? You can get your stuff from the hotel later?'

It bought me time and I was grateful. 'I have to go now,' I told her. 'Homepage is a mess and some breaking news coming in. But I appreciate it. You have no idea how much. I'll buy you dinner soon. Say thanks.'

She dismissed it. No need, no need. We dialled off.

The relief was enough to mean I could get on with work, block out real life, even as I saw a call come in from Eleanor, then one from Alice. Patrick must have told them. Now they were phoning to lecture me, or check on me, or persuade me, none of which I could cope with now. So I turned my phone off. Ten minutes later, Douglas called my landline. I'd turned my mobile OFF? I'd turned my fucking mobile OFF? And I called myself a fucking *journalist*? Not only that but I had got the name of a football manager wrong in a story. I was a fucking *idiot*, thank God they had found a new night editor before I ruined the whole fucking website, etc. etc.

It had been a while, now he was starting to trust me, since he had given me a bollocking of this magnitude and my body couldn't handle it. I shook like I was in a blizzard, and it opened me up to the rest. Patrick was no longer my fiancé. My boss was screaming at me so loudly I couldn't hear the rest of my thoughts. The world was chaos.

'Rosie? Are you even fucking *listening*?'

It ended eventually, as everything does, but I needed to recalibrate before I was calm enough to handle work. It's not okay, is it, for someone to affect your physiology like that. The most fucked-up relationship of my life: the one between me and this place. But it's my dream job, right? I'm lucky to have it.

When I turned my phone on, it pinged with a voice-mail from Officer Parmar. I felt my breath quicken again.

'Just checking in, Rose,' he said out loud to the empty newsroom on speaker on my phone as I copied, pasted, replied to an email. 'Since we haven't seen you for a while. Don't forget, if anything crops up or you think about why Will would have written that note, do call us day or night.'

I stopped typing. There was an assumption now, when I messaged Pete or Keiran or Richie who brought me news from my colleagues on real time, that Will had, simply, 'done a runner'. Maybe made a mistake at a major level: upset a politician or a celebrity with an inaccurate story and knew we would get sued. Even used shifty methods, perhaps. Everyone was united: Will had fucked up, somewhere, somehow and then disappeared so that there would be no consequences. Perhaps that trip to the roof had been plan A, but it had been plan B that had won out in the end.

'Mmm,' I would say, doubtful. 'Maybe.'

But I didn't buy the party line.

'Call us back, Rose.' Officer Parmar's message came to an end.

I sat back into my chair. Sighed. I didn't get the impression the police bought that party line either. But then again they – unlike my colleagues – knew about the note. My breath pulled in sharply again. They couldn't honestly believe I was at the centre of this. Could they?

I don't know what made me do it, because I had been through it before. Frustration, perhaps. Desperation. But when I checked Will's drawer, it was the same as before. Notebooks, pens, a phone charger. I opened the notebooks, but I'd done that before too. Lists that looked like my lists. Reminders that looked like my reminders. Day editor, night editor, two sides of the same coin. I had seen it all before. Hadn't I? Had I delved fully into those notebooks? A work life, minutiae, the mundane. This time though, I kept going. More minutiae. More mundane. Except right at the end, when there it was in caps, underlined and next to a phone number. CALL RANIA.

Which was okay, wasn't it, I thought, as I ignored the feeling in my belly, because it would have been about a physio appointment – I knew now Will had them. But the number next to it wasn't our in-house physio's internal line, which we would call for appointments. Even I still did that, it was procedure.

But no. This wasn't that.

I check my phone contacts.

That number was Rania's mobile.

I hadn't had Rania's mobile number until we were going out for drinks together, until we were telling each other our secrets.

I thought of the conversation I'd had with her in that toilet in Surrey. How she had told me so much but still, *still* I had the strongest feeling that Rania had been holding something back.

Chapter 29

'Chicky!' she shouted at me, ushering me into a Hackney third-floor flat I had never visited. I looked around. Not an inch of space was unaccounted for. Fairy lights were strung across the walls and on the floor was a jungle of houseplants. Incense burned and candles were crammed onto surfaces, next to bottles of nail polish and the tins which I soon discovered she kept her weed in. The floor was a mishmash of rugs and floor cushions and there was a coffee table so low that your chair could be the floor.

On the wall were pictures, framed and not, posters, Frida Kahlo, Rania's – I presume – family, some seventies psychedelia, a mishmash and an explosion. In between them hung beads. None of it had ventured near a spirit level. I smiled. It was like the interiors version of her body, which was layered with tattoos, jewellery, nail art and giant curls.

'Sit down and warm up,' she told me, rubbing my arms like they were firewood. 'I'll get the tea on.'

A message pinged in as I sat down. It was 6 a.m. I had left my shift fifteen minutes late and ridden the forty-five minutes to Rania's on my bike with eyelids only able to stay open because I was so unbearably cold. I had had two pairs of gloves on; my fingers, when I got there, were still numb. The ride hadn't warmed me up, the wind was too icy for that.

I took my phone out of my rucksack. *Been up all night*, typed Patrick. *Thinking about something I can't believe hasn't occurred to me before.*

Then another.

Was there something between you and that night editor? Why else would this affect you so much? Break up our relationship? Ruin our wedding?

I shook my head. Sighed.

Another one.

Everything seems to come back to it. What's the story, Rose? Why are you so obsessed?

I sighed. We had moved to a different stage today then. Not the understanding and kindness of a fresh break-up. Instead, the paranoia and accusing of the later stages. I didn't want to go through this. Not with Patrick. For the hundredth time, the doubts crept in. Was I doing the right thing? I glanced at the door, to where Rania was shouting to ask me if I took sugar.

'No thanks!' I yelled back. Then I thought. 'Actually yes please. One. Today.'

I would sleep soon, which is why I was avoiding coffee, but to hold a conversation, to cope with feeling this sad, I needed something. 'Have you got any food, Rania? Anything with sugar, too?'

I thought of that note. *CALL RANIA.* The mobile number. And I thought of Rania's new lover. I had barely taken notice of her when she'd mentioned that she was in a relationship, so preoccupied with what was happening to me, me, me.

Rania walked back into the room, holding two steaming mugs and, tucked under her arm trailing on the floor, a tassled Moroccan throw. She draped it over me, then she nipped back in, came back with a cold pain au chocolat. 'Thank you,' I murmured, then ate it in three bites.

Rania smiled at me. 'Wow, you were hungry.'

A pause.

'You okay, chick?'

I thought of Patrick's message.

Was there something between you and Will?

I wiped a flake of pastry from my chin.

A question for me? Or a question for Rania?

Chapter 30

Rania drained the last of her obscenely milky tea then kissed me on the cheek. Afterwards, it felt like the musk of her perfume lingered on my skin. I hadn't asked the question. How could I, when she was letting me stay and when I had no evidence and when I sounded as paranoid as Patrick?

'Right,' she said. She looked a little awkward. We were friends, but not in a space like this. We were friends in her treatment room, at the pub under our office. We were not friends who kissed goodbye and shared sofas.

'Are you sure this is okay?' I asked. 'Me staying here?'

'Oh, of course! Of course!' She looked alarmed. 'Please don't leave. Stay as long as you need. There's not a lot of food in though, so you may have to pop to the shops.'

I nodded. 'Of course. And I'll give you some money too, cover bills and . . .'

She waved a vague arm. 'We'll sort it later.' Then she nudged a nail varnish up to put her mug onto an already full coffee table, and it snuggled up to a vegan baking recipe book, what appeared to be some knitting needles and the start of . . . something knitted plus a two-week-old supplement from the *Observer*. I smiled.

'I'll see you tonight, chicky.' She blew me a kiss. 'Seriously. You're welcome. I'm not good on my own anyway.'

I heard my phone beep in my bag and the reaction came. Whoever it was at the moment, it wasn't a good conversation. Patrick, angry. The police, suspicious. Alice or Eleanor, sad and confused.

'Oh! I've just noticed that you're in red!' said Rania, before I could grab my phone. When I looked up she was framed in the doorway like art. If you ignored the navy tabard and leggings of her physio uniform. Her smile negated it though; wide mouth, gleaming white teeth. Her nose ring gleamed too, under the spotlights of the hall. Her finger went automatically to her lips – nails and mouth matching in glossy scarlet.

I looked down. My jumper, bright scarlet too.

She sighed. 'Single. Red. Rose. How can that be wrong? Single red roses are the most perfect thing there is. Fully formed. No need for anything else.' She pulled on a bobble hat that matched her mouth. 'You're going to be absolutely fine.'

Next, she shrugged into a giant yellow faux fur that she had told me she was currently renting, having avowed to turn her back on what she called 'fast fashion'. 'Call me if you can't work anything. Enjoy the shower. Enjoy the sleep.' She waved a hand around her head, indicating her flat as a whole. 'Enjoy the space.'

When the door shut, there was just me. Single. Red. Rose. Fully formed? God, the irony. I went to the bathroom, started the taps running for a bath. Then my phone beeped again and my heart speeded up. If Patrick was angry, it would hurt. If he was sad, it would hurt more.

But it was Officer Ford: 'Did you get earlier message? Wanted to catch up.'

My chest pulled tighter. No one else – from what I knew from the colleagues I'd had messages from – was being hounded like this. The voicemails and texts that the police left for me were daily at least, the frequency upped since I had stuck my head above the parapet and visited Will's place. Sometimes, they were so clearly convinced I knew more than I did that I would find myself feeling foggy, and wonder if somehow, they were right. If I wasn't to be trusted, even by my own mind.

'Need to sleep now,' I texted back, a slight shake to my hand. 'But will call before shift.'

Except how would I sleep now, the pull across my breast bone, the feeling of dread below it? I read the next message. From an old work colleague inviting me to her birthday drinks. I deleted it without replying. No. That wasn't my life anymore. *This* was what I had wanted and now, it was what I would get. Rania and I would cross over like we had today, half an hour here, hour or so at the other end of the day, some days, but mostly it would be just me.

'Shit!' I had been staring into space. I twisted the hot tap off as fast as I could. Not ideal to flood Rania's bathroom on the first day she let me stay. And then, the silence. Rania lived in Hackney so outside the

192

window there was still an angry man who wanted his taxi *now* and there was still someone playing loud rap music with the windows down and there were still children, laughing then fighting, fighting then laughing. *I've a feeling we're not in Foxlands anymore.*

But I was on the side of the flat away from the road. The door was closed. This was silence, or as near to it as I was getting. I sighed. Yes. Slowly, I removed my clothes. The bath was too hot but still I lowered myself in. I lay still. I tilted my head back so that my dark brown hair was saturated.

Something had to fix it, didn't it? Something had to fix the feeling I had had since last June. It felt like physical pain to leave Patrick and I had no idea if it was the right thing. But *something* had to fix that terrible feeling. And if I could just quieten everything down, I was sure that's what would do it. I slid myself under for a couple of seconds. And I thought of those bodies of water, just outside our office window, where divers had swum looking for the thing no one wanted to find. And I thought about people, and how they could disappear in there, in a way they couldn't disappear many places. Not in the Docks, perhaps. But once you got out there into the Thames, the scale was too big.

I only got out of the bath an hour later when I realised I had fallen asleep, and half of my face had already slipped under the water. I came up to the surface swiftly. Gulped the air like it was a tequila shot. I transferred myself to bed, phone still off, world still quietened. Yes. Yes. This was what would do it. Single. Red. Rose. No need for anything else. But I saw Patrick's face, broken, every time I closed my eyes and I thought, *You did that*, and so I took sleeping pills that day, and on many days afterwards.

I didn't call the police back.

Chapter 31

Three days later, I had spoken to a total of three people. Douglas, the takeaway guy and Rania. Though between her social life, stays with her new lover and my sleeping, that was brief and infrequent even over the weekend.

I was still avoiding the police, though I knew I wouldn't get away with it for much longer. I was twitchy, wondering if they would turn up, if they knew where I was living.

'This is getting ridiculous now, Rose. Call. Me. Back.'

I knew I was getting myself in more trouble but I couldn't face it. Couldn't face their suspicion. Though I still couldn't work out what they thought I knew. How they thought I was involved.

My sisters called and I ignored them then texted later to say I was busy at work. Patrick had stopped calling, after I had told him I needed some space. Once, when a friendly takeaway driver asked me what I had planned for the morning – that's when I have my main meal, of course – I noticed my hands, clutching my sushi, were shaking.

'I'm sorry, I have to . . .' I gestured behind me to empty space. My voice sounded odd. I shut the door quickly. Sighed with the relief of being alone. Opened a bottle of wine. I glanced at the clock. 9 a.m. But I was going through a break-up and I did the night shift. When else was I supposed to switch off? My rules were different now. I finished the bottle of wine in an hour, eyes closing, sushi uneaten. I tried to sleep. Failed to sleep. I missed Patrick so much it hurt and picked my phone up to message him, started writing, at least five times. But hadn't I told him to give me space? I would be sending mixed messages, and that wasn't fair on a good man. I sat on my hands to stop myself, and looked around for a distraction.

The next thing I was wandering in my pyjamas, blackout mask shoved up onto my forehead, right into Rania's room. Distraction. Anything to get Patrick out of my head. I looked around. If Rania's flat was a maximalist's paradise, her room was the epicentre. The bed exploded with Moroccan blankets and at least fifteen pillows; the place had never heard of a colour scheme. A pair of black tights lay on the floor. Her mirror had a postcard pinned to it: YOU. ARE. BEAUTIFUL. How could Rania need a reminder? I looked at the pictures of her, everywhere in this room. Her curls thick and dark and proud, in a way mine never were. That's why they were stymied now. Why I came at them with the straighteners daily until they gave in. But mine weren't as good as hers. Look at her!

In one of the pictures Rania posed with a group of friends, men and women. In one, a single man. I looked at him closely. Blond and happy and large enough to obscure most of the background of where the picture was taken, I wondered if he came from the Amsterdam chapter

196

of Rania's life. I was vague on the details of that but I knew she used to live there, with her ex. Could that be him? Did anyone keep photos of exes on their wall? Rania, I thought. Rania probably would. Unless he was the new lover?

My eyes flicked back to the bed – a smallish double. Above it were half a dozen dreamcatchers, on the wall a hotchpotch of beautiful canvases, Dalai Lama quotes, postcards from every continent of the globe and Post-its, reminding her of appointments, arrangements. It was like a room-wide mood board, if the mood was everything, ever. Where did Will fit into this tapestry? And why hadn't I – now we were *living* together, when she had told me what she'd told me – asked Rania why Will had her mobile number yet?

I shook my head. Stifled a yawn. I looked more closely at the Post-its but they were names I didn't know, numbers that meant nothing. Appointment times. Thoughts. Specialist references.

I hadn't asked Rania *because* we were living together. I hadn't asked her because it's not a good look, is it, to return a favour someone does for you with some suspicious-sounding questions about a missing person. And because I thought, perhaps, I would be better finding out on my own.

It's not a good look to return a favour someone does for you by rifling through their drawers when they are at work, either, but that, I did do. I was in there for an hour, when I should have been sleeping, looking now at home for exactly what I spent my time looking for at work: a tiny trace of Will Frost.

Perhaps I am obsessed, Patrick, I thought, *if I can still be like this when I am grieving the end of us. If I can be here, hands in Rania's drawer, when all I should be thinking about was the wedding I have cancelled, the relationship I have ended.*

But I had no idea how not to be obsessed.

Had I really believed I would find that trace? Perhaps not. Because when I did, I gasped so hard I felt like I couldn't breathe.

Chapter 32

Outside there was rain but inside our building, you can't hear it. I pressed myself up against the window and watched it, silent. I was a mouse, being tested on in a controlled environment. No weather could come in. No temperature, other than the one it was regulated to, in here on the thirty-fourth floor. Perhaps it was another way too to help us forget where we were. I clawed my nails down the glass. To help us forget we were high up in the sky. Regulate, regulate, make us more comfortable than anyone could be, no sound, no temperature, no outside influence. I looked at my nails, normally groomed, now too long and untended and I pictured them scrabbling onto a wheel. Little mouse. Copy. Copy. Paste. Don't feel the rain. Do your job. No need to feel cold.

When the phone rang on my desk, I jumped like someone had touched me, from nowhere, on the shoulder. I ran back over there and leapt on it.

'Where the fuck were you?' said Douglas. 'Sort the homepage out. It's a fucking mess. And stop wandering away from your desk. What do you do there in the middle of the night by yourself anyway? Sneak that fella in for a shag, is it?'

I dragged my teeth over my bottom lip to stop myself from crying. The hand that wasn't holding the landline was curled into a fist.

'Get some tits on there too. A wardrobe malfunction. Someone falling out of Mahiki pissed. Whatever.'

I took my teeth from my lip and winced. They were on the inside of my mouth now, the moist fleshy parts peppered with mouth ulcers.

Two weeks until I would have to face him in person every day again. Days of Douglas punching the air with joy at people's misery. People, everywhere. They would want the gossip: *why was my wedding cancelled, why had I ended things, did someone cheat, who was shagging around Rose, come on.*

I craved a glass of wine.

In truth, the drinking hadn't stopped with the night shift, as I had told Patrick it might. The drinking had increased, actually, on those days alone in Rania's flat. I hid the bottles under my bed; sneaked them out to the shared recycling when she was at work.

Another reason I couldn't see my sisters, despite Florence's repeated attempts to get me to come and stay with her and Nell for a weekend. My sisters know how I am, the second they see me. They look at eyes, eyebags, flushed cheeks, pale skin. At plump happy thighs or sad skinny arms. Their eyes are on me, knowing. And at that moment, they wouldn't like what they saw. I felt weak suddenly and leaned my head forward. No, not my sisters. Not my parents. My belly hurt with how much I wanted to call Patrick. But that was the last thing I could do. Mixed messages.

The sobs were loud, and echoed around the room. They sounded lonely. It took a minute to realise they were mine. And then my phone rang again. Mobile, this time. An unknown number.

'Rose! Well, you've been elusive.'

Officer Parmar. God. Was he so deperate to speak to me he was using other people's phones now?

'Not exactly.' But if I sounded snippy, it belied how I really felt, which was nervous and, somehow, guilty. 'But I'm sorry I didn't get back to you.'

'Not a problem. Didn't want to hound you at work and I know you're busy but I had a night shift anyway tonight and it was getting to the point where I was a little concerned you may have left the country, so . . .'

'Why would I leave the country?'

A beat. 'It was a joke, Rose. That night shift isn't good for the old sense of humour is it?'

I didn't say anything. Just tried to remind myself to breathe. But why were they talking about me leaving the country? Was I not allowed to leave the country?

'So, all okay? Anything else turned up? Remembered anything? Thought of anything else?'

'Nothing, I'm afraid,' I said. I saved what I'd been writing with audible clicks and tried to sound brusque and busy. Together. 'Anything else come up with the investigation?'

'That's confidential of course, Rose.'

Even though he couldn't see me, it seemed important; like he was watching me. Like he would know I was faking understanding if I didn't look the part. 'Of course.'

He left the silence that followed, I think, to give me an opportunity. I thought of what Rania had told me on the phone. I should tell them. But how could I? I would drop Rania in it. An ultimate betrayal of trust. Plus, it wasn't my story to tell.

It meant that things had changed though. Now, I was actively lying to the police. There was something else I knew, and I wasn't sharing it.

'Rose? You there?'

'Did you ever speak to Will Frost before all of this?' I asked, impromptu. 'About . . . anything else?'

Officer Parmar left a pause. Then he repeated himself. 'That's confidential too, Rose.' A beat. 'Odd question though. Can I ask why you would have wondered that? It sounds like you have something on your mind.'

It wasn't just the phone call. I should have told him then about the picture I found at Rania's. My friend, a little lipstick on teeth that were bared in a wide smile, in Lizzie's flat at the party. I already knew Rania had been there, my memories from the beginning of the night had always been clear. But the person standing next to her was a complete shock. Even from that glimpse I had had, I knew for certain. It was our night editor, Will Frost.

'I'd better go,' I told Officer Parmar. 'Lots to do. The night shift, you know . . .'

'Ah, I know the night shift, Rose,' he said. 'Or I'm starting to, at least.'

The picture could have been taken on a different evening, of course. Except it couldn't. Because in the background is me, in a dress I only wore once. I binned it afterwards. When you are sexually assaulted in something, you don't have much of an urge to slip it on and head out into the night wearing it ever again.

Chapter 33

When Officer Parmar hung up, a stapler fell off the desk on the other side of the office and landed with a harsh thwack on the floor. I jumped. Then I watched my bony hands shake for hours as I wrote, edited, tidied, replied to emails. Elongated headlines, added in images.

The panic attacks had multiplied, coming in waves in Rania's flatmate's bedroom, in the queue for self checkout at Tesco. On the night shift, often. Twice now, I had come out of them and found myself curled in a ball under my desk.

Now, all I could think about was what I had found in Rania's drawer. What it meant. But my work to-do list had thirty-five undone things on it so I tried to block the picture out. 2 a.m. Time was running out.

My phone rang. I pictured Douglas, tongue moving over his lips as he lectured me on the other end of the phone. I thought of the police, with more questions. How I seemed to make them more supicious of me with every bit of contact we had.

But the word on the screen was less menacing than either of those: *Patrick*. Still, I ignored it. Let it go to voicemail then played it on speakerphone. 'How is this better, Rose?' His voice sounded lazy, like he had been drugged, and I wondered if he had. His father was a doctor and could have prescribed him something, if he was struggling. It couldn't have been anything less formal: this was Patrick. But the fact I was even considering that . . . My heart hurt.

Two o'clock in the morning. Midweek. Was he out, drunk? That wasn't like him when he had work the next day. Was he okay?

Another beep. Patrick again. 'You never answered me last time. *Was* there something going on? With you and this night editor?'

I heard every syllable of the desperation for some explanation – *anything* to help him understand – in his voice and tears sprang up. I could give him that, if I just told him what had happened at Lizzie's. But that would mean acknowledging it out loud, and I had never done that. Couldn't do that.

Beep. 'Something doesn't add up. You're obsessed. What is it?'

I made a drink, downed it, and my stomach made noises that sounded alien. I ran to the toilet and threw the coffee up.

I was obsessed, he was right. But what I'd seen last night confirmed it – there was something to be obsessed with. My story and Will's . . . they converged. I had thought Will hadn't been there that night but I had been wrong, and that changed things. I felt my hands ball into fists and a swell of rage. Fuck you, Will.

In the toilet again shortly afterwards, I looked at my complexion closely in the mirror. Pale. The type of spots

I'd last seen on my face when I had posters on my wall of Keanu Reeves. My hair was no longer its sleek self; frizzy curls popped up around my temples. The only make-up on my face was mascara from a day or two ago, smudged beneath my eyes. The holes in my ears that normally wore hoops or huggies were bare. There was no space for extras in my life, whether they came in the form of people or jewellery. I thought of Rania, adorned head to toe with those extras.

I stared at myself. *Who are you?* I wiped away the mascara half-heartedly, because really who cared? It was one of the benefits of being alone. No performance. No show. I could exist in the shadows, as ghostly almost as Will. Back at my desk, I messaged Patrick. Tears poured down my face as I typed, going against every urge to run to him.

'Nothing was going on. I know it hurts but I think we still need space before we talk again. Please take care of yourself though, and make sure you're with friends. Love, Rose xxx'.

It took a few minutes afterwards to recalibrate to work mode but there was no choice. I replied to a panicked, drunk email from a news writer who had not obscured the face of a celebrity's child who wasn't in the public domain and thought they were about to get sued. Pixellated the image myself. I was starting to calm down, with the work, with the silence. But it was less than two weeks now until the new night editor started and that made my heart race. I wasn't there yet.

I reached down then, to get my purse out of my bag to go to the vending machine, and my eyes locked onto the familiar sight: Will's shoes. No one had mentioned taking them and it seemed weird to bring it up but I also couldn't move them because then was I . . . I don't know, tampering with evidence? Or just being disrespectful? So there they stayed. Even though every time I saw them, those shoes caused a little earthquake in my gut. Even though every time, I remembered. Those shoes were all I had seen as I looked up, half awake, half passed out, starting to come to and starting to realise what had happened to me on that morning at Lizzie's flat.

I had been lying on my side on the very edge of the bed. I had looked down and seen those shoes before my eyes had fallen closed again. I have no idea how long it was after that that I woke up properly.

Now, like always, when I saw the shoes, the wave came; it was how Annie had described contractions when she gave birth to Robin. I gripped the desk and felt the palpitations come. The horror. The feeling that something bad was on its way. When it passed, I kicked the shoes further under the desk. That could be accidental; a cleaner who got enthusiastic with the Dyson.

I thought about Rania. For the last few nights, she had come home late, got up last minute, or stayed at her boyfriend's.

'How's the lover?' I would ask when we did cross paths briefly. Eyes on her.

'All good!' she would chirp, skipping out of the door, no detail.

We barely exchanged two words.

'Like normal flatmates now,' she laughed, pulling her bobble hat onto her head one morning with one foot in a boot. 'Hardly seeing each other.' She had laughed, shoved the other boot on. 'We'll catch up properly soon, chick. When you're off that bloody night shift.'

And my mouth had gone to open, to ask about that photo. But how did I start that question? 'When I was snooping around your room . . .' 'You know how you kindly let me stay here rent free . . .'

Rania, what was there between you and Will Frost?

Why did Will have your mobile number?

Why was Will there, that night at the party?

Why wasn't Will on the night shift?

Rania, how far does patient confidentiality go? Why did you tell me anything if you believe in it so deeply? Why are you only telling me half a story?

I kicked the shoes again, deeper into the mess of wires and stuff that sat beneath the interconnected desk puzzle in our office, until my toes lost contact with them and they were gone and then I crawled under there and pushed them deeper, deeper, deeper until they were about to pop out on Pete's side, and could finally be someone else's problem. And then I stayed under there, until the wave passed.

Chapter 34

It felt like the night I came undone, that shift. The waves kept surging. Sweat poured down the small of my back. Moments when I would have to run to the toilet. A heartbeat that wasn't normal. Working at a slow speed because my hands shook so violently. At times the screen blurred in front of me and I would realise I was crying again. Then the voices would start.

You're so pathetic, Rose.

In between the messages from my own mind, messages would come from colleagues up late, up early. They needed this, they needed that, they were pissed off, they were drunk, they were impatient. I flitted between tasks but didn't complete them. They chased me. I forgot things. They got angry.

I went to message Patrick over and over to be rescued, but then I remembered how unfair that was. *Time to rescue yourself, Rose.* Except that wasn't possible. I was drowning. Drunk news writers phoned and shouted at me again. I sat silently as they yelled, some of them junior to me, younger than me, fuelled on the confidence of six Peronis. I didn't answer back. I unravelled further.

I tried to eat a bar of chocolate from the machine – those good lunch habits had waned quickly – but the sugar hit my stomach like the caffeine had and I threw that straight up too. I didn't know what was happening. I stood up to get some fresh air, thinking that would help, then I remembered I couldn't leave and I sat back down and I googled: *Am I dying.*

I started messaging Florence, then I remembered it was 3 a.m. and she was at home with her wife and the dog and she would get up at 7 a.m. and walk on the beach after drinking a hot water and lemon, slowly, measured, and how could I disturb that life with this, whatever this was, that was in no way measured but was charged and flailing. I thought of Florence, and how she would never eat chocolate bars for meals; how she would eat spinach and fresh fish and roast potatoes and lentils and good things, because she believed in herself as something to preserve and she wanted to keep believing in herself as something to preserve. What was I doing then? Rotting something that was already rotten?

I turned the radio on because the quiet was too much but then the noise was too much, and Florence's happiness was too much, and I was too much, for me, and where did that lead you, so I panicked because when you were too much for you, what did you do then?

I turned it off, and sat on the floor, the carpet scratching the back of my thighs through my tights. I thought of Will again, on that roof. I thought of the water that surrounded us here on our island. Highest highs, lowest depths. I sagged back on the seat. The exhaustion tonight was worse even than normal. I looked at the clock. 3.30.

I couldn't even will it to pass faster because what was I willing? An awkward exchange with Rania, who I didn't want to speak to and who was hinting to me now, *remember, remember, my flatmate is back in eight days.* Trying to resist the urge to fall into a bottle of something. Gruelling insomnia, if I did manage to resist it. Then a temptation, when Rania left, to search her room, putting my hands on things that were private and tucked away.

I didn't cycle home that day, or the next, and instead I got the tube, glass-eyed with tiredness as I ended my day opposite commuters who were starting theirs. There I was, back to front, upside down. A shadow to the rest of the world. That, or a wonky reflection. The people scared me. All of them, everywhere. I could smell them, hear them and all of it seemed too strong, too loud. Too much. Sometimes I would jump off at an earlier stop. Wait for a quieter tube. Try again. It could happen over and over and over. Journeys took twice as long as they should. But I had no choice. In the same way that making lunch, planning food, was too much, the cycle was too much. Everything was too much. I had to go to work though. Because how else would I figure this out?

I had accepted defeat really. And now I just waited to see what that would mean, and where eventually it would lead, and I wondered if Will ever felt like this, or if I was projecting, or if the boundaries were becoming blurred again: Will, me, Will, me. Wherever Will had gone, I would, I accepted, eventually go too. Whatever the repercussions.

Chapter 35

Weekends are funny things when you're the night editor. It had been different when I was with Patrick. But now, alone, there was no need to break the pattern so I slept during the day and woke for the long, dark February nights. Nowhere to go then, of course. Nowhere I would want to go at least so I watched films through the night in bed with my headphones on. Once, I went for a walk but the streets of Hackney at 3 a.m. were full of noise at best, fear if you were feeling fearful, and I ran home clutching my keys, past the kebab shop that was just closing its doors and man after man who wanted to tell me I looked beautiful, where was I in a rush to, cheer up babe.

I dropped my keys on the floor and got back under the duvet and stayed there. Sometimes I braved a trip to the supermarket on those nights but it was a lot. The stark lighting, teenagers swerving at me with four-packs of Stella. I couldn't remember what I bought in supermarkets either. Shopping in them seemed like something I had done in another life, with Patrick. Now I ordered Deliveroo or pressed F3 for the KitKat. Often, when I did go to the supermarket, I left with three disparate items, and couldn't fathom what I had been planning to do with them.

The police left messages, I replied to them when I started to get worried I had left it too long and they would turn up and that would be even worse. It was always the same, of course, had I thought of anything useful – no. The only difference was that every time I said it, it felt more and more like I was lying.

Then one day, just over a week after I went to stay with Rania, I got a message from Richie. 'In your neck of the woods picking up something from eBay. Pint later?'

I didn't know if he knew I was staying with Rania or thought I was still in Stoke Newington but either way, he was in East London. Close enough.

'I could do about 5 p.m.?' I messaged, working it around sleep like a toddler on a nap schedule. 'Where are you?'

Why did I say yes, when I was avoiding people and places? I could say it was because Richie was my friend but that wouldn't have cut it. It was because I felt like I had stalled finding out what happened to the night editor and that wasn't helped by having no contact with my colleagues. I needed to move this forward; make some progress. Maybe Richie knew something new that could help me.

We met at The Three Compasses. When I arrived, he had ordered me a large Pinot Grigio, which he nearly knocked over when he jumped up from the table to hug me. I was shrouded in my parka and I kept it on.

'Not stopping?' he asked with a smile as I took a gulp of wine with my gloves on. I felt the cold lately more than ever.

I didn't laugh. Just glanced around. Bodies, everywhere. Like the tube, with added alcohol, and everyone seemed to feel the need to be so loud. Someone moved close to our table to let someone else pass and my body leapt and then recoiled, like I had been pounced on by a Doberman.

He leaned forward over his pint. 'Rose?' he said. A frown. 'You okay?'

I got myself together then, or faked it enough to be convincing. We exchanged the basics: how was the night shift going, how was everyone in the office, until we got to it. What Richie had come here for. He reached out for my hand before he said it, which felt weird. We were colleagues. We had an ease about us which was entirely non-physical; we were kept apart in the way that desks kept you apart all day long.

I flinched and he looked alarmed. Pulled his hand back. 'Sorry,' I muttered.

'No no, I am. I was only trying to . . .'

I nodded, impatient. Let's get to it. He returned the nod.

'There's some chat in the office, the blokes, you know . . .' He trailed off, awkward.

I raised an eyebrow. I was listening now, he had got my attention away from scanning the room to check how busy it was, what time it was and if I could leave soon, where the toilets were if I needed to lock a door behind me suddenly. A tiny hint of pink flushed across his cheeks. He took a large gulp of his pint.

'That you have a direct line to the officers who are looking into Will's disappearance. Like, a special relationship. They speak to you more than anyone else?'

I stared at him. Thought of the many, many late night calls and visits. Of the endless texts and voice-mails. Officer Ford if they were sending in good cop, Officer Parmar if they were starting to get irritated with me. If that was a special relationship, I didn't want it.

'Someone even said you're looking into what happened yourself. That you went to Will's *place*?'

I was still staring at him. He repeated the question from earlier. 'Are you okay?'

I ignored it. 'So the problem is that I care? That I haven't just moved on from the fact that one of our colleagues has disappeared off the face of the earth?'

He puffed a little air out between his lips. 'Not a colleague exactly though, Rose, only—'

'Only the night editor? And what does that mean? That it makes a person not real, like a vampire?'

Richie was shaking his head then and talking over me: 'Oh God, I know that Will was a human being, Rose, obviously I know that, I didn't mean that.'

'Then what?'

He leaned forward. Rested his chin on one palm. Looked me right in the eyes, his watery blue onto mine, the eyes that Patrick used to say were the exact colour of his favourite chocolate. Which came from Selfridges, of course. No corner shop Dairy Milk eyes for Patrick.

'Did you?' Richie asked. 'Go to Will's flat?'

'Of course I didn't,' I murmured but it was a half-hearted lie. Richie frowned. 'Rose,' he said then. 'If I were you, I really would leave this alone.'

I stared at him. Thought about how Richie – and Pete and Keiran too – would get this, if they knew what had happened to me. How I had known that it all tracked back to that, somewhere in my gut, as soon as I heard the words *Ask Rose*.

And then, everything that followed. What Rania told me, that weekend in Surrey. The shoes. The photograph. Despite the night shift, somehow Will *was* there at Lizzie's midsummer party. I could call up no true memories of what had happened but that didn't stop my brain from creating them. In my sleep, awake, they were relentless.

I saw Richie look up in alarm as a shudder ran, visible, through my whole body, as though we were sitting outdoors in a frost but people were in here in T-shirts. We drank up soon after that and though I asked him why he was so sure it was the best idea for me to abandon all hope of finding Will, he never did deliver an answer.

As I left the pub and walked up Dalston Lane, I had a gut instinct that I was right, whatever my colleagues said, and that I couldn't leave this alone. That I had to find our missing night editor. Not anyone. *Me*. That that was my role, whatever people thought.

I felt those fists ball again as I turned into Mare Street. Past a supermarket and a swathe of students, swarming around me. I felt my arms move closer to my body, trying to pull myself inwards and away from them.

I shook all over when I went into public places and couldn't bear people coming near me. I weighed barely eight stone. I had the pallor of a Victorian child. I was having panic attacks every day, more, some days almost hourly. I barely saw daylight. I had lost my home, my fiancé and all of my friends – albeit voluntarily – and I was doing a decent job at pushing my family away too. There wasn't a lot left. But the little there was? I would use that, I thought, as I shook this time with rage. I would use that to find Will. And finally, to have my questions about that night at Lizzie's answered.

Chapter 36

It was 1 a.m. A busy night shift, following a busy news day. For the last few hours I had been getting calls and texts from everyone on the team who thought their issue was the biggest. It was Friday, so I was simultaneously trying to put up the newspaper stories from a bigger weekend paper tomorrow so that we were there, ready, when the first readers logged on. It was a lot.

It would be impossible to do it in time but I would do as much as I could to incur the least wrath from Douglas, which meant I wouldn't stop for food or coffee or anything that could ease the hangover I was suffering from after drinking too much white wine in bed this morning when Rania left for work.

At 6 a.m. when I'd walked through the door at her flat, I was so exhausted that I was snappy with her, the only person there to take it out on.

'Morning chicky!' she had chirped, opening the door of her bedroom in her dressing gown. 'Now. Not chasing. But you know that Lucinda comes back in four days? You know you will need to be—'

'I've got it, Rania. You need me out. Message received.

Can I at least walk through the door after my *gruelling* night shift before you start reminding me I'm about to be homeless? I haven't even taken my shoes off.'

Her mouth dropped open, cartoon shock. 'Oh.' That was all she could manage.

I knew I should say sorry but adrenalin was charging through me. I looked up at her. Taller and stronger than me with skin that shone with health, even at this hour of the day. Curls that pinged. I felt a layer of grease across my face; the throb of a spot beneath the skin. My eyes were still on her. 'I wonder,' I said before I could stop myself, adrenalin pumping the words out, 'if before I leave you will tell me the truth about you and Will. Or if you'll let me move out, and go wherever the hell I find to go, and you'll drip-feed me tiny bits of information but you *still* won't give me the whole story.'

She stared at me at first. And then she nodded slowly. Tightened her dressing gown belt around herself.

'I don't think that counts as tiny, what I told you, Rose,' she said, looking down at her slippers.

'But there's more to know, isn't there?' I hit back. 'Will you ever tell me?'

She was heading for the shower now, starting her day as mine ended, as I was about to shrug myself into some pyjamas, but she stopped and turned to me. 'No,' she said. 'The sooner you grow up and realise that not everything revolves around you, the better. Get out of my flat, please. And take all those wine bottles you've hidden all over my lovely flatmate's room with you. And then *get some help for your bloody drink problem.*'

* * *

She arrived when I was lying on the hotel bed, two rooms up from my old one, same corridor, and waiting for the room service I had ordered. 'Can I come in?' Rania said. 'I've told work I'll be late.'

I stared at her, confused. 'I thought you were wine.'

She raised an eyebrow. *See.* It was the day after she'd kicked me out and I was back at the hotel I had stayed at before, nowhere else to go. Different identikit room. Same feeling of being non-existent, flailing around in a part of the world not frequented by other people my age who were at weddings or hen dos or parties or dinners or that new Korean place on the high street or anywhere, as long as it wasn't here.

I walked back to the bed and she followed. She sat down next to me. 'Sorry,' was all she said. She had slipped her boots off and her legs next to mine were long, in her loose blue work trousers. Between those and her socks, I could see a nick, from shaving her legs. I stared at it and eventually her legs began to blur, before I spoke.

'I don't have a drink problem,' I said, quiet as a mouse, and then I let myself fall into her side and sobbed into the crook of her arm.

Eventually, I pulled away. 'I found a photo in your room. From that night we all went back to Lizzie's. How can Will have been there? Will would have been on a night shift.'

I didn't tell her why I cared. Still I had never told anyone what happened to me that night. It felt impossible for the words to leave my mouth; the reality that would confirm. But sometimes Rania looked at me like she could see it.

And she was staring at me now, watching how my body reacted as I talked about that night, hearing my voice shake and seeing my shoulders do the same. Boring into me. Getting it?

'It was midsummer, Rose.' She spoke very slowly and carefully. 'Remember how late that party went on? Will had *finished* the night shift. Maybe knocked off an hour early or something, I don't know. But anyway. Came afterwards.'

As I said, we didn't do moderation. That night at Lizzie's, the party had gone on so late that for once, our night editor had been able to join in. Given the usual lack of sociability, God knows why. But it was round the corner from work. There was a novelty, perhaps. A text from someone saying: *We're still out! Come!* Being able to 'go out after work' like normal people. A curiosity: What were we like, after dark, with our guards down and the shackles of work removed? What were we like full stop, these unseen colleagues, when we didn't just exist on email?

And so Will came along in a crumpled work shirt, straight from the office. Spotted Rania and was relieved to see – from their physio appointmeents – a familiar face. Slung an arm around her for a picture. Grabbed a beer, yes, but was way behind the crowd.

It was 5 a.m.: everyone else who was there at Lizzie's flat was out of it. But not Will. No. Will knew what was happening.

I felt it again, that fury.

Chapter 37

4 March, 2010

Tonight is brutal in its coldness – which has not been helped by me having to come straight from the hotel to Canary Wharf, without any of the comforts from home that could ease going to work in minus two degrees. I picture thick wool scarves that I would have wound round and round my neck if I had come here from home.

From my former home.

The lift opens and I should be warming up by now but still, I'm shivering. I fantasise about my favourite beanie. Think dreamily about the black tights in the second drawer down in my bedroom that are so thick they are almost leggings. The wool socks I bought for a ski holiday with Patrick's family which have seen me through many a cold morning cycle across East London to work. The jumpers, the boots. Oh God, the ear muffs.

I swipe my pass. Sigh. I will get my stuff – tights and socks and beanie and earmuffs included – at some point. But first, I need somewhere to transfer it to. And where would that be? I can't keep everything that makes up my life in the cupboard of a very average but competitively priced hotel in Canary Wharf.

Into the office now. As I get to my desk, I look down. There is a thick ladder beneath the knee in the flimsy hosiery I picked up at TK Maxx and the cold has stung the exposed skin. I lean down and examine it and find that my knee is almost blue. Seeing that makes me colder and I feel my teeth vibrate against each other. The walk from the hotel is only twenty minutes but that's been long enough to let it set in, for the cold to bury itself deep within me. It's refusing to leave now, a squatter.

I keep my gloves – something I had with me at least – on while I start up my computer. Rub my hands together like sticks. It makes me think of fire, blazing high and wild. Mmm. A fire would be nice. My computer springs to life just as my phone beeps.

'You're late,' says a message from Douglas.

Tonight is going to be brutal in other ways too, by the looks of things. How can he know that I am late, all twenty minutes of it? I've checked the news en route; I know nothing major has happened. Paranoia creeps in like that cold. I spin on my chair to take a 360 view around the room. Is he *watching* me? But no, of course not. Jesus, Rose.

Ping.

Again. Him.

'I know you're not here because you always email me within two minutes of arriving to prove you're there,' he types like he is reading my mind.

Ping. 'I know you better than you know yourself, Rosie.'

I can hear his voice, the snark to it. Unease vibrates through my whole body. I stick my tongue between my teeth to stop them bouncing against each other. As if he knows me. As if he fucking knows me at all.

'I'm here now,' I type. 'Sorry.'

One emoji back from Douglas: the watching eyes.

I hug myself, my parka zipped up, not going anywhere yet. The hug is to warm myself up but also to shield myself. I look around again. Nothing. Now, I delete emails from yesterday on autopilot, generic PR spam calling me Rachel, whole team messages about who could make it for the 'better social media' training day. As usual, I have the best excuse not to attend: *Can't. Am sleeping.*

I delete the emoji message from Douglas though it's pointless, but it makes it feel less real when it's gone. He watches me though, whether I can see it or not. It's not new to me, in this place, feeling watched. There are the phone calls checking in on me, the bollockings yes, but they are not the worst ways. I think of Douglas laughing as I walk past, eyes on my back until I am through the door and I can let my held breath go. I think of Will, trolling me with those stories of sexual assault.

It had to be a coincidence, I used to think. Will couldn't know anything. Will wasn't even there that night at Lizzie's. Will was on the night shift.

But now I know differently.

I think about it. Our night editor was a ghost. Ghosts don't come to you directly, over a cup of tea. They send you clues, don't they: they hint from a distance. Keep out of sight. Usually. Except I know now the ghost was in the real world that night, the night my life changed, and that alters the picture. That makes the picture darker, by far.

224

I start writing the first story of the night: snow forecast for the weekend. Save. Publish. I push off against my drawers so that my chair wheels backwards. Sit in the limbo between the desks, the thin gritty carpet beneath my boots. And I think, or I try to.

I slip my gloves off, finally warm enough to brave typing in bare hands. I inch forward on my seat and there it is again, brushing up against my boots, that Tesco bag. Pete must have pushed it back through to my side, his long legs stretching out languorously at the end of his shift. I reach down, and shove it back under, and feel the shape of those shoes. I need them gone. I stand up and walk around and fish them out.

But now I am back at the party, in the dulled snapshots that night always exists in. There is me, slowly opening my eyes. There is my underwear, crumpled on the other side of the bed. There is the throb, throb, throb. And there are those shoes.

I walk across the office and throw them in someone else's bin.

They wonder, these colleagues of mine, my fiancé, my family, the police, why I am obsessed with finding Will Frost? It's because I have to quiet my mind. To piece together this picture and make it whole. It's because I have to find Will to get the answers I need for myself.

It's 10.45 p.m. I glance over my shoulder. When I start typing again, it sounds louder. Too loud. I try to go lighter, so I can hear around me, if I need to, and that sounds so crazy in my head that I stop and type normally. I think of those eye emojis. My head swims with the paranoia. With the exhaustion.

Just over a week until I leave the nights behind and the day shift resumes and then, I think, I will *have* to look for another job. A decent one, too, now that I need to find somewhere new to live, not to mention a bunch of wedding outgoings: most of them baulked at refunds when we tried to cancel with only weeks to go. And how could I let Patrick's family money pay for that?

There is another reason I need to look for a new job, of course. Because while I have tried to block it out, through drink, through work, through banter, the truth is becoming impossible to ignore. I was sexually assaulted by someone I work with. And when that thought creeps in, it is everywhere in my body, crawling around. I think about it as I type. I wish I could tell my sisters. Tell Rania. Patrick. Tell *somebody*. But still, I can't get the words out. I think about it as I try to breathe normally. I think about it as I reply to emails. I think about it as I hear a noise. The door, opening, at a time when the door never opens, when it is resolutely just me here. My head swivels towards the door. I am not imagining it. There is a noise. Two noises. A door opening first, and then a voice, saying my name.

It's Will Frost, of course. Who else could it possibly be?

Chapter 38

Coffee runs down my arm and I am aware of the scalding, somewhere, on some plane. I must have jumped when the door opened. When I saw Will standing there. Now, my arm burns. Some part of me knows that. But what happens on the outside of my skin is incidental really. Because what is happening inside takes over.

We stare at each other, Will and I. Fear has wings and they spread just below my rib cage, out out out to the furthest reaches of my middle and then they flail and settle, so that they cover me in my entirety. Now, it is just us, night editor, day editor, back on the see-saw. Now, I have to face the truth.

When I go to speak, I can't. When I go to move, I can't. It has been coming, it now seems clear to me, my complete paralysis. My movements have been becoming smaller, smaller, smaller. From work to Rania's, scurrying back and forth to each, taking up my position, static and small. Often at work I am so intimidated by the vastness of the space that I can't move around it. I wait until I am in pain to go to the toilet so that I don't have to move and remember how big that floorspace is; so that

I can sit still, only my fingers moving quietly across the keyboard and pretend that the space is only as wide as me, that I am in a box that is the width and height of my body.

At Rania's I rarely sat in the living room. When I ventured into the kitchen or to the bathroom for showers that became less frequent, I headed quickly back to the bedroom. I moved to eat mouthfuls of pasta. Pressed play on the iPad. Tiny movements and a miniscule life.

There are no longer weekend trips to Paris or Bruges or feet bouncing around a dance floor or filling in for a friend's netball team or the matinee at Sadler's Wells. Now, there is almost stasis.

Will still stares. I feel the coffee burn and sting. From outside of myself I can see me, frozen, staring back into those watery pond eyes. I hear a voice say: 'I'm sorry.'

A reply: 'Are you?'

I look now at our night editor, standing in front of me in the office. It's not Will who is saying sorry, it's me.

'Are you?' A beat. 'Even when I am in front of you, Rose . . . even now, I bet you still don't have the balls to call me by my own name.'

I duck my head, shamed. And I feel a sob rise up from my throat. They call her Will, you see. Like Douglas calls me Rosie.

But her name is Willow.

Chapter 39

Before, I hadn't remembered any of what Willow had told me that night on the bus. Hadn't remembered talking to her at all. I was telling the truth to the police, or what I thought was the truth, at least. I sometimes wonder if my own trauma was protecting me from taking on more; if that's how I blocked it out.

But after Rania told me that Willow had been assaulted, as I leaned against the door in the end cubicle of that old country pub, it was like she eased a door open for me. Something was able to pass through and my memories of that night Willow went missing started to come back.

There I was, slumped drunk on the back seat of the 73 just over six weeks ago, moving slowly down Essex Road, from Eloise and School Friend Sam's in Angel to my own flat in Stoke Newington. The vibrations of the bus made me sleepier. We picked up pace as we left N1 behind, zipping past inviting old Victorian pubs, lamplit and tempting and then less tempting. Myriad late-night supermarkets. I had seen it a thousand times but I barely noticed any of it that night, scrolling on my phone, eyes drooping.

Too drunk to be shocked when my phone started ringing in my hand, even though it was two o'clock in the morning and the volume was set to the loudest it could be. Of course it was; it always was. Douglas could call at any moment and you had to stand to attention like a major: *you are a journalist, Rosie.*

But that time it wasn't Douglas.

'It happened to you too, didn't it, Rose?' Willow had said to me during that phone call. The second time was a statement: 'It happened to you too.'

I had sat up straight and held on to the pole even though the bus was still, regulating the service with a two-minute wait. I had felt everything blur, and thought I would faint. I remembered catching a glimpse of myself in the window. A mouth, stained with red wine.

I had known what she meant straight away. I didn't know how the hell she had this information, but I knew in my gut what she meant. And I knew what she was telling me.

What had happened to me at Lizzie's party, at the hands of someone I worked with, had happened to a colleague of mine too. It had happened to our night editor. To Willow.

Instead of answering her though, instead of asking her questions, instead of being a human being who cared and listened, instead of any of that, I hung up on her and played Nicki Minaj at full volume because I didn't want to hear it and I didn't want to *think* about it.

I had never told anyone. Never said it out loud. And now, here she was, calling me about it. Knowing. Making it real. It was buried so deeply, and I was terrified – truly terrified – of taking a spade to it. I even deleted Willow's call from my log, like that would delete it from existence.

Like that would delete that night. Just like I did tonight, with Douglas's watching eyes. I didn't let her talk when she needed to. And then look what happened.

'You put the phone down on me,' says our night editor now. 'I tried to talk to you.'

I nod. Feel tears begin to roam down my face.

And then she had tried again with the note: *Ask Rose.*

But back then I couldn't remember and none of it made any sense to me. When I saw the shoes and found the photo, though, something started to form. Not yet a whole picture. But a surety: that note, Willow's disappearance, was something to do with what had happened to me that night at Lizzie's.

And yet, even then I didn't speak up.

Even when Rania, that day on the phone when I was in the pub with Patrick's parents, filled in more gaps and the memory of my phone call with Willow on the bus started to come back. *Still*, I didn't speak up. Because I was too worried about having to confront what had happened to me.

I feel tears threaten as I stare at Will.

Willow. What is wrong with me?

Chapter 40

Willow dressed in androgynous clothes and wore no make-up. Her hair was cut in a beautiful pixie crop. She was smart. Capable. The nickname was a power grab. She never called herself or signed emails as anything but Willow. Calling her Will was one of the ways in which Douglas tried to belittle her. It was not a nickname she had ever chosen or used, and that scored a point. But he made it so ubiquitous a moniker that everyone used it. Including – shamefully – me.

I look up at her now. 'I was worried you—'

'Were dead? And who did you think killed me, Rose? One of those colleagues of ours? But you're still here. Still working with them. Weren't you worried?'

'Not quite working with them . . .' I manage.

She puts her head in her hands. 'Please don't tell me you think the night shift will keep you safe.'

She sits down on Richie's chair and swivels round and round and round in circles until I am dizzy watching her.

'I was drunk that night,' I tell her eventually. 'When you called, I should have listened to you but I had been at a friend's house for dinner. I'd had too much wine.'

She puts her foot down and stops spinning like a car screeching on the brakes. Her stare is an X-ray. 'You're drunk now too, aren't you?' she says, head tilted, and she is right. Only a little; sometimes a whisky in my coffee helps. I'm not sure what it helps but it helps. I duck my head, shamed. While I am staring at that gnarled, thin carpet, I feel the breeze of someone walk past me. I look up. Willow has pulled up a chair, and now she is at my computer. She is still logged in as me. Whatever she is doing is under my name. Sweat tickles my top lip. I am definitely no longer cold.

'What are you doing?' I ask.

When she spins round to me, her watery blue eyes are intent. 'The night shift,' she says. 'What else would I do? I am the night editor, Rose.'

She clicks and saves and I am terrified because Douglas will think it was me, and what if she is making a mess?

After a minute, Willow's head snaps backwards to stretch and I see the line of that dark pixie crop. Growing out slightly now. I doubt haircuts have been high on the agenda for her recently. Her hand comes up to run along the nape of her neck and her nails are bitten so far down that the skin appearing at the top looks like it belongs on her insides, red and fatty and exposed.

'What are you watching me for?' she asks over her shoulder, though she can't see me.

'I'm covering the night shift now, remember,' I say, nervous. 'I'm . . . the night editor. I need to know what's going up. That everything is okay.'

Still, despite everything, I am scared to let them all

down. 'You are such a *people pleaser*, Rose,' she laughs. She does turn then, fleetingly. 'I used to be like you.'

She pulls her bottom lip over her top lip. Thinks. 'But like I said, Rose. I am the night editor. So I can manage the night shift. Go and get yourself a coffee or something. Have a doze. Chill out.'

I wait for a few seconds, willing myself to argue but eventually my body moves and I do walk away from her, trying to work out what to do and trying, again, to please someone. Her, this time. I circle the office like a fly. Try to think. Should I call someone? Tell them she is back?

But how can I let her down again? She is here to exorcise some demons: best, perhaps, to just let her get on with it. I look over at her though, intent on the screen, and my stomach lurches. I can't see what she is doing.

Most likely, Douglas will call me soon. I am resigned to the fact that whatever Willow is doing to that home-page can't be good and I expect my phone to ring any second. And what will I say? *Will is here, blame Will.* People pleaser, people pleaser.

'Where did you go?'

She flicks back to another document. Finishes what she is writing and saves before she answers me, the consummate professional. Always the night editor, at her core. Then she swivels round. I lean awkwardly on a desk opposite her. And she frowns at me. 'Go?' she asks, a look of genuine bemusement. 'I didn't go anywhere.'

'But you . . .'

'Yeah. I didn't come *here*. And I wasn't at home. But I didn't go anywhere.'

I nod. The eyes are intent but they are glazed a little too. Am I not the only one who has been drinking?

'You didn't intend to come back.'

Nothing.

'That's why you cancelled your physio appointment. Tied up your loose ends. You hadn't planned to come back to any of this.'

A laugh. 'I didn't cancel my physio appointment. Jesus. Who the hell would do that, in the midst of what was happening to me?'

But Rania said . . . An unsettled feeling creeps across my middle. Then something else occurs to me. 'Did you come back here another time? During the night shift?'

'Once,' she says. 'But I couldn't go through with it. I wasn't ready. I stood outside the door for a few minutes, then I called the lift. Left again.'

I picture myself standing on the top floor, the lift being called away at such a quiet hour. That was Willow, so close by. I could have opened the door and walked straight into her.

'The thing is, Rose, that I didn't know how to be anywhere else. So I came back to sit in this seat. I hated somebody else being in it. I hated seeing you in it tonight.'

A note has edged its way into her voice that tells me to tread carefully. 'I didn't even *want* the night editor gig.'

'And yet you took it.'

The effects of the whisky have worn off now and I feel hyper aware. 'To help *you*,' I say but it is barely audible. 'To try and find out what had happened to you.' I look up. '*Ask Rose*. You left the note. I felt like it was up to me.'

Her back is still to me when she speaks. 'I shouldn't have put that on you,' she says. 'The note. It wasn't fair. I just . . . I wanted someone to pay and I didn't know where to start.'

I think about the way the police have buzzed around me more than anyone else on the team the last six and a half weeks and the heaving weight of that attention.

But who could blame her? I hadn't listened.

'I'm sorry I hung up when you called me that night. Do you want to talk about it now? What happened to you?'

She swivels back around while I am still talking but it is cautious this time, like she is in slow motion, and her voice when it comes has changed tone again, a false lightness to it. 'Nope!' she says. 'I don't. I wanted to talk then and you didn't and that was your prerogative, I suppose. And now I don't want to talk and you know what? That is my prerogative too. What is the point anyway? It's too late, Rose. Too. Late.'

Another switch flicks, and the tone is different again. Weary. 'Now why don't you just go home? I can handle things here. Leave the middle of the night behind, if you didn't even want this gig anyway.'

'I like the middle of the night now,' I tell her quietly. 'Everything else scares me.'

She is the wrong person to break down to because she is missing, presumed dead and that cannot say great things about someone's mental state, but she is all I have in front of me at the moment that wave comes, and she is there, and so I do, and she simply stares at me. When it lets up a little, she walks wordlessly to the kitchen and makes me a coffee.

'There. Black. Without whatever you normally put in it, I'm afraid.' And I know it then: she isn't drunk. Just wired. High on adrenalin. Not like me. I feel my face flush, she sees through me to bones. People pleaser. Burying my head in the sand. Ignoring people when times get tough and they need me. Running, at the first sign that things have got hard. Sleeping pills to switch off; caffeine to switch on. Throwing whisky in my work coffee while convincing myself that the night shift has solved my drinking problem.

I stare at her face and then the rest of her. Long legs end in the awkward juxtaposition of black trousers, black socks and very basic white sports trainers. On her top half is a crumpled shirt, no shape to it and no love. Not a shred of make-up or jewellery, not a sign of anything but what is necessary. I think of the engagement ring.

'The police have your ring,' I tell her, to stall her, to stop her sending me home.

She sits back down in her chair. Checks the homepage like a reflex; I notice it because I do the same. Usually. Now she is firmly positioned in front of my computer and I can't get close.

'You were going to get engaged.'

'I *was* engaged.'

'But . . .'

'I was engaged, and then I wasn't engaged. It wouldn't have worked anyway, but the night shift finished it off.'

'Now that's ringing a few bells.'

She looks surprised. 'Why do it then?' She answers herself. 'Ah yes, to help me. How did that go, Rose?'

I am silent. Our eyes are on each other.

'I put your shoes in the bin,' I tell her. A large swig of coffee. Here we go. What we have skirted around. We edge closer and when she replies, her voice is level.

'Why did you put my shoes in the bin?'

My eyes are right on hers. 'The first time I found them under the desk, I knew I'd seen them before, when I woke up at Lizzie's party. My whole body went into shock.'

I watch her for a reaction, but there isn't one.

'It was the gold buckles. They're so big. Distinctive.'

Blank.

'I never saw a face but I remembered those shoes. And now I knew whose they were.'

I had thought I must have had it wrong though, and I told myself that over and over. Because Willow would have been on a shift. But then I found the picture of her with Rania at the party and knew I had been right.

'You *were* there. It was your shoes I saw.'

For two minutes, Willow moves stories round, adjusts headlines, scans her eyes upwards to the chart and fixes typos. I sit patiently, like she is a doctor finishing a prescription for the patient before me while I sit opposite waiting to get my mole checked. When she turns it's in one sudden, swift movement and I jump and then I see it. She hasn't been doing site maintenance; she has been composing herself.

Her voice cracks when she says sorry to me. 'I didn't know what had happened to you,' she says. 'But I went home from that party with an unsettled feeling in my stomach and I should have come back. Taken you to the police station. *Anything*, instead of walking away and leaving you there. I had a gut instinct something was wrong.'

Willow was the colleague Lizzie had mentioned, the one who had come in to check on me. That is why, every time I duck down low to put something under my desk, those shoes cause an earthquake in my gut. Those shoes were all I saw as I looked down from that bed. Thick soles. Large gold buckles across the front.

She pauses. 'I shouldn't have had a go at you about putting the phone down on me. It's only what I did too, that night, really. Buried my head in the sand, because I didn't want to think about it either. But afterwards, I couldn't stop thinking about it. About you.'

'The stories?'

She nods. 'Trying to prompt a reaction from you, I suppose. I didn't know you and I didn't feel like I could ask, in case I had got it wrong, or made you uncomfortable. But what we did have was our handover. I thought . . . I don't know, it seemed like the way I always communicated with you. It seemed to make sense. It was what we did.'

In that moment, I realise something else that has percolated in my subconscious: our night ghost sought them out, those stories, because they weren't commonplace. These women, in her stories, all got justice. Most women do not get justice; we all know that.

'It did prompt a reaction,' I grimace. 'Just not the one that I'm guessing you wanted. I never reported it.'

She does it again, with the site. Turns away and uses it for what she needs. For a break. Maybe when she was trying to tell me to report it she was also saying: if you do, I will too.

Willow checks the wires, and there is breaking news of a motorway pile-up so she does the story, and I twitch to check it, but she is the night editor so I can't and she posts it under my byline so they don't know she is back. 'There,' she says, calm.

'I didn't report mine either,' she says then.

And we move on, to her half of the story.

Chapter 41

'What happened to you?' I reply, barely a whisper.

I feel my heart speeding up. I know some of it, the part that Rania told me that day, but not the whole story. I steel myself.

'Willow,' I manage to croak out as she remains silent. 'What happened?'

Next to me, she looks up from the screen. She lifts her index finger, with its bitten-down nail and she points to Douglas's office across the room. My eyes follow and I am still looking at it when she speaks, which helps, not to see her eyes.

'On the night shift he came in drunk, tried to kiss me then when I said no, started insulting me. *Fucking dyke* this, *prick tease* that. The usual shit. But my God, the snarl on that man after a drink . . . the loathing . . . When I answered back . . .'

I hear my breath quicken. 'How did you answer back?'

God, her face. 'I snapped. I was trying to do my job and he was preening round the room like he owned it. Owned me. Owned everything. I stood up. And I asked if he knew who it was, Rose. Who had hurt you

241

at the party. It had been torturing me ever since that night that I hadn't helped you and I thought fuck this boys' club. Fuck it. I would ask him, and see if he knew, or had heard anything.'

'Did he answer?'

She speaks so quietly now that you can barely hear. 'Not with words.'

A ghost, haunted.

'Sometimes, when I was at work alone, I slipped off my shoes,' she says. My insides harden, even though I know what is coming. 'I kept catching a glimpse of my socks and bare ankles and I thought from that angle, it was weird, I didn't even look *human*. I had the feet of a rag doll.'

She looks up. Nods. 'I was raped at work,' she says. 'And yet here I am, back again. How messed up is that?'

I stand up and lean down to her in her office chair, pull her in close. I try to ignore the wave of terror that's started to submerge me. Rania had told me, that day in the pub toilet, that Willow had been raped. But she hadn't told me that it was one of our colleagues who'd attacked her, just like it was one of our colleagues who'd attacked me.

Willow Frost. My work twin. My fellow survivor. I hug her thin frame tighter, as much for me as for her.

'Was it that night?' I ask her. 'The night you phoned me? The night you went missing? Was that the night you were attacked?'

'No.' She shakes her head. 'That would make sense, wouldn't it? It wouldn't make sense to keep coming back in night after night to the place where that happened. That wouldn't make any sense at all. But I did. It happened right back in September.'

'It makes complete and absolute sense,' I assure her. 'To me, anyway.'

I think of my own reaction. Running, changing the picture makes it seismic. Staying still, keeping going makes it small.

'What *did* happen that night then? To make you call me? To make you disappear?'

Willow pulls her legs up to her and sits with them under her chin; a small child on an adult work chair. Her eyelids sag. 'He called the work phone late, threatening me. Very, very drunk. Or high. Maybe both? If I told, this. If I said a word, that. He knew it was unsafe having me around now and he was nervous. There was an edge to his voice that . . .' A shudder runs through her body. 'I knew he was serious. He told me it might be an idea if I *disappeared*. I think he meant more like handing in my notice than this but still, I followed orders. I was scared, absolutely to the bone terrified. And I ran.'

She looks up at me. 'I knew I had to speak to you first though. Warn you, apart from anything else. That he was still angry, still cruel. To watch out. Steer clear. Because I knew it must have been him that . . . But you were . . .'

I apologise, again.

She shakes her head. 'So I left the note instead.'

I pull my arm away from her. Sit back. 'I want to talk to you now, Willow. Can we talk now?'

And this time, she nods. Those pale eyes are almost out of my view, she has been exhausted by the truth and the return to this world. But she does begin to speak.

'I went up on the roof that night,' she says.

Willow went up there to that roof even though she was terrified of heights. Even though she could only work in this giant tower by sitting in the middle of the room, never straying near an edge, and convincing herself she was on the ground floor of a building a couple of storeys high in Clapton. The night shift meant she never had to go to meetings in the offices with the 'amazing views'; the kind that her old school friend Marcus told me would have made her vomit up her lunch.

'I was just in socks again, when I went up there,' she says now, twirling round and round in circles in my chair so that every time her face goes past I see the tears. 'I went up there four months after someone I worked with turned up at the office in the middle of the night and did that to me. Because I wasn't coping with it and couldn't think of anything else that would fix things.'

I fight back tears. Hold her hand and stop her from rotating. But she takes her hand back and circles, again.

'On the roof, I really did think about it. Ending things.'

'But then what?'

She puffs out air through her nose, a semblance of a laugh. 'I came down and wrote a story about a dinosaur-sized shark instead.' She pauses. 'But then I sat, staring at a picture of this shark while looking over my shoulder in fear and I thought what the hell am I doing. So I put my trainers on and walked out of the building. He told me to disappear. I would disappear.' She stops circling. Turns to me.

'After that, instead of thinking about ending my own life,' she says, 'I thought obsessively about ending his.'

That does seem like a better idea.

'Are we going to talk?' I say. Because the dots have joined and everything has aligned. 'About who he is?'

That colleague who attacked us both.

When Douglas calls, at that exact moment, we both jump. I answer like a robot. Put a finger to my lips so that Willow knows to stay quiet. I keep my eyes on her, as she starts typing. I try to see what she is doing but the screen is too far away from the landline I'm speaking on and everything is charged and it is like we are holding our breath.

Willow does what she is told though. She stays quiet.

'I know, I know, it's totally my fault,' I say into the phone, amending the tone of my voice to pliant, everyday and trying to ignore the adrenalin coursing through my body. 'I had a migraine. Haven't got as much stuff up as usual.'

A beat. Yes Douglas, I do know a good journalist wouldn't get a fucking migraine on a fucking shift.

When I hang up, I turn to Willow, who is visibly shaking. Thinking about Douglas, hearing his voice, ranting . . . it's too much for her.

'Get out of here,' I tell her.

I dig into the depths of my bag. In amongst the chocolate bar wrappers, the cycling helmet. The miniatures. I feel it poke into my palm. I hand her a key.

'I'm staying at a hotel at the moment,' I tell her. 'Long story. But it's close by. Just next to the river. Go there and wait for me. I'll finish this shift and then we'll talk and make a plan and you can stay with me, if you want?'

She looks lost. I wonder again where the hell she's been for the last six weeks. What she has been doing. The threats, the fear. Being on the roof, in her socks. Willow has had a breakdown, that much is clear. But I'm still in the dark on the specifics.

'Lock the door,' I tell her gently, as I write down the name and directions to the hotel. 'Order room service and put it on my bill. Just try and relax, sleep until I get there.'

She hesitates but then, decisive, snatches the key out of my hand, shoves it into her khaki jacket pocket and stands up. She looks at me, wide-eyed.

'Come now,' she whispers, like she is begging and she is so childlike, despite being my age, that it makes me hurt.

I smile at her sadly: 'I can't, Willow. I have the night shift.'

And she understands that. She of all people understands that. She is the night editor.

Chapter 42

Willow

Perhaps I try to persuade Rose to come with me to stop me from doing it, to stop me going through with a plan, like a child who wants rules and is acting up to push a parent to discipline them.

Maybe.

Or maybe it's because I know she won't leave so I just say it, like I take the key, to pretend that something else is happening. To pretend that I don't already have a plan. That that's not why I left: to escape the night shift for long enough to work this out from a hostel deep in South London.

In a couple of minutes' time, when the cache updates on the website, Rose will realise what that plan is. Rose, and, of course, everybody else with an internet connection in the rest of the world.

Chapter 43

When Willow leaves, I jump back on to my computer to check everything she did and bang out some news stories. I will update our social media feeds, scan through email and start to work through the endless list of amends people need from me.

I take a deep breath. No one knows Willow is back. To them, tonight is like any other night, and the best thing I can do for her is to make sure it carries on looking that way and then go back to the hotel and speak to her, and figure out what's next without any other eyes upon us.

If it occurs to me to be frightened, to wonder if I am being watched, then I can push it down easily. Type. Delete. Calm. I am within my tiny radius, my desk, my small world. And even now I know what happened here, it's nothing new. This place has always played host to a monster and I am used to navigating that. Two a.m., 3 a.m., they contain a safety net of silence and alone time. *This is*, I repeat to myself, *the best thing I can do for Willow.* Before I can begin though, my phone rings.

'It's after midnight, Patrick.' But my voice is soft. I know why he is calling.

'On what should be our wedding day.' His voice slurs and then, quietly, he begins to weep. I hear that rarely, and my insides sting at the rawness of the sound. 'We had done the table plan, Rose. I had written my speech.'

'I'm sad today too, Patrick.'

But I am also, if I'm honest, distracted. I think of my wedding. But then I think of *him*. The man who did this to me and Willow. Of how I know, now. I picture him. Mean little chin; skin like Play-Doh. I think of what Willow said. Of both of us still coming back here, of him thinking, *I got away with this*. And then: *I got away with this, again.* All of the hairs on my body stand on end. We know who did it. We know who came for both of us. Willow has always known while for me, it was slower, more gradual. But now we know and we are united.

'You don't sound sad,' says Patrick, permeating my thoughts. 'Are you thinking about someone else?'

'Willow is a woman, Patrick, you know that.' He knows I am straight, why is he doing this? I sigh. 'I'm at work. I have to get on . . .'

'You have to get on? Wow, Rose. Wow.' I hear the bruise form. Then, defeated. 'It's meant to be our wedding day. I'm downstairs in your building. Can't you just let me up? Be a human being.'

'No Patrick,' I sigh. 'I am honestly so sorry, and I know today is hard. We can talk soon. But tonight I can't be a human being, I have to be the night editor.'

When I get off the phone, I glance at the time on my

phone. Willow should be almost back to the hotel. About to do what the normal people do at half past midnight, and sleep. Before I see her, and we can drink some coffee together and eat breakfast and make a plan.

Now, I wiggle my mouse, and look at my screen. Blink. *No!*

I see what Willow has posted on the homepage, and fear charges through me. My eyes dart around the office. I can't keep her hidden now. There is no chance. All I can hope is that she is back at the hotel, safe, and the night-time has bought her enough minutes.

Willow Frost, *what the hell have you done?*

Chapter 44

Willow

I message him as I leave Rose which, of course, is at exactly the right time. There is no element of chance to tonight, I have been planning this and watching him for six weeks. Oh God. I have watched and watched and watched. Most of it has not been easy to see.

But he is a creature of habit, I now know, just like me and Rose. Thursday nights, he will fall out of a painfully edgy bar on Old Street when it closes at midnight. Right now, he will be trying to find a woman even drunker than he is to pretend he is having consensual sex with. Perhaps he has found her already.

All I send him, at first, is a link. I have already posted the story, there in clear sight without Rose realising, and now I go direct: bait him like a fish.

Next, a message. *I know it wasn't just me you attacked. I know you attacked Rose too. Two of us: we can get you with that.*

I never make it to the hotel. I never had any intention of making it to the hotel. Instead I wait at a quiet spot next to the water. One of the coldest winds I have ever felt slaps my cheeks and I bury my chin into the top of my coat. I tell him where I am.

'If you don't want me to write the second story, about what you did to Rose, I would come here. It's all ready to go. Saved to drafts. It could blow the fucking roof off the chart.'

The wind whistles. The rain transitions to sleet. I shove ungloved hands deep into my pockets and jump up and down. Minutes roll by and the sleet comes down, heavier. A beanie sits over my short hair but on my bare neck, the ice pours now down the back of my coat. My back is soggy and my hands are numb. I pull my hands up inside my coat. Inch nearer to a closed office building to try and get some sort of cover but this isn't the kind of weather that observes boundaries; it'll come in anyway, it is tricksy, angling itself sideways. My socks are damp, even my underwear.

But suddenly it doesn't matter. There it is, that tread. Male. You always know. But this time I won't be cowed by it. I finger the knife in my pocket. A ghost. A robot. And soon, I'll be something else.

The tread gets closer. Thud, thud, thud. Closer, now. Running. And then the tread stops and instead comes heavy, panting breath. A face, close to mine. He says it with satisfaction; sitting down for a meal he has been looking forward to. A wolf.

'Will fucking Frost.'

Chapter 45

How dead is the dead of night? Willow Frost has logged into our national newspaper website and posted her final story. The story is another one about an horrendous sexual assault, a woman who was raped while she was at work by one of her colleagues.

It is filled with more detail than we would ever normally report and she hasn't buried this one, not like she did the others: she has put it top of the homepage. Headline emblazoned across it. I AM A RAPIST. And there, underneath, his full name and picture. Fuck. Fuck. *Fuck*. Willow has written her own story.

I am trying to work out the chance that no one has read this yet, that I can get to it before Reader Zero clicks on it, eyes widening at the realisation of what this is, and shares. I picture data, charts. And then human beings, in rooms, picking up their phones and logging on. The two converge. There is Reader Zero. And then there is beyond. There are lots of people, at once, insomniacs, posting it; this scandal on a national newspaper site. It's shared over and over. They know it will be deleted and they have to get in fast before that happens. It will propel itself up the chart. Head abroad, across oceans. They will screen-grab it, for the time when they can't access the link anymore which they know will be soon because when does anything this scandalous not get taken down, snuffed out? It's a ticking time bomb, and how lucky are they that they saw it before it happened. But if I can snip it at the roots then maybe I can stop all of this. My mouth is dust, and my hands shake on my keyboard as I log on and unpublish the story as fast as my fingers can go. Delete it entirely.

But when I turn to the chart, it is too late. Willow's story has gathered massive traction, far bigger than anything else we post in the middle of the night. It is building higher and higher, even now it has been deleted, as the internet catches up.

Incredibly though, my phone isn't ringing yet. I stare at my screen. The oddest limbo. Wait. Things move slowly online. The cache will take a while to catch up and render it non-existent and in the meantime, it is there for everyone to see. Refresh.

So now, there is nothing to do but wait. I notice my arm sting and remember the coffee I threw all over myself when Willow arrived. My hands go up to my neck and it feels pinched and sore where I have been scratching at it. Refresh, refresh, refresh. *Come on*. And then, inevitably, my phone rings and even though I am steeled for it, I gag.

'Hello,' I say carefully. I am about to be destroyed. I know what will happen. I know how this will go. He will think, of course, that it is me who did this. It's done on my login.

And he will come for me.

But it is not Douglas. It is Officer Ford. 'Rose, I just had a call about someone in the river near your office.'

It seems incomprehensible that someone is talking about anything except this story that I am still picturing, travelling at pace around the world. I had been so sure it would be Douglas on the phone. But they *are* talking about something else. Something important. Officer Ford is almost gasping for breath, and I can hear an effort to stay professional through it.

'I'm running down there now,' she says and I can hear a whistling wind too; rain that is hammering the ground. I glance at the window and see how bad the weather is. In here, we hear nothing. 'But I needed to know you're okay.'

Still, in the midst of this conversation, I refresh. But wait. What? 'Someone in the river?'

It takes me a second to catch up. 'A body, you mean?' Why is she checking I'm okay?

Pant. Pant. Pant. 'I don't know yet, Rose. That's the honest answer.'

I catch a glimpse of myself in the glass skin of the building. I have aged, a decade. And then I get it. 'She came back,' I say, deadpan.

I listen to the silence. 'When?' She doesn't sound shocked, or ask who I mean.

'Tonight. She has been with me, in the office. And she did something that could have made people angry. Oh God. I'll send you the link.'

'I'll look at it as soon as I can. Are you okay, Rose?'

And I feel a heavy sob rise up in my throat. Emit it loudly, and another, and another. I know they will come

255

for me soon, asking questions. Willow came here. She did this. What do I know? How much of it was true? And then I will have to start talking too, won't I, about what happened to me and what happened to her and what the hell has been happening in this place in the days and nights since.

The time for silence is past.

'Rose?'

'Her name was Willow,' I hear myself saying. 'She never used Will.'

I picture that river, how unforgiving it is at the best of times but in the middle of weather like this, whipped into a frenzy by the wind . . . 'You call her Will.'

Officer Ford sighs. 'Everyone seemed to, Rose. Nobody said Willow. We thought . . . it seemed liked a nickname she used all the time.'

'She never did,' I tell her. 'She never used it. It was just other people who used it for her.'

Silence, except for the heavy breath as she hurries down there. 'I'm sorry. But you never corrected us. And . . . even you used it, Rose.'

She was right. I did. I might have called her Willow when I messaged her directly, but other than that, it was Will. Somewhere along the line, without her presence in the office to challenge it, Will had become her accepted name. My boss had defined her, named her. And the rest of us had blindly copied. I feel deep shame.

'Make sure you don't use it now,' I tell her, on a sob. 'If it's her, and you get her out, call Willow by her name.'

It's Officer Ford who calls me again, just after I have finally gone to sleep, at 8 a.m. The night has been fraught. On the phone, as she told me somebody had been found in the river, Officer Ford instructed me to go back to the hotel and stay there, and that she would call senior management at the paper, tell them about Willow posting the stories. Explain it was nothing to do with me.

I didn't have to do a thing, she said, speaking in a hurry. Just leave. She wanted me out of the way. Officer Ford sent a police car to pick me up and spirit me back to the depressing four walls of room thirty-seven in the Premier Inn, Canary Wharf. I stared at those walls, too wired to sleep. But finally, I climbed into bed.

I have just drifted off when the phone rings. Now, I lie in the anonymity of the hotel bed and I hear her say the words.

'I'm so sorry, Rose. The person in the river was Willow. It was too late to save her.'

My wail sounds like a colicky baby. Not this. Not this. I think of Willow and her watery blue eyes, asking me to come with her. Of her leaving. And then what happened? I think of her, up there on the roof that night. It had crossed her mind before. Had she done it this time? Or had someone else got to her first?

'What happened?' I ask Officer Ford in a croak.

'We don't know yet, Rose. As soon as we do, and I am able to, I'll give you more information.'

There we were, sharing a chair, sharing a desk, sharing a screen, yet we never met each other until last night. And now. Now. I am the one still here. Push, pull. And the other one is dead.

Chapter 46

Her nails are painted with tiny marijuana plants as I stare at them, her hand in mine. I didn't know where else to go. That smell of her – the lemon from her armpits; the slight body odour – drifts up towards my nostrils.

'I know this is such an obvious thing to say but how can it be that *final*?' I say, with a fury. 'How can there be nothing left of her now? It is so. Fucking. Monstrous.'

There is nothing to say to that though because it's the simplest and the most complicated part of being a human being and so we sit, contemplate, in nothing like silence, as buses hurtle past Rania's window and her next-door neighbours play nineties Madonna.

'I'd sent her back to the hotel,' I tell her, when she comes in a few moments later holding two mugs of coffee. Sits them down in front of us on the low table. I slide down, onto the floor cushion. 'That's where she was heading to.'

I wasn't fast enough, and overnight the story has gone viral. I am trying to avoid my phone but still I know that it's the biggest news story of the day; screen-grabbed and shared more than anything in recent tabloid memory. Oh the irony: our own story, for once, and we can't even take the traffic win.

I go to the kitchen then and drink glass after glass of water, like I have the worst hangover of my life. Then I sit back down and turn to Rania.

'You always said we had a lot in common. You were right.'

And so, finally, I tell her my story as well. About that night at Lizzie's party and what happened to me. When I stop speaking, Rania reaches for my hand. 'I didn't know what it was but I thought something had happened to you. I'm so sorry.'

I nod. 'Well, it's out there now. They can charge him. And I can do something for Willow at least, and try and get him convicted.'

Something odd flickers then across her face, and she asks me a question. 'Was it the same person?' she says. 'Who attacked you both?' Yes, I clarify. We had a lot in common. Including the same attacker.

Rania stares into the middle distance. She reaches behind her head and coaxes a curl out. Leans back. She puts her hands, fingers threaded, behind her head. I watch her. Try to work out what is happening. Something is off.

'You did have a lot in common. This life was a bit . . . much for you both, I always thought.'

I think back to being in that bar with Patrick. How I'd wanted to turn the volume down there, and then slow it all down, but how, as I walked to the bus stop that night, I realised it went beyond that; that I wanted to do that everywhere. Mute people. Put soft cushions underneath me and close my eyes. Close the door. How strong that urge was, after what happened to me, to retreat from life. She is right. 'It was too much. It is too much.'

And look at us, Willow and I, both ending up on the thirty-fourth floor, at night. Alone. The quiet only disturbed by a ringing phone, by Douglas screaming at us. And then, when he hung up, we could take a deep breath and step back into the silence. I even learned to type quietly.

'You had the same odd relationship with the night shift too.'

She gently takes hold of one of my wrists. It slips out of her hand, and I look at my arm and realise how little I've eaten lately, since things started to change with Patrick and especially since I moved out, how often I just forget. Or the panic attacks come, and it is too overwhelming to make a meal. Or I have wine instead.

'Then there were the relationships that were wrong for you. That you were trying to get out of.'

The ring. 'You *knew* who Willow was engaged to?'

She is defensive. 'I told the police! Of course I told the police. I didn't know anything but her first name but I told the police that. I wouldn't have kept information like that from them.' She pauses and I think about that cancelled appointment.

Wouldn't you?

I think of Patrick then, in so much pain last night. It is difficult, isn't it, to say where the night shift sits in our problems, where its role comes in our lives. In some ways it gives us an out. But it's there too causing problems, making things unfixable. It rules us out of life, that shift.

'I doubt the night shift helped either,' says Rania. 'Willow had been doing it for eight *years*. She was only thirty. Most of her adult life, living like this . . .'

I think of different days here, me coming in from a shift, Rania heading out. A brief chat, about her day, about her plans, that she wouldn't be here tonight, 'am at the lover's, chick'. And suddenly, something occurs to me. Rania has always been private about her love life and Willow's sexuality was utterly unknown to me.

'Were you and Willow—'

But Rania cuts me off with a shake of her head. 'No. We just talked. You know what it's like. Therapy. It was the same with Willow. Nothing else.'

The tears start again, heavy rain. Eventually I look up.

'So who is your lover then, Rania? If it's not Willow, who is it?'

And her face loses its usual light.

Chapter 47

She doesn't answer me, and eventually it gets awkward.

'You were right about the alcohol,' I say, changing the subject. 'I thought it would help to cut back on the social life, the pubs.'

'It didn't, I take it.'

I shake my head. I think about the wine bottles. About how I could convince myself it was better because it was less public. I think about what Willow said to me. I think about getting better, for her. Trying to, at least.

'I've taken it too far,' I say to Rania through tears that have now made tiny puddles on my cheeks. I curl up, foetal. 'I just wanted things to be slow. And calm. The wedding, the office, I couldn't, I couldn't . . .' I struggle to catch my breath and Rania grips me, vice-like, as though she is stopping limbs from detaching themselves from my body. It isn't there that I am coming apart though, I know that. I have known that for a while.

'Shhhhhh chick, shhhhh,' she says as she holds me close to her like I am a homesick toddler. 'Shhhhh shhhhh shhhh.'

She repeats it for seconds, minutes, I have no idea, until something starts to still in me and the mantra stops. What is left behind, though, is a feeling of such sadness that it might be worse than the panic, perhaps because it feels like it could last so much longer, without any let-up.

Rania stands up and walks to her bag, by the door. Takes out her water bottle, a long swig. She doesn't come back to sit next to me but sits at the other side of the room on a chair.

'End a relationship that's not right for you, sure,' she says. 'Easing back was a good plan. But we all need conversations and someone touching us, even if it's just on the arm or brushing past us in the kitchen or shaking our hand in a meeting. We all need human beings. We all need love. Or we lose it, like Willow did.'

I reach up to the table to pick up the coffee Rania made me but when I sip it, it makes me gag. Cold now. I nod. 'Patrick wanted this life that was so . . . public that I can't fathom it anymore, since what happened to me. I think I need to start again. Figure out who I am now.'

'I know that, chick.' Rania nods. 'I think that's perhaps why you let Willow Frost come along and form you.'

Something strange is happening to my friend's voice. 'Why you morphed into her. Why you let her write your narrative for you.'

'Willow didn't write my narrative. What are you talking about? Something happened to me, which also happened to her. We were both assaulted by the same colleague.'

Quietly, she says: 'The night shift can make you imagine things. Get things wrong. And then look what happens. Lives, ruined.'

I repeat it. 'What are you talking about?'

But she says nothing else. And now I am confused. Can't think straight.

'I have to sleep soon,' I say. 'I have the night shift.'

But is she right? Has the night shift made me imagine something?

She looks at me in shock at first, but then she nods. She knows. 'You will quit it though, won't you?'

'I won't have a choice,' I reply. 'Someone new is coming. The new night editor.'

'If it doesn't work out. If they don't turn up. If anything. You will quit it, and you won't go back?' She pauses. A haunted expression crosses her face. 'The night shift leads to bad things, Rose.'

I stare at her. 'Did you call her Willow? In the office, no one did.' Why did I go along with it, that nickname? Not to her face, of course. I didn't see her face. And on email, in messages, I called her Willow. But to the group, to my colleagues, she was always Will. I let that happen. *People pleaser.*

I will leave the job, of course I will. Tonight though, there's no choice. Soon after, I pack my bag, get on my bike, and cycle back to the hotel to sleep. I'm the night editor.

Chapter 48

I work, but all I can think about is what happened in between Willow leaving me, heading to the hotel and her being found in the river. Suicide, people say. Rania says. Everyone says. The real people, and the online people, who are now heavily invested in this, having seen a screen-grab and reading a few speculative tweets and so knowing everything there is to know.

They are investigating and the post-mortem is pending, but all of that feels like a technicality. Willow had disappeared. Posted explosive allegations online about one of her colleagues. And then she walked along the river, past Canary Wharf pier. It's happened before, there. It's sad, they say. But it's common. Plus once, you know, she was spotted on the roof?

I wonder though. *He* would have seen the website, of course. What she had written about him, there, with a large photo of his face. The word she had used.

I try to calm down. Take in the quiet of the thirty-fourth floor in the deepest well of the night.

I am not Willow.

I am safe.

I am alive.

Willow used my login but removed my name. I didn't post anything about anyone.

Except . . . something niggles at me. Willow was angry that night. She wanted the truth bared, whatever the consequences. I didn't get a mention in her online piece but that didn't mean she didn't tell someone in real life what had happened to me.

Something pulses in my belly. If someone did push Willow into the river that night because she wrote that piece, they may know there is a second victim, who has access to the same system Willow did. They might know that before Willow died, she and I had joined the dots. They might know that the second victim, now, knows more than she used to.

I glance around the room.

Two o'clock in the morning.

The stark lights are bright and the computers hum. There is security downstairs, CCTV. And surely, surely, no one would do anything *now*, after what has happened.

I am safe here. While my heart still hammers hard, I remind myself of that. I am safe. *But look what happened to Willow here*, a voice niggles. CCTV doesn't cover everywhere. He doesn't follow normal rules.

When my shift is over, I tell myself, I will call Officer Ford and tell her exactly what happened to me at Lizzie's party, and who did it. I know I owe that to Willow, and I have learned to say it out loud, and whatever happens, it is time for the truth.

I stand up, to get coffee. To calm me. Sort of. To do something to me. But it hits me again like a punch, that

266

this was supposed to be a night that looked so different to this. I should be scooping up the dregs of my wedding now. Bleary and bright-eyed, I should be saying goodbye to the last of the guests, the party crowd, the ones who stayed with us for *one more song, one more song.* There would be dust, by now, on the bottom of the obscenely expensive dress that I still have hung up in my wardrobe. Sorry, Patrick's wardrobe. Instead, it is preserved, never to live the life that was intended for it.

I am in shock, at where I should be, at where I am, at how this has happened to my life and to me in the last six or seven weeks. I glance at my hand. There would be a ring now, there, on that finger – two rings. Rose Rivers-Hart, I would be, and wasn't it a lovely moniker, didn't everyone say? Some double-barrels don't sit as well. This one hit the spot.

I sit back down, winded. I picture the luxury suite that I should be in now, exhausted, curled up close to Patrick in expensive bridal lingerie.

But then I hear the door. Footsteps. And thoughts of the wedding are wiped out. He pushes me backwards and backwards across the room so that eventually we are at the window and my head and shoulders hit the glass. A small sound comes out of my throat. He tightens his grip. He tightens, again. And then, he snuffs the sound out.

Chapter 49

I keep still, like he is a wasp I am trying not to anger.

'Did you let her post that stuff yesterday?'

I can't say a word, but I can meet his eyes. Shake my head. He answers his own question. 'I know you fucking did. You were here, the whole time. I've been into the system. It was done under your fucking login.'

Deep lines between his eyebrows; a mean set to his chin. Doughy skin, like a caricature, like a puppet.

I had figured out who'd attacked me a few days ago now. But I had it confirmed by Willow's story, by everything lining up. That night when she came back, we said his name. We nodded at each other. Yes. That was him. We had our guy.

I feel my body try to curl up away from the glass, a reflex.

The glass has to be thick, when people walk around this building all day, doesn't it? It wouldn't be possible for him to push me through it? I feel my heart rate speed up, up, up until it pulses at the base of my throat. I don't have a fear of heights but I do have a fear of dying, young, by being shoved through glass 250 metres in the air. Don't all fears come from logic? That seems like reasonable logic to me.

'Do you know that after she wrote that shit, she started sending me messages?' he says.

'She didn't even have a phone,' I manage.

'Clearly she got a burner from somewhere.' And then he carries on. 'But the most interesting bit was that she was saying I had done this stuff to you too. That you knew it. What the fuck, Rose? You're the one who was steering this really, letting her post this stuff. Will has lost her mind, clearly, who's going to take her seriously?'

'But you! You're different. So I came here for answers, instead of going to her like she wanted. Except you had gone hadn't you?' I am rigid now.

'So you came back tonight.'

He is that wasp again and I am ready, to respond in whatever way he wants.

'She's a crackpot. A fucking loon. Hanging around on the roof? She left work in the middle of the night and went off radar and no one would believe a word she says. But *you*. You're the one who let her come in here and blow my fucking world apart. How could you do this to me?'

A little spit lands on my cheek. He is very drunk. His eyes are unable to focus at all.

The dough of his skin glistens with sweat. 'She left a note, saying to ask you where she had gone.'

I try to move my head within the constraints of his thumb and finger. It doesn't move far.

'I came in early that day. I saw the note.'

Ask Rose.

'You and her,' he carries on. 'You were in this together.'

Laughter sounds odd when it comes up through a constricted throat and when no one feels any mirth. 'Why would we be in this together?'

He stares at me and I feel fury. The idea of him removing my underwear while I was unconscious, of him having that memory where I have none . . .

Perhaps he was drunk that night too. But he was not as drunk as me. He was sober enough to make choices. Sober enough to act.

The stare keeps going, and going, and I think I forget the glass behind me, forget the fear. 'Is it because you raped Willow?'

The anger makes my skin smart. 'Is it because you assaulted me too? Is it because you did it to us both?' The anger sears my insides. It is everywhere. It is all of me now. Everything. 'Is that what you think we have in common? Knowing the truth about you? Knowing that you are a sex offender and knowing that we could smash your world to pieces any time we wanted?'

'What the hell are you talking about, Rose?'

And I know I should be placating that wasp again but I cannot stop. 'I am talking about the fact that you are a rapist. I'm talking about the fact that you—'

He slams my head backwards, hard, into the glass. Then again, again, again.

Stung.

The room starts to spin and I think, *don't black out, don't black out, whatever you do, don't black out*, but it is becoming difficult. This room where I spend so many of my hours, this room that is so stark, blurs at the edges.

I still try, to tell him what he is. The room smells of his aftershave. I gag. He has been out tonight.

'Attacked you? If Will says she was raped, then sure, she was raped. But not by me. And I don't doubt something happened to you, Rose, if you say it did, probably by the same guy who did it to Will.' His words drip in, then retreat. 'But that *was not me*. Posting about me on a fucking national newspaper website, while you sat there, and let her *use your fucking login*, Rose. You've ruined my life.'

I feel my head, tipped back and back and back. Again. And there they are again too, those wings reaching for my edges, meaning I can't be strong, or brave, or even just okay, but that I must now face this man with my weaknesses written all over me. When he stops, I ball shaking hands into fists to still them.

I stare at him and feel the warmth of blood on the back of my head. I have not got long; I can feel myself losing consciousness.

'When someone has that written about them, Rose, what you and Will did . . .' A sob comes out of his throat, but there is rage in it and I have never heard a sound so guttural. His face moves closer to mine.

But I manage one word: 'Willow.'

Something soars from that. I think of my sisters, and I think of this one day, a few years ago, when I cycled through London as the sun was going down and I felt full of the knowledge that I was happy and how far away that feeling is now. But I hold on to the memory of that happiness. The knowledge that if that could happen then, it can happen again. I think of a hot bath, I think of warm gloves on cold fingers. I think of my niece curled onto my chest and I think of how I love the 360 view of my city from the top of Primrose Hill. And I think, clearly, I am not ready to check out. I need to make tweaks or possibly enormous seismic shifts to my life, yes, and I have so much to deal with. But I do not want it to be over.

My phone rings again, and we see it there, both of us. The name Officer Ford, ringing out.

'Looks like they've got an update on our friend Will.' I hear him through a fog, talking in a stage whisper. And then, that snarl in his voice. 'I'm glad she went into that river last night, Rose. So. Fucking. Glad.'

I can't speak because my head flicks back, back, back, like a soft toy in the hands of a toddler. My eyes droop. My arms sag. The thought becomes woollier. All thoughts become woollier. But I can see that smirk. And then my head hits the glass one too many times, harder, harder, harder.

'Did you go to her, last night?' I ask him, though my voice sounds odd. Distant.

Again.

'Her . . . name . . . is . . . Willow.'

And then he slams harder than ever, and as I have done so many other times in my life, I black out. This time though, I am sober. But that will not help me.

Chapter 50

He walks in screaming.

'Do you want to tell me what the fucking FUCK is happening? It's not bad enough that we had all that shit on the homepage yesterday and that I am fielding calls from the CEO, from investors, shareholders, all fucking day but now there's radio silence on our site. No fucking news. FUCK.'

He rounds the corner.

'No concept of what this could do to people's lives, to all of our livelihoods,' he rants. 'No concept of the magnitude of this role. What is this, a joke to you? A prank? A national newspaper, the only person around and you do this? Do you want to explain? Rose? Why you're not answering my calls? Are you even fucking HERE?'

But then he spots me, on the floor behind a desk. Blood trickling from my head. Barely conscious.

'SHIT! SHIT. Rose!'

He shakes me, and I stir. Hot breath hits me. He hasn't brushed his teeth.

Douglas is vile. That's not up for debate. But Douglas was not my attacker. Not that night at Lizzie's party, and not earlier, slamming my head against glass. He is not the one who did this to me.

I am lying on the scratchy carpet next to the window. London is still there, reliable old bird that she is, but she has been my only company as I have drifted in and out of consciousness for an unknowable length of time.

'Rose? Answer me, Rose.'

His voice has fallen down a notch. He is worried. He crouches down; rests a pudgy hand on my arm. The top of his belly rests on my side. Douglas in his civvies: the conscious part of me registers this on some level as noteworthy.

'Don't move,' he says. He takes his phone out of his pocket and stands up. 'I'm calling an ambulance.'

I don't know if it is the rugby shirt – and its tiny smear of tomato ketchup next to one button – that makes him lose his power, or the knowledge I now have that it was not him who attacked me.

I had, of course, always wondered. But now, I know, his worst is using unliked nicknames and calling his wife the missus and making people shake with fear, just to wield the power. A pantomime villain, really. His worst is not the worst. It is someone else who is the worst.

'Willow is . . .' I start to cry.

'Oh it's Willow now, is it?' His voice is relief, that I am talking. 'I know, Rose, I know. Ah. So you two *were* close. No wonder the police were so interested in you.' He waits. Expectant. Then he changes his mind. 'Just rest, Rose. The ambulance will be here soon.'

But when I start to drift off as we wait for the ambulance, he keeps talking to me. In the only way he knows how. 'This is pure bollocks, Rose. You have a job to do and you've missed most of your shift already.'

'Call myself a journalist,' I manage, with half a smile.

He gives a weak smile, too, and down here on the floor when he is smiling, even with those ludicrous white teeth, he passes as a human being.

'Can you call Officer Ford too?' I say, the words difficult to get out. 'Tell her I have some updates.'

Willow confirmed it with her own story but I had already figured out who had attacked me. A week ago now.

He didn't wear that aftershave in work, just for special occasions. You know the kind of thing. Parties. Meeting up at the weekend with your mate at a pub in Dalston. I walked away from our drink that day with a smile, but it had fallen off my face by the time I rounded the corner from the pub. I ran all the way home.

The first time we had physical contact: when I was passed out and he assaulted me.

The second time we had physical contact: when he reached for my hand in the pub, so sure – I presume – that he had got away with what he'd done to me; then focused on making sure he had got away with what he had done to Willow too. That no one tried too hard to find her when she had done what he had suggested to her and *disappeared*.

The third time we had physical contact: when he spread out the thumb and index finger of his large hand and pushed me backwards until there was only glass between me and the whole of my city and I felt my body brace against it.

Did Richie know I had no memory of that night? He must have done, to have that front. Must have known I never woke up.

So, Richie and I stayed friends. Became better friends, perhaps. I wonder sometimes if I knew in my subconscious. If our friendship was my attempt to rewrite history; to reduce the size of what he'd done to me. If he was my friend, he could not be my attacker. If he was not my attacker, I could not have been attacked. If I had not been attacked, I didn't have to deal with what came next. Nobody told my body or my mind that though, so the trauma landed anyway. It does that.

Chapter 51

One Week Later

'Mum and Dad are on their way,' says my sister Florence and I sink down deeper into the crunch of the hospital sheets. How to know you have failed as an adult: when your parents are heading down to hospital to fetch you and take you home, to sleep in your childhood bedroom and be given jam on toast for breakfast and to stare at the walls that had been painted magnolia over the many marks from my collection of large, yellowing posters of Keanu Reeves.

But where else would I go? I have closed off the bridges.

My head throbs, despite the painkillers that come regularly, four at a time in their dinky little pot.

Patrick tried to tell me to come home. Through thick, dripping tears I told him no. That's not home. I can't pretend it is or mess with his mind when I know that it's not right, whatever has happened now.

'Have they found him yet?' I ask Officer Ford, speaking slowly. The words take all of my effort.

I am relieved it's her that's here, not Officer Parmar or anyone else. She sits at a subtle distance from Florence and I, on a blue chair in the corner of the cubicle. Her mouth sets into a line so straight it could have been drawn. 'We're working on it.'

She will never say it, as I never said it, but I know she had eyes on Douglas. Wondered if he had something to do with Willow disappearing; this nasty boss who disrupted the silence of the middle of the night with his shouting and screaming and his swearing. She glanced down, saw my hands shake when he spoke to me, and wondered if Willow's had done the same. If he had tipped her, perhaps, over the edge. It's not like I hadn't considered it myself. At times convinced myself: it must have been him, mustn't it? He was The Bad Guy.

Meanwhile Richie, on the surface, was docile. He wore a smile and Nikes. His hair would always be called boyish, however far into his thirties and beyond he descended, when it greyed and receded.

But true badness is more than performance. It is more than a snarling face, in being appalled about what's happened to your overpriced, fancy new shoes. All of that happens on the surface. True badness sits deep next to organs and pumps around with blood.

I look up.

'I think I'll head off for now,' Officer Ford says. I nod, relieved. Saving my words. Because I have used a lot as we have been over it all – what happened the night that Willow came back and what she told me and everything right back to my attack. It's been a triathlon and I need recovery. 'Unless there's anything else you want to tell me.'

Officer Ford pauses. And I think. Anything else.

'Just that I'm sorry,' I say, quietly. If I had spoken up, if I had reported what had happened to me when it happened, then at best Richie would have been arrested and at worst, he would have stayed away from people we worked with, knowing eyes were on him. Could I have stopped Willow being attacked? If I had just done something so simple as opening my mouth? And if I had stopped that, I could have stopped her going missing, stopped her being killed, stopped all of this like a big red traffic light . . .

I realise I am speaking out loud, Florence's hand on my arm.

'Can you tell her to stop saying this?' Florence says, looking pained, and she turns to Officer Ford like they know each other well. Clearly they have been speaking outside this cubicle. My sister necks her coffee and winces: my poor Flo, used to what Nell brings her in a cafetière in their garden with the long grass filled with wildflowers in Devon. Now here, drinking Homerton's machine finest. 'She's driving herself crazy.'

Officer Ford's phone rings. 'Just need to get this . . .' she murmurs and slips out of the room.

I look at Florence. The hand that is not on me is wrapped around her coffee. Her country girl rouge has departed her cheeks.

She grips my upper arms. Gets close up in my face. 'You are not bad. He is bad. He is terrible. You . . .' She stops to compose herself. To touch my cheek. 'You have never in your life been even a tiny bit bad.'

And then a sob lets itself out from her throat and I see its force shock her and it sets me off but for me, the effect is quiet. I am weeping. A tear, and then another, then another.

When the curtain pushes back again and Officer Ford walks in, the sobs fade and my head stills and we both try to get ourselves together. Florence's hand is on me, clutching tight. I mop my eyes with the heel of my hand. Florence reaches in her bag, passes me a tissue. Officer Ford looks between us.

'It's okay,' I tell her. Nod. 'Go on.'

Officer Ford folds an arm across her middle. Her fingers are in her mouth. She is uncomfortable, knows this isn't the best time to bring us news and that we are in the middle of something. But what choice does she have? I nod again. Go on. When she speaks, her voice is pure professionalism. 'They've found a lanyard in the river,' she says. 'From your place. Name of Richie Molloy.'

'Is he dead?' Florence asks, cold, and I look up in surprise. My wispy sister and her floaty dresses and her wildflowers: I have made her speak in a language that's not her own, of cold dead bodies in dank rivers. I am glad Nell isn't here, that one of them can stay cocooned, and that when Florence goes home, she can welcome her and comfort her, without being tainted by today.

'I can't tell you that from a lanyard, Florence.'

'But what do you think?' I ask.

Officer Ford locks eyes with me. 'I think that he had been publicly accused of rape in a way that would be difficult to ever wipe from the internet. There aren't many things that people can live with less than that.'

She pauses. 'But you know this. He told you that himself.'

I have given a full statement now. I have relayed it all, through the relentless pounding headache that won't shift.

'So he killed himself?' Florence asks. 'Is that what you're saying? You think he killed himself too?' Her eyes flit across to me.

Officer Ford holds a hand up. She sounds impatient. 'I'm not saying anything, Florence. Like I say, it's barely anything, this stuff we've found. Certainly not evidence of clear death. But I'm saying that as of right now, Richie is missing and if another body were to be found in there . . . well, it wouldn't surprise me, after what's happened. And yes, suicide would – again – be a possible explanation to look at.' She clasps her hands together. 'Right. I need to get back to the station, Rose, but I'll be back soon to check in. And I will update you, of course. Florence, you're staying? You'll be with her?'

Florence nods and Officer Ford scoops up her rucksack. She rips back the curtain, and leaves.

One week after that, they find me trying to get into the office for the night shift. My pass still works, so I make it all the way to my desk where the new night editor – the permanent one, who has started now – is wearing a crisp shirt, shiny shoes and has six tabs open at once; fingers darting across her keyboard. She screams when she sees me.

'I could help,' I say to her, with an attempt at a smile. 'I used to be the night editor.'

She backs away on the wheels of her chair and grabs her phone. I see a Lion bar wrapper on her desk. Two empty coffee cups.

'Oh hello, New Me!' I laugh, as she waits for Douglas to answer. I am not sure why she doesn't find it funny.

The new night editor says my eyes are dazed and I am slightly hysterical and that I scare her a little, and that that is why she is calling her boss.

Douglas contacts my parents, down as emergency contacts from a form filled in another lifetime ago, and they come to get me, and late that night they drive me back to the Hertfordshire countryside and my childhood bedroom again. It is where I had made my escape from when I headed into Canary Wharf earlier, the jam on toast and the 'are you okay' frowns and the hands on my forehead getting too much. I had felt like I had been encased in plastic wrapping and I needed to take scissors to it and slice myself out, whatever mess I caused. All of that daylight too. All of that daylight was unsettling me.

But back in my childhood home, no one cares if I am going crazy, as long as I am *resting*.

Rania calls at just the right moment. It is the most perfect timing, that her flatmate has moved out, for good this time, getting a place with her boyfriend, just as I need somewhere to live. Just when I need to slice myself out of the plastic and be an adult. To work out what is next.

My flatmate Rania doesn't let me out of her sight. Now I'm here, under a duvet with a cup of tea that she made me just before she left for work. A large, neon-green cushion is propped up behind me.

She cooks me meals with six different types of vegetables in. She sits with me as we talk through different options for my career, for my life. Googles courses, makes notes – how much they would cost, how much we think my skill sets match them. We don't have any more of those conversations about Willow shaping my narrative.

She's never mentioned it since. I put it down to trauma, in the aftermath of our colleague's death. Instead, Rania signs me up for yoga. Walks next to me around Clissold Park, an arm reaching out to still me as we go past the paddling pool, telling me it's time for a break, let's get some tea.

But the most important thing Rania has done for me? The most important thing is persuading me that I was imagining it when I thought I saw Richie outside our flat one day, boyish hair stuffed under a baseball cap. Clearly my mental health was in a bad way then. There may still be no body, but there is no trace of Richie anywhere. His lanyard was in the river. Richie is, surely, dead.

Rania left for work ten minutes ago.

The front door opens.

I scream before I see him.

That *smell*.

Chapter 52

We lock eyes and I have an awareness as sharp as knives of complete terror, an automatic reaction. The last time I saw him, he left me for dead.

And now, Richie is here. Richie is going to attack me again. This time, why would he leave, until he was sure? But first, what? My whole body shoots fear through its skin and the scream comes so loudly, so quickly, that it hurts my lungs.

But then, nothing. Richie turns. The door slams. I lock it behind him and then I manage, my hands vibrating like a drill, to call the police. While I wait, I call Rania and tell her what has happened. She gets there faster than Officer Ford. When she walks into the flat, she looks everywhere but my face. And I realise something in slow motion, staring at her the whole time.

'You're looking for Richie.'

'He didn't come to hurt you,' she says, as she falls onto her sofa like a teenager spent from school. 'He wouldn't have . . .' A hard, guttural sob.

My phone is clutched in my hand. I look down. My

bare feet have chipped nail polish on them and the skin is dry and pale. 'So why would he come, Rania?'

I am still staring at the floor as I think back. The way she looked at me when I talked about getting justice for Willow and making Richie pay. Keeping things from the police. The suggestion that Willow had pedalled me a narrative; that I wasn't telling the truth, even though I was her *friend*. The drip-feed of anti-Douglas propaganda to pass the buck to him, instead.

There's a relief in her voice when she speaks, which is the most shocking thing. She wants to tell me. She needs this out. She sighs. 'Because he's my boyfriend, chick.'

The lover. The man she was supposed to go to Berlin with. Richie, Richie, Richie. My heart speeds up. Jesus. What is this?

She puts a hand up. 'Hear me out.'

I am standing up, heading for the door.

But she follows me. 'Don't you want to hear me out?' she says, through a desperate sob. 'Don't you want to know the truth? Or are you running away, like she did?'

Chapter 53

I stay, of course, because I'm a journalist. I have lived through the opener of our story, and the bulky, sprawling middle. And now, I need to know the end.

'Go on then. Tell me.'

'You've got the wrong guy, Rose,' she says, one hand grasping her hair like a rope that will pull her to safety. 'I swear to you. You've got the wrong guy.'

Our eyes meet. 'So who is the right guy then, Rania?' I say, carefully. 'Who did Richie – the man who left me for dead, remember, in our office – tell you it was?'

She winces. 'He was broken and terrified, Rose. I know it doesn't excuse it but that wasn't him, you know that.'

I ignore her. 'Go on. Who did he say it was?'

'Who do you think?' she says. 'Who do you fucking think?'

I realise now why she told me what had happened to Willow in the first place. She had picked up on things I had said, hinted at: she thought the same thing might have happened to me, at the hands of the same colleague, and that I could help prove who it really was.

She thought that Willow was – whether from malice or confusion – blaming the wrong guy. If I said I had been attacked by Douglas, maybe that would exonerate Richie. But I shake my head. No. Douglas wears his awfulness right up his suit arms and down his suit legs. My attacker was a different breed. He stacked layers on top of the badness. He had the gall to sit next to me and rib me about my lunch choices.

I have figured this out. Haven't I? For a moment, I think I might throw up everything in my stomach.

My head is still shaking, back, forth, back, forth, keeping time with her words. No. It was not Douglas. Stop telling me that it was.

'But you used to believe it was Douglas!' she pleads. 'You told me that, when you told me what happened to you. That you thought for a long time it was him that did that to you. So what changed?'

'I met up with Richie, in the pub. His aftershave . . . It just came back, Rania. That smell.' I see her face. 'Scent is one of the most powerful triggers for memory that there is, Rania.'

She interjects. 'And you knew then?'

I duck my head.

'No. You didn't know then. You knew the smell reminded you of something bad but you also thought no way, because Richie was your buddy.'

I can't look at her. It wasn't like that. Not exactly. Except I *had* thought that, hadn't I? That he was my mate. That a smell and a Pavlovian reaction alone couldn't convince me that my friend could do that to me.

Rania is looking at me closely. 'Thought so. It wasn't

the smell, it was because of what Willow said. Willow told you Richie attacked her, so you thought that you would jump on her bandwagon.'

'What a word to use, Rania. Jesus. What's wrong with you?'

She holds a hand up. 'But my point is right, yes? How could you believe this just because of a vague . . . *smell* and because Willow said it? You can't make such an important call on something unless you know it and I mean really *know* it yourself, Rose. That's not okay. What if she has it wrong?'

'That wasn't the only reason,' I say, but my voice trails off and it's difficult to enunciate.

It wasn't just the smell of his aftershave that afternoon in the pub but the warning shot in his eyes: Don't pursue this.

Why not, Richie?

And yet she's right, isn't she? I still thought I was being crazy. This was *Richie*. Until Willow said his name.

'Whatever Richie has told you, he's trying to shift the blame,' I say. 'It wasn't Douglas.'

'You sure?'

A beat.

Was I?

Chapter 54

I stare at Rania, now, sitting on her sofa below a sketch of a naked woman's outline. It's beautiful. I think she drew it. I had loved it when I first came to stay here: art, everywhere, on the walls, on the shelves, in the coffee table books, the pillows, even the mugs. All the stuff, this colour, everywhere, was reassuring.

Everyone else our age – Eloise and School Friend Sam are the worst – lives in these minimalist homes where shelves are for display of one lone candle and an artfully placed and unread Penguin Classic, not storage, and there is the impression that no one ever takes off a jumper and puts it on the sofa arm or leaves the dregs of a cup of tea on the table for a couple of hours. Perhaps because they are too busy tending to the gallery wall. There is no life. Just display. We are the display generation.

I sit down opposite Rania in a large yellow armchair. I thought the stuff made her a greater whole. That she wasn't trying to scrub parts out and make her life beautiful but she was here, in full, on show to me. How wrong you can be.

'Everyone who comes to see me hates Douglas, Rose. *Everyone.*'

'Me included,' I reply. 'Doesn't mean he did this.'

'I got close to people in our building.'

Didn't you just. Close enough that I became her flatmate and Richie became her lover. 'Too close.'

'Yes. Maybe.' She sighs. 'I knew a lot of their secrets. Tended to them on my sofa. Listened to their problems. Healed them.'

'*Healed* them? It sounds like a fucking God complex, Rania.' I never minded the fact that she spoke like this before; I bought into her alternative therapies and loved her talking to me about crystals and reiki. Now, she has become a cult leader peddling lies and danger and the whole thing feels a lot more sinister.

She ignores me. But it's true. I think of how she has bloomed the last week, pottering around me as she fixed my cushions and took me out for walks and signed me up for vinyasa flow and told me, always, what was good for me and right. God complex sounds pretty accurate.

I shiver. 'Rania, you are dating a man who left me for dead. And you are dating a rapist.'

She takes a sharp breath in and is shaking her head. 'That is not what he is.'

'It's exactly what he is.'

My fingers are tensed around my phone now, and a rage is kicking in.

'Did you know?' I ask her. 'That he was around, while I was here? When I said I thought I had spotted him outside, and you persuaded me I was going crazy?'

She lowers her head.

'Did you *tell* him to come?' My mind considers something dark and permissive.

'God no!' She looks horrified, and I find relief in that at least. 'I never would have wanted to scare you like that. He's off radar, isn't he? We aren't in contact at the moment.'

Her eyes fill with tears. She shakes her head, down low. 'Okay yes. I knew he had been here that day, when you thought you saw him. But I didn't want you to tell anyone, and for him to get caught. It was just a goodbye.'

'So why was he back today?'

'I really don't know.' She looks pained. 'Maybe he was struggling. Maybe he needed me.'

I recoil. 'But he knew I was here?'

She looks up. 'No. I never told him you were here. He'd have gone mad, to be honest. He'd have thought it was weird, when you're accusing him of all of this.'

And wouldn't he have been right? 'Why *did* you ask me to stay with you, Rania? Surely that would be pretty inconvenient? When you couldn't have your boyfriend round? Why *would* you want me living here?'

She keeps her head bent low. Doesn't meet my eye. Doesn't say a word.

'Ah,' I say, getting it. That God complex. Move me in, weakened, control all of me. Ending, presumably, with my thoughts, so that she was able to exonerate her boyfriend.

'If I was close, you could work on me. Persuade me it wasn't true, as my friend. Wow.'

Look Richie, I can even fix this. Watch me make this disappear, like a crick in the neck or lower back pain. Ta-da!

291

'What he did to us both. Do you care?'

'How can you ask that, Rose?' she rages. 'Of course I care. Or I would care, if it had happened. But it didn't.'

'Did Richie tell you that?' I ask.

'Yes,' she replies, voice grit now, stone wall up. Even her accent sounds different, the sing-song gone. 'Richie told me that. While he was weeping, that six-foot grown man, about his life, his career, everything being ruined by Willow posting online that he was a *rapist*. While he was saying goodbye to me, because he is running, scared of what he is accused of. I know he came into the office that night and I know he said and did some stuff he shouldn't have to you but he was broken, Rose. Terrified. Do *you* care? Do you know what that does to a person? To their future? That stuff, on the internet forever. He was your *friend*.'

'He nearly killed me, Rania.'

She winces. 'I know. And he is devastated about that and sorry and he will get help but you nearly killed *him*, Rose, doing this to him. He is human. It was wrong and he's sorry but he's human and he flipped.'

'And what about Willow?'

She hardens.

'She had chronic pain. One of the worst cases I've seen. So I treated her a lot. She told me what she thought happened to her, that she had been raped in the office. She didn't say who, at first, but she started to treat me like a therapist. People do, I've told you that before. She asked for my mobile number in case she needed to talk and I said yes, how could I not? Then, we talked even more often. She opened up.'

'And one day, she told you it was Richie who did it. Not realising you had started dating him.'

She locks her eyes on mine.

'When, Rania?' My voice is pretty hard too, now. 'When did she tell you it was Richie?'

A beat.

'The day she went missing.'

So she told Rania, and then she told me. And no one gave her the response she needed.

'And what did you do?' I ask. 'After she told you?'

It's like she's squaring up for a boxing match, her body at sharp angles. 'I told him! Of course I told him. I told him that she was accusing him of rape.'

And that's when he called Willow and threatened her. Made her think that he was coming back for her. And that she had no choice but to run.

'He said he didn't do it. But that he had colleagues who were misogynists. Did she definitely see the face of whoever did this? Or did they creep up on her? He was sure that was it, it had *happened* – he would never accuse a woman of lying about that, God no, that isn't Richie – but that it was one of them.'

She sounds so unlike herself. Rania, but Richie really.

'But you have validated this bollocks by putting something that happened to you in a box with her, of all people, like you want – I don't know – a *teammate* in this or something. You've been swept along.'

I think of that smell. No.

I picture myself sitting with Rania, only hours ago, me crying, asking her if she thought Richie had found Willow. If he could have been the one to hurt her. To put her in the river. I pictured that news story. Dear God, he had motive.

She had shaken her head, firm. 'No. Everyone is saying suicide, Rose. That's clearly what it was.'

And I hadn't thought it was odd, why she was so sure, when I knew the police were keeping an open mind about the possibilities. I just thought everyone else was more sure of their convictions than I was lately.

Now, I glance at the door. Touch my phone in my pocket. Where is Officer Ford? I told her Richie had gone; that I wasn't in danger. That I didn't believe he would come back. He'd have to be an idiot to come back. Am I sure though?

Rania turns to me, then. 'He sees that chart every day, Rose. He knows everything is data. He didn't want to be data. There, online, forever, with that against his name. Even if – best case – he was cleared, there forever for any future employer. Any future kids.'

And it's only then that I notice. Her work tunic, normally loose, pulled tight across her middle. Beneath it, a slight round to her stomach. The bottle of Pepto Bismol I saw in the bathroom earlier – I remember Annie drinking it neat like tequila during her first trimester.

That is why she's defending him like this. That's why she can't hear the truth. Because he isn't just her boyfriend. He's going to be her baby's dad, and she is scared and desperate. And that has raised the stakes.

Chapter 55

When I meet up with Douglas three days later, I think about telling him what Rania said. But there's no point. He is already angry. Knowing that Rania is telling people that *he's* the predator, that Richie is pedalling that too, that who knows who else believes it, is not going to help that.

'She says they kept the fact they were a couple secret because it was unprofessional,' I tell him instead, filling him in on the rest of the conversation. Omitting.

He bangs the table in front of him with one large pudgy fist. Scoffs.

'FUCK. OFF. More likely he told her to keep it quiet so he could do whatever he liked and no one would bring up his girlfriend,' he says. 'Snide fucking bastard.'

I watch his face, carefully. 'A snide fucking bastard who will hopefully now be charged with murder,' I murmur.

'Fucking right,' he says. 'Nail the bastard.'

I ignore the bombastic rhetoric. I agree with the sentiment, anyway. I sip my coffee.

They haven't found Richie. I glance again at my phone, out on the table in front of me. Douglas raises an eyebrow briefly, but says nothing.

He takes a large gulp of green juice and winces. 'The missus has got me on a health kick.'

I nod. I already know that, from a very amused Pete who saw him choke on something in his Graze box earlier that week and spit it out, appalled. Word is he carries a yoga mat into the office now so he can go straight to Pilates after his 5 p.m. exec meeting. Pete and Keiran, cheese and onion Greggs in hands, cannot get enough of the whole thing.

Pete told me all this earlier in the week, to try and shift the tone after we'd had a very awkward conversation about our mate Richie, and what the hell had been going on beneath the surface of our friendship.

'Richie though, man. Seriously? Richie. God Rose, I'm sorry.'

I didn't tell him what Rania had said either. Didn't tell him that her take on the bad guy was that it wasn't our good pal Richie but that one with the yoga mat under his arm and the cashew nut flying from between his lips. The one who is sitting here now, in front of me in an East London coffee shop where a toddler is having a full-scale meltdown over a babycino.

'And Will—' Douglas corrects himself. 'Willow saw this physio often?'

He gives the two-year-old a death stare.

'Yeah. Rania said she confided in her. About the attack.'

I feel myself flush red. I know that my boss has been told about what happened to me now. That the police have spoken to most of my colleagues, including him, about that night at Lizzie's party.

'She thinks I am being "swept along with it". Because something happened to me, and I think it's easier to be in a "team" with Willow than to be honest about the fact I don't know who attacked me. Or I know that it's someone else.'

I don't know why I feel so embarrassed. Other than thinking how pathetic Rania must think I am, that I would do that. And how the fact she thinks that about me taps into something I fear: that that is how people view me now, someone who doesn't know who I am, someone who doesn't know what I think, someone who throws everything at the wall to try and make something stick, to be happy, and then watches it all peel off, land back on the floor. Someone who remembers, one day, knowing who I was, what I loved, what I would stand up for, the hills I would die on, and since that night, knows nothing, least of all myself.

Douglas nods, stern. But he doesn't meet my eyes and I am paranoid: does he think it too? That I'm lying about remembering more? That I'm lying about the whole thing? Or does he understand what's going on beneath the surface? That Rania is trying to persuade me that he is my attacker, not Richie.

'So what's the plan work-wise, Rose Rivers?' he says. He has stopped the Rosie thing.

He waves a hand. 'I know you're not coming back. I know. I don't mean that. But you're a good journalist and I wondered if you wanted a reference, a word . . . I know a couple of people at the *Standard* are hiring . . .'

I don't realise that I am shaking my head, but he stops talking and it must have happened automatically, like a tic.

'Thank you, but no. I'm not looking. I'm going to have some time off. I've moved out of Rania's, obviously.

I'm going to stay with my sister in Devon. Figure out what's next. It is also absolutely hilarious that you have just said I'm a good journalist, by the way. Comedy gold.'

He looks confused. Bollockings are so normal to him he has no idea of the terror he's caused me; the racing speeds he has caused my heart to beat at. I realise that he treats everyone this way. I thought I was special, but it was only my reaction that was.

'Anyway . . .' I say, looking down towards his feet.

'Yep. Yep. Sorry, yep.' He reaches down for a large bag for life under the table. 'This is it. Your stuff from work.'

I nod my thanks. I hadn't been able to face going back to the office. Now I have what I came here for, I swig the last of my coffee, and watch him battle through another swig of his juice.

'It was good to see you,' he says. 'And everything crossed that they find Richie soon.' He grimaces. 'We've all seen women passed out in a spare bedroom after an all-nighter. You don't go and touch them up. I'm so sorry, Rose. Horrific.'

He picks up my things.

'Thank you.'

Then I lean in towards him to take my bag from those pudgy hands, and I know I haven't hidden it. I saw him notice, that moment of realisation, the second it crossed my face.

Chapter 56

We say goodbye like normal, with good manners, because that is being a human being, that is what we do. And because he is the king of bravado, Douglas, the king of putting a face on it and I am the world's biggest people pleaser.

I thank him and I pick up my things, and I leave the coffee shop behind St Pancras station and I walk through the throng of people, outdoors in their coats sipping wine or marching past on their iPhones, without making a fuss.

My heart thumps, hard, at its limit. I don't mirror it on the outside though, and I walk slowly and carefully still, while I can feel his eyes on me, until I'm round the corner on to the Euston Road. But when I am there, I break into a run, just as I did when I left Richie that day in the pub in Dalston, and I don't stop until I am on the 205 to Paddington, when I call Officer Ford from the back seat, and leave a voicemail, and tell her it's important and to call me back the second she gets this message. And then I sit back, and I try to slow my heart rate but how is that possible now?

'You don't go and touch them up.'

I am floored.

I didn't know that.

I didn't know what my attacker did to me, and what he succeeded in doing to me, despite hours of trying to picture it, battling against a brain that was telling me: why *would* you try? Why would you try and remember *that*? *Against tiny faceless snapshots that were nightmare-like, unreal.*

But Douglas, it turns out, knew. And how could he? I walk away, slowly, and the smell, Richie's out of work fancy aftershave smell, comes back to me. And then, other things come to the fore. Seeing Richie and Douglas huddled together over a table outside the pub as I walked past, days after what happened to me. Seeing something fly across Douglas's face then, as he clutched his beer and quickly stopped speaking. The moment before, his face had been contorted into a smirk. He had been telling a story. It wouldn't have been called what it was, of course, but the details would have been there.

She was out of it. Did it anyway. Yeah I've seen her naked. Big laughs. More beers. Good times.

Goose bumps prickle on my skin as the bus lurches to a standstill. I glance over my shoulder at the pavement outside.

I know now a little more about what happened to me. The big picture. But I will never know all of it. A specific kind of torture, that, so you can invent version after version after version, and all of them can hurt you in different ways.

The bus pauses at a red light. I stare out of the window at a city hotel; one-night-only visitors leaving for the office with briefcases and intense expressions.

And something else dawns on me. Douglas didn't come to the office that night after Richie left me for dead because there wasn't enough news on the site. He cares, yes, but at 3 a.m.? Whatever I told the police, even he sleeps. At most, if he couldn't sleep and saw it and couldn't get hold of me, he'd have no qualms about waking up a junior reporter and telling them to log on from home and *write some fucking news.*

At the five-bed in Kent with the Range Rover and its personalised registration plate outside, no one would be calling a hundred-quid cab just to chivvy me along on my story count. No. Douglas came because Richie came. Because he followed him.

I think I have found Richie's hiding place.

And then, tears in my eyes, as the bus roars forward towards Baker Street, I think about how I still said thank you to my boss, even after I had realised what was happening. She was right, wasn't she? Willow was always right.

People. Pleaser.

I said thank you to him even after I leaned in close for my bag and realised what had been niggling me through the whole conversation. I could smell it properly then: that same expensive aftershave that Richie wore, doused all over Douglas's face.

Chapter 57

Six Months Later

I take my tea outside and tip my face up to the sun, eyes closed, knowing it is crinkling the skin around my eyes and not caring.

I would have cared, once. Now, Florence and I swing in the hammock, rocked like babies. Everything here is gentle. Nell teaches painting courses in a nearby college but her hours are odd and often evenings, so she is with me a lot during the day, lounging in the hammock or weeding the flower bed or taking Bella for a walk on the beach. Florence is my main ally though. She is a teacher and is happy, she says, to have somebody to spend this long summer holiday with. She has also become my second – unofficial – therapist.

I am recalibrating. Days are days, nights are nights, and there's a reassuring simplicity in that.

I thought Richie attacked me because he attacked Willow, and there couldn't – surely – be two of them. I was wrong. We were unlucky enough for that. Except it wasn't luck. In our world up in the clouds, misogyny was as contagious as a cold for Richie and Douglas. It was Pete who asked the police to look again at the internal chat history, the main thing I had been trying to get to that day my boss caught me on his computer. I didn't know exactly what I was looking for but I knew there would be something – everything happened on the internal chat. We had completely stopped remembering that the system was run by the company and used it like we were messaging on our phones.

Pete had seen evidence of it when he first started – grim, old-school sexist banter. The men who fostered it had quickly realised he wasn't into it, wasn't one of them. Most of my colleagues weren't. I was surrounded by good men, husbands, partners, dads, human beings. Men who made me laugh until I cried. Smart men. Interesting men. Men I rooted for. Kind men. My friends.

Pete had thought Richie was part of that same crew of good men. Me too. But maybe, Pete said to the police, now, knowing what he knew . . . Could they just look again? One more time? So they did. It still makes me sick to describe it. There was a competition, see, between Richie and Douglas. The police hadn't spotted it on first look because it was in code. Ostensibly a fantasy football conversation, but really about women in the company. Kiss them after a few beers in the pub, one point. Have sex with them, many more points. No one seemed to mention consent.

From what I can gather, this is how it happened. Douglas told Richie that something happened between us at Lizzie's party – leaving out the part where I was unconscious and never consented – and Richie – younger, more popular with women, competitive, single – was aggrieved. He didn't like losing. Douglas taunted him about it and then, one time, Richie came back to work after a night out to pick up his laptop and there was Willow. Not interested when he tried to flirt; she just wanted to do her night shift and get home. He didn't care. He was drunk, and he did it anyway. We were goals. Points. It was teenage boy stuff. Or would have been, without that contagion of violence.

When Richie tried to persuade Rania that it was Douglas who liked to sexually assault his colleagues, he was convincing because it was true. And that helped with the part of his story that wasn't true: that poor old victimised Richie, his life ruined with the stories that were plastered over the internet, was innocent. Could never be like *him*.

As if I walked into an office and raped someone. Look at me. Look at Douglas, sure, you can believe that, but then look. At. Me.

Rania did look at him. She saw a young, attractive, tall, confident man. Boyish hair, sticking out at angles. This season's Arsenal shirt fresh on with his Nike trackie bottoms. She didn't see that doughy face, that snarl. She saw what she wanted to see – the good bits of the man she was falling for.

Not knowing that the whole time as she supported him, all she was was the ultimate points win: make them fall in love with you, jackpot. They played for money, Douglas and Richie, and with what he did to Willow, then forming a relationship with Rania, Douglas was on track to owe Richie *a grand and a half*.

Rania didn't know that. Instead, she knew her own narrative, more simplistic: Woman meets Man. Woman gets pregnant. Woman and Man stay together, without Man turning out to be a rapist and a liar. Man can be a dad.

I am sorry for her, that her narrative – and that of her unborn child – has gone so awry. That it was just something else on the grim points system that played with our whole lives. That someday, she will have to figure out a version of that to tell their unborn child. Where do you even begin?

'Have you heard anything about the case yet?' Nell has just got home. She bites into a strawberry she has picked from their patch, a little red juice dripping down her chin. Sits down on the grass in front of Flo and I.

I watch her wipe it with the back of her hand. Shake my head. 'Not yet. Officer Ford said she should have an update for me next week, on both cases.'

They found Richie. He wasn't dead – he'd just thrown his lanyard in the river, rightfully presuming he would never work at our place again, livid about that, when he left me unconscious in the office.

No. Not dead. But, like I thought, hiding out in Douglas's garage – the one Douglas put a sign on the front of declaring it a man cave last year. We'd all heard that story, at least twenty-five times. I wonder, briefly, if *the missus* knew that Richie was staying there. Or perhaps she was busy shagging the tennis coach. I do hope so.

Rania believes the truth now and she has broken up with Richie. She keeps saying sorry. I am sick of hearing it, as though it makes everything better, and for once, I am not trying to please people. One day, perhaps, Rania and I will talk again, but not now.

My own nails, unlike Douglas's talons, were down to the quick after the attack but they are starting to grow back, like all of me.

For a while, at least, I will sleep in Florence and Nell's box room. Until whatever is next. The therapy I've been having for the last six months should help figure that out too. My therapist and I talk about alcohol and blocking things out. We talk about people pleasing, and how sometimes, people just can't be pleased. We talk about my panic attacks, and slowly, slowly, they are easing. I think I will die far less regularly now.

I don't drink anymore, so my head is clear enough to communicate with Patrick when he will come, tomorrow, to visit me. Where sleeping pills had become a nightly habit, I now rarely take them.

I don't have a job, or a plan, but I am lucky that I have a sister who'll let me be here without either for now, just taking my time. Popping strawberries so sweet they could come in your bag of pick'n'mix into my mouth; earning my keep by deadheading her flowers and batch-cooking for their freezer and walking their beautiful collie.

Inside the house, I look at my face in the mirror. My cheeks are pink, even without blusher, and my eyes shine. I have freckles, just a handful, over my nose. I can't stop looking at it, this face. It will be strained again, when the trial comes and I have to talk about what happened. But for now, it's my face again. Rose Rivers. Definitely no longer the night editor.

Chapter 58

I got something wrong when I left Patrick.

I like space but I don't like it in giant, empty air-conditioned offices at two o'clock in the morning. I like it in fields where the grass has grown so tall you have to wade through it, and a collie is racing fast after a ball thrown overarm. When I take people away, I should swap them for a field of cows or apple trees.

I haven't said that out loud to Patrick since he arrived a couple of hours ago for a visit. I know it doesn't sound great and it's a little offensive to suggest I traded our relationship in for cattle.

But he is here now, and I am trying to explain, better than that, better than I could have done before. We do it while we walk, across a long, wide beach that helps me remember to breathe.

There is more than that to talk about too.

'Why did you never tell me you were attacked?' he says.

It has been months now since I told him, just after Willow died. He still winces when he says it though, like he is in pain and I reach for his hand. 'I didn't tell you because I knew how much hurt it would cause you.'

I pause. 'And because I thought it was my own fault, and I didn't deserve sympathy.'

'You can't still believe that?' he says, stopping and turning to me.

I think of the weeks and weeks with the therapist. 'I still mostly do.' But a tiny door has opened up, and maybe there is a sliver of me that doesn't and maybe that sliver will get bigger. Imagine that. It's difficult to comprehend.

'And because I felt like I had cheated on you.' Sometimes you can only elucidate thoughts when you say them out loud; that was this one. I hadn't grasped fully that I felt that way, until the words were being formed by my mouth.

'Rose. God.' He looks appalled. 'No. God!'

I carry on.

'And because I didn't know what had happened, or who it was, and how mortifying is that? How could I expect anyone to believe me?'

He looks pained. A ball lands at his feet, and he kicks it back to a group of kids playing by the water's edge.

'And then the way I dealt with being so drunk I blacked out enough to be attacked was to keep getting so drunk I blacked out again.' I shake my head. 'I just got lost in a stupid, destructive cycle.'

He is shaking his head now, over and over and over. 'Please stop it, Rose.'

'But do you get it?' I say, crying now, hard, as the sun dips behind a cloud and a chill drops like rain. 'Why I had to figure some stuff out about myself and how I am, before I could be married, start a whole new life?'

He ignores that.

'I was your fiancé,' he says like he is only just realising the timeline. 'To come home after something like that happens. To carry on as normal and not tell me . . .'

We walk in silence for a few minutes and fall into the same step. The mood begins to feel less charged. I change the subject. 'Are you feeling nervous?'

He digs the toe of his Nikes into the sand and looks down. Shrugs. 'A little, I guess.'

I hold his hand, without thinking, and we stay that way as we walk. I squeeze my palm into his as we watch the waves bring in their flotsam and jetsam. Two teenage girls preen, lying on their fronts in bikini tops and shorts that show the whole of their bum cheeks. I smile at them as we pass, feeling something almost maternal. It's seventeen degrees with a decent wind chill. They have headphones on and phones in their hands and I am as invisible to them as the cold, as the future. We are mimicking Miami here, and a teenage lifeguard rides a jeep across the sand towards the sea, red shorts on, top off, just to complete the scene.

Patrick laughs, murmurs to me: 'I feel very old.'

I look at him and think what I have put him through; what he is doing for me, now. Maybe I have overcomplicated things.

I glance at a couple in their sixties putting up a windbreaker and unwrapping their sandwiches. Perhaps Patrick and I could be old together, like that. Perhaps we could figure it all out. Perhaps being wrapped in a blanket and listening to jazz in a wing-backed chair at Foxlands is all I need.

Early next year, Patrick will be the main witness for the prosecution to convict Richie of Willow's murder.

Douglas will also stand trial accused of sexually assaulting me. I hold very little hope of a conviction. I know the stats. I have no memories to help. It was also, now, over a year ago, any physical evidence long gone.

But I will do it for Willow. Because there will be no posthumous trial to hold Richie to account for raping her; it was thrown out, made unviable by a report that was posted on a national newspaper website that named him, and contained a lot of bias. Willow knew all of this; she had done her journalist legal training. But she wanted to blow up the Houses of Parliament that night, and she was thinking as long-term as a child in the sweetie aisle.

The murder conviction is different though: for that, there is the key witness. After Patrick came to see me that night at the office, he hung around Canary Wharf, hoping I would change my mind and speak to him if he texted me enough, pestered me enough. Even when I stopped picking up and replying, Patrick stayed, waiting it out perhaps for my shift to end. I think of that night, freezing, rain turning to sleet, icy wind whipping around the river.

But, he says, he wasn't giving up. He smiles at me when he says it: *See. Look how much I love you.* And while Patrick waited, he saw two figures, from a distance, arguing at a point near the water where the barriers are low. And then he saw one figure push the other up against it, a short tussle, and then it go backwards like a doll over and down. A brief flail of legs and then nothing, the figure moving too fast from him – still a good fifty metres away – to catch, despite how fast he ran. The sleet whipped into his face. Stung. Visibility was bad.

Richie is bigger than him, taller. Richie plays football twice a week with the fifty-something 'lads' from the paper and runs to and from work. He is strong, fit.

We have paused now, Patrick and I, and we are staring out to sea. An old man, long beard and a wetsuit, stands on a paddle board with his dog and rides the choppy waters impressively. He raises a paddle in hello.

Imagine if you knew, I think, what this conversation on a Saturday afternoon on a windy beach, entails. What that man and woman, holding hands, trainers on, strolling on the sand, are speaking about. What they have been through, and are about to go through. Murder and revenge. A body in a river. Missing, presumed dead, but then not dead, except then yes: dead.

I raise a hand back to him.

Imagine if any of us knew what all of these conversations entail, going on around us all the time over a ham sandwich, a beach walk, in hushed tones at the table across from us at the pizza place. Inconspicuous settings containing the horrifying twists and turns of a life.

'If only I'd been that little bit nearer,' Patrick says, so often. If only, if only, if only. Tiny words that have the threat of becoming bigger than any reality.

'If only I'd got to speak to her that night,' he carries on now on the beach, same mantra. 'Persuaded her to keep going, to wait for you at the hotel.'

I shake my head. 'There's no point going over this, Patrick. Don't do it. You didn't get to speak to her, and that's it. It's done.'

A pause. 'I do it myself though,' I admit quietly. 'All the time.'

Patrick puts an arm around me and I lean in, automatically. 'I'm here,' he says. 'Not going anywhere.' I realise I feel safe.

I glance behind us, at the old couple and their windbreaker. 'Remember when your only involvement with Willow was thinking that I was obsessed with her. God, you hated her.' Then I realise that's inappropriate. She's dead. 'Sorry. I mean not hated . . .'

The lifeguard runs past, to help someone who is in trouble in the water and the next group of teenage girls sing loudly to the Little Mix song that's playing through someone's phone.

I look again at Patrick. Down. Our hands are still joined. I cling to him like a life raft. Dependable. Reliable. That feeling, safety, comfort, comes flooding back.

I turn to face him but he is looking away from me. Out to sea. 'No, that's fair. Some days I did hate her. Or the concept of her. For taking you away.' He says it like he's dreaming. 'Yeah. Hate is fair.'

Epilogue

Willow, That Night

I look at him. Blink sleet out of my eyes. Wipe it away with the sleeve of my coat. Maybe that will change the picture.

Because I have practised this moment over and over in my mind so many times but now that it is real, something about it is skewed. Something pretty fundamental.

'You're not him.'

I take this man in. Unsure what is happening. Unlike the one I am expecting, who tops six foot, this man is not that much taller than me. Hair that is naturally blond by the looks of things, though don't quote me on that, it's pretty dark there by the river. Above his frown lines, his hairline shrinks back a little.

'Will fucking Frost,' he repeats. Louder. More confident. He doesn't seem to be noticing the weather.

'It's *Willow* fucking Frost, actually,' I correct him loudly to make myself heard over the wind and rain, and my voice surprises me with its steel. Too many men have called me Will, too many times, and I have made too few corrections, and I've had *enough*. Especially from this one, whose very presence is irritating me now because *he is not supposed to be here*.

Suddenly though, I get it. Peer a little closer. Ah. I loosen my grip on the knife. 'Are you looking for Rose?'

He's Patrick, of course. I saw his bright-eyed, fortunate face on Rose's screensaver every evening, when I arrived at work. Why could she never just log out?

'I was going to go and see her at work,' he says and it's only then that I notice he's slurring. I feel my shoulders stiffen. Drunk, angry, rejected men: the worst kind.

'She wouldn't speak to me, it felt like the only way,' he carries on. 'But she doesn't want me here. There's no point. I saw you come out. Have you been with her? Everything, *Willow*, seems to lead back to fucking *you*. Ever since you went "missing" it's been the beginning of the end for us. Today would have been our *wedding day*, and still she is with you. She won't see me, when she is supposed to be married to me now. But she will see you, her colleague, not even that, just her . . . well actually Willow, you tell me, what the fuck are you? What are you to Rose?'

I realise he thinks he is making an impassioned and emotive speech but honestly he just sounds like every drunk, hard-done-by bloke who won't take no for an answer that I have ever met and *I do not have time for that shit*.

I look over his shoulder, distracted. Where is the man I am baiting? I've caught the wrong fish and he could turn up any second and none of this is how it was supposed to happen. After I have planned so carefully, too, for so long.

'I need you to go.' I can't hide the impatience in my voice. Don't even bother trying.

'Why are you here, Willow?' he says, persistent, voice picking up the volume. 'What is it with you and Rose?'

I look at him then, and I open my mouth to speak. Tell him, and then it's done. Tell him, and then you can get rid of him. But I stop myself. Pull across the zip.

I can tell my story to whoever I want. But this is Rose's fiancé — her ex-fiancé — and it is not up to me to tell him that Rose was assaulted. Even after six and a half weeks of living off grid in youth hostels and the unreality that has left me with, I can see that.

Push, pull, she said to me earlier with the hint of a smile. Work twins. This is our story.

'Come on, Will,' he snarls. 'Spit it out.'

Again.

'I'm waiting.'

I feel a surge of something rise up through my belly and land in my throat. It's adrenalin. Rage. A lack of all control, I swear, if he calls me Will one more time. If anyone ever calls me that name again. But I push it down. Patrick isn't where my attention should lie tonight. Focus, Willow, focus.

'It wasn't the night shift, you know,' I say, the last thing before I walk away from him, while he is still asking his questions but I am tired of him and I can't do this now. He looks up. 'The night shift doesn't cause things. It just exacerbates them. The issues we already have; the people we already are. That's what the night shift does. It takes our problems and it magnifies them all and it forces everything out into the open.'

I laugh at him. 'What I'm saying is that you and Rose were fucked anyway. Don't kid yourself you weren't the problem.'

315

I start walking, then shout over my shoulder.

'You're just a bog-standard jilted fiancé, Patrick. Don't try and persuade yourself that there is anything more to it than that. Take your suit back. Turn your honeymoon into a lads' holiday. Move. On.'

I don't know why I'm being so mean except that I am so annoyed he isn't the right fish, and I'm soaking and I am so angry at the world and this isn't how it was meant to go and look at him: his face is annoying. He is annoying. He called me Will.

Patrick says nothing in response and I roll my eyes as I walk away. Pathetic. That is it now. He will move in the opposite direction, wake up with a terrible hangover. Stay angry but, eventually, move on. Not me. How wrong this has gone.

Where *are* you?

I quicken my pace. And something dawns on me. I hyped him, my fish. Drunk. Angry. But he has not come for me. And if he is not coming for me, there can be only one other person he is going for. He would think, wouldn't he, that we are in on it together. That while I'm the mad one, the livewire, the missing presumed dead, it's Rose who is steering this from the inside, who let me in and sat back as I posted the story online.

He blames Rose. Oh God.

I turn, intending to run fast back to the office. But I never make it. He takes me by surprise, and my knife is no longer poised and I am bones now; a month and a half living off grid has seen to that.

They presumed me dead, when I was missing.

They presumed me alive, when I came back.

But soon, they will be able to confirm it: I am dead. No presumptions needed any longer. A body sees to that.

He is stronger and more muscular than he looks but mostly I don't fight back because I am taken – utterly – by surprise as he pushes me backwards against the low barrier. Does Patrick *mean* to do it? Or is it a moment of such all-consuming rage and blind fury, a snap, on the day his life should have looked one way and didn't, to a man who had a plan and a trajectory and couldn't handle it going off course, and could have been punching a wall?

When I go into the water and it thunders into my ears, my insides, my lungs, I think only about survival, but on the edges of my consciousness I see Rose, too, and I wonder if she has made it.

Work twins, push pull.

What happens when one ceases to be?

Acknowledgements

I will start off with my agent Diana, since that is who this book – book four! How's that happened? – is dedicated to. You are the most supportive, engaged, patient person anyone could have on their team and the only one who can talk me round when I'm having a 'too many hours on my own at my desk self-doubt arrgggh-hhhh' meltdown.

You are my mentor, my advocate but also now such a good friend. I can't imagine what we have in common ('Is that Diana?' 'Yes that'll be Diana because she's got two drinks in her hand' or 'ProsecNO Caroline, we're having champagne'). Thank you.

To the rest of the team at the inimitable Marjacq. Leah Middleton for your TV and film expertise, Sandra Sawicka and Catherine Pellegrino for your amazing work securing foreign rights deals and still being lovely to me even when I have sent you 57 emails about the same certificate of residence request and the gist of every single one is 'I don't get it.' Guy Herbert, whose name is always my favourite to see in my inbox. Definitely not because you're the one who pays me, Guy, I promise.

To everyone at Team Avon! Firstly, my editor Thorne Ryan, for your super smart suggestions and edits, for coming up with the name that we all love so much for this book and for without a doubt having the coolest name in publishing/ possibly the world. To the rest of the Avon crew, especially Oli Malcom, Elisha Lundin, Ellie Pilcher and Becci Mansell, for all your hard work publishing my books and getting them out there over the past four years. And Helen Huthwaite, of course; even if you didn't work on this book with me, your wisdom and editing advice is never far from my mind when I write.

To my brilliant copy editor Fran Fabriczki for making the book better and sorting out my messy tenses. Tenses are my nemesis.

To London, for being such an incredibly rich tapestry for fiction. I love writing place, and London is one of my favourite places to write. But zooming back up north… for the local support, thank you to Sue at my fantastic local indie bookshop Linghams, to Beckie at Waterstones Liverpool, to Cheshire West and Chester libraries and to the book club that taught me why people like book clubs, via Louise Beach at Real Food Kitchen.

A big thank you to the super-talented author, and my very good friend, Tabitha Lasley, because who else wants to talk about certificate of residence requests when you've met up for a nice walk on the beach?

To Diana's Dames, Lucy and Daisy, for voice notes that make me cry with laughter or stop me from crying with empathy, kindness and a team spirit that is so precious and special when you work at home alone with only your computer to speak to.

Which brings me neatly to the Mac dictation tool. Sure, you think that when I say the word editor I actually said the word hamster and there are those instances when I forget to turn you off and you transcribe – of a sort – entire conversations of mine, but still! We're getting there, aren't we?

I have a history of writing epically long acknowledgements and when you're thanking the Mac dictation tool, it's probably time to wrap it up but I saved the most important people until last so I'm still here for a bit, sorry.

So, to my family and friends, especially Mum, Dad and Gem, for their excitement about this whole journey that has never waned, even now we are on book four. Being able to share my dream coming true with you really is a special thing.

To my brilliant, hilarious, loving boys, for giving me buckets full of joy and perspective on all things in life, even certificate of residence requests (I'm sorry, I literally can't stop talking about them).

And to Simon. I lied when I said I only had the Mac dictation tool to speak to when I'm writing. I have you, and you are far more engaged and far more accurate than the Mac dictation tool. Plus, you bring tea and Welsh cakes to my desk and do pre-school pick-up so I can hit my word count. Infinitely superior to the Mac dictation tool in every way, and if that's not a note to end on, I don't know what is.

'I did this. The most awful thing . . .'

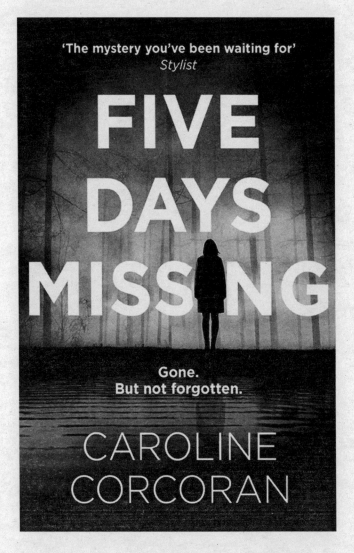

'The mystery you've been waiting for'
Stylist

FIVE
DAYS
MISSING

Gone.
But not forgotten.

CAROLINE
CORCORAN

A twist-filled, emotional tale of dark pasts
and even darker secrets.

Her life was perfect. Until the video.

She thought she could trust them.
She was wrong.

THE BABY GROUP

'Addictive'
Stylist

'Twisted'
Cass Green

CAROLINE CORCORAN

The deliciously twisted thriller from the
Sunday Times bestselling author.

Lexie's got the perfect life.
And someone else wants it . . .

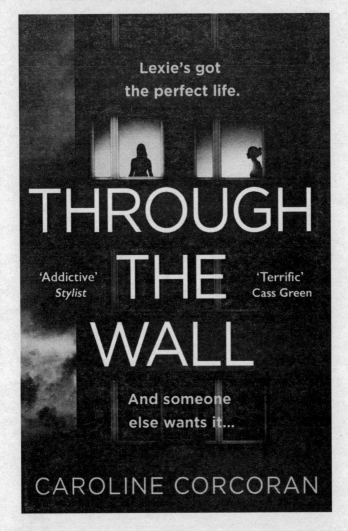

Lexie's got
the perfect life.

THROUGH

THE

WALL

'Addictive'
Stylist

'Terrific'
Cass Green

And someone
else wants it...

CAROLINE CORCORAN

A heart-racing psychological thriller perfect
for fans of Louise Candlish and Adele Parks.